"*Inheritance* mimics the form of a Babushka doll, with the Singh family's tale sitting within the larger microcosm of Singapore's Punjabi community and further encircled by the narrative of a newly independent state's shifting identity."
—Tali Levi, *The Melbourne Review*

"Jaswal's prose is pellucid and evocative. It drops the reader easily into the mind of her characters and their dilemmas and captures wonderfully the paradox of order in the tropics."
—Ed Wright, *The Australian*

"This is a novel with large themes including identity and multicultural-ism; repression and individuality; superstition and the stigma of mental illness; shame, disappointment and regret; desire and mania; and love and grief. Ultimately about defiance, survival and self-acceptance, it is surprisingly hopeful."
—Paula Grunseit, *Bookseller and Publisher*

"A tender and enlightening read."
—Emily Laidlaw, *Readings*

"With *Inheritance*, Jaswal makes a debut of an imaginative boldness and assurance."
—Peter Pierce, *The Monthly*

"Jaswal's complex and tender portrayal of a bipolar personality and the stigma of mental illness are the highlights of *Inheritance*. And her descriptive language, whether about character or setting—of HDB flats, of Iowa—is evocative. A dazzling novel."
—Pooja Makhijani, *Notabilia*

INHERITANCE
BALLI KAUR JASWAL

A NOVEL

EPIGRAM BOOKS
SINGAPORE · LONDON

Epigram Books UK
First published in 2013 by Sleepers Publishing (Australia)
This edition published in Great Britain in May 2017 by Epigram Books UK

A CIP catalogue record for this book is available from the British Library.

ISBN
978-1-91-209800-2

Printed and bound in
Great Britain by Clays Ltd, St Ives plc

Epigram Books UK
55 Baker Street
London, W1U 7EU

10 9 8 7 6 5 4 3 2 1

www.epigrambooks.uk

For my parents, Sohan Singh Jaswal and Ajit Kaur

PART I
1970–1971

Narain

IT WAS AN established rule in their household that books—and all documents containing pages and words—were not to be stepped on. Magazines were tucked away under the coffee table lest somebody's feet touch them. Stray newspaper sections were always neatly arranged, folded and stacked like fresh laundry. But in the days leading to his departure for America, a distracted Narain left brochures and forms all over the floor. He got from his door to his bed by tiptoeing around the edges of the room.

One afternoon, his sister stood in the doorway, her own toes perilously close to his papers. "You look like a pondan," she said. It was a word people used to describe men with shrill voices who walked like they were dancing, hips unhinged.

Narain ignored her. Amrit sang the word and mimicked his movements. He made a sudden leap to hit her but she moved out of the way with a squeal. Stepping back to regain his balance, his heels grazed the Iowa State University course catalogue.

"I wasn't bothering him." He heard her protesting outside as he knelt to kiss the catalogue. If somebody stepped on the printed word, house rules required a tender apology. The rules were inspired by Father's view that stepping on education was the ultimate display of disrespect. It brought terrible luck to a person. In his childhood, Narain remembered watching his brother Gurdev kneel and pray for accidentally knocking a Holy Book onto the floor. "You never put sacred words where somebody could trample on them," his father had shouted. Not even Amrit was excused from breaking this rule.

Narain gathered his papers and pulled the two old suitcases out from under his bed. He still had a week; it was not necessary to pack now, but there was little left to do. Father would enter the room occasionally to read through the brochures and murmur words of encouragement. Gurdev's wife Banu had helped by doing her own sorting— she searched the island for its weight in bay leaves, padded clothing and powdered drink mixes. Every week she arrived at the house to deposit items that would only add bulk to his already overloaded luggage. "They're for you to take there," she said. She showed little care to know the name of the state he was headed to; like everybody else in the family, she spoke of America only in vague terms. There.

In secret, Narain had allowed himself to be more sentimental about his departure. He had purchased a book of photographs of Singapore, and made a project of fastening family photos to selected pages. A portrait of his unsmiling parents was placed against a bare sketch of crammed shopfronts on the banks of the Singapore River. A candid family shot taken during Gurdev and Banu's wedding was clipped to close-ups of mangosteens and papayas bursting with festive ripeness.

Amrit was allowed to help fill a smaller suitcase kept in the storage closet. The night before Narain left, she came to his door and reminded him not to forget it. The note of concern in her voice was touching. She lingered outside the room, her eyes roaming over the bare walls. Narain knew he would miss her the most, but he caught himself before saying something. This was exactly the sort of weak behaviour he was expected to shed in America.

A smirk formed and spread across Amrit's lips. "When you're gone, this room will be mine." He glared at her but decided against taking a swipe. Amrit giggled and dashed down the corridor. He heard her feet slapping across the wooden floors for a while before the house settled into a gradual silence.

Narain had already picked out an outfit for the aeroplane and Father had made arrangements for a bus to bring family and friends to see him off. Leaving for America would be a grand occasion but Narain could not feign pride or excitement. The only reason he was going so far away to study was because of what had happened when he was in the army. There was no way to undo that shame but he could disappear for a while and return with a degree, a form of recompense for the damage he had caused to Father's reputation. "You will go to America to study engineering." Father had pronounced this fate with such certainty that Narain could only accept it.

Evenings mellowed the Naval Base streets. Palm trees hunched closer to the ground, burdened by heavy shadows. In the distance, stray voices flashed through the air like lightning, followed by the hum of crickets gathering to a steady harmony. The wind sighed through a crack in Narain's window, making the loose pages of the catalogue skitter across the floor. He picked up the pages and brought them to the living room to add to the stack of old newspapers. The karang guni man would arrive to collect them tomorrow, the coins in his pouch jingling to the staggered rhythm of his walk.

Narain had to arrange the papers carefully, placing thicker stacks on top of the single sheets to avoid scattering. On his hands and knees in the dark of the living room, he glimpsed two feet, darting like fish beneath the curtains. "Who's there?" he called. No answer. He inched closer to the window and saw the shape of a teenage girl. "Amrit, come out."

Amrit stepped out from behind the curtains, grinning. "I'll get to keep all the money from the karang guni man when you go," she said. A streak of moonlight illuminated the panic she failed to disguise. She had been trying to sneak out of the house through the window again.

"You have to stop this," Narain said, quietly. "Whatever you were about to do, you have to remember you're only fifteen. You're a *girl*." He looked away, embarrassed by this fact.

Amrit brushed past him, leaving behind a trace of jasmine perfume. It was a gift from her girlfriends, she'd insisted when he caught her spraying it at her throat. He had seen her sneaking off into the night to mingle with boys who smoked cigarettes and pinched her tiny waist. Since she turned fifteen, it was disturbingly clear that she enjoyed the stares of men and the taste of the night air. She had become less discreet as the family's concern shifted to Narain, but he was still the only one who had noticed.

He followed her into the room. "Amrit," he said. "You're old enough to take care of yourself now. If you need anything while I'm away—"

"What will you do? Fly back here?" she challenged. Spinning to face him, her heel squeaked against the floor. She began to giggle at the awkward sound.

"No," Narain said firmly, remembering the man he was expected to become overseas. He straightened his back and looked past Amrit's shoulder. "I have to focus on my education. You have to learn to take care of yourself." As he turned to leave, he was about to say something to soften the harshness of his words but then he noticed she was still laughing at her feet. Her shoulders were shaking and her hands were cupped over her mouth so that nobody would hear.

• • •

While Narain was in America, Father wrote long letters, which Narain kept scattered about his dorm room. Father's careful English script betrayed the attempts of an adult learner trying to perfect the roundness of his o's and sharpen the edges of his e's. As Narain read the letters, he ran his hands over the words in search of traces of forgiveness but Father's only intention was to provide updates on recent events. The only tenderness apparent was when Father enquired after his feet. "Keep them warm. You'll get sick otherwise." And then, "Do well, son."

The same three words concluded every letter and as the first months passed, Narain became increasingly irritated with Father's assumption that success could be so easily attained. He was ignored in Iowa, just as he had been all his life in Singapore, for his slight frame and effeminate gestures. Although he had spent his primary school years reciting every idiom, synonym and gerund in the *Comprehensive Guide to Queen's English*, the language spoken here seemed foreign. He drew curious looks for his turban and his beard. As a young boy in Singapore, he used to complain that people stared and his classmates made jokes, but Father never tolerated whining. "You are Sikh and you are showing this to the world. Be proud." But pride was measured no differently in America. Classmates didn't invite him to parties or include him in their study groups. They cleared their throats and lowered their voices when he passed them on the quad or in the library.

One day, Narain had to go to the university registrar's office to confirm a change in his elective subjects. The plump, red-haired clerk cheerily asked for his surname. "Sandhu," he said absent-mindedly, watching a fog settle on the tops of bare branches through the window.

The clerk chatted about the weather as she pulled out a heavy metal drawer. "It's getting colder out there," she said. "It's a shame we didn't get to savour fall this year." Her smile faded as she picked through her folders. "Would you spell your last name again?"

Realising his error, Narain apologised. "It's Singh." He spelled it out.

Exasperation rearranged the clerk's features. "I don't understand why it has to be so complicated with foreign students," she muttered. By reflex, Narain nearly launched into the explanation he had repeated so many times back home: "Sikhs are all supposed to have the same surname, for the sake of equality. Kaur for women and Singh for men. But it becomes confusing, with so many of us, so we use a family name specific to our region in Punjab. Officially, my surname is Singh but informally I use Sandhu." Generally, this speech was received with indifference, with more astute listeners reminding him that there were too few Sikhs in Singapore for identities to be confused. The clerk would likely say the same thing about his existence here in Iowa so Narain offered another apology and hurried off, feeling the familiar shame of an intruder.

The weather became similarly unfriendly. A rusty autumn turned into winter and stripped Narain's surroundings of colour. He dreaded going outside. A pair of thick-soled shoes that he thought he remembered packing had gone missing and when the temperature dropped in the evenings, his toes felt like blocks of ice. Engineering classes were difficult; he found himself drifting in and out of his own thoughts and thinking about home. Amrit's suitcase remained unopened under his bed. He knew what was inside—he had seen the other foreign students. Thin sweaters that began to unravel and stretch the minute they were worn. Packets of Ovaltine, which looked and tasted like sand. Dial soap and Darkie toothpaste. Mint oil to soothe those headaches from studying all night. A box of tea leaves that tasted bitter unless mixed with condensed milk and spices that he would never find in Iowa.

Narain vowed not to turn to the bag to remedy his homesickness. As a child, his cousin Karam had teased him about being a mummy's boy. Karam said that Mother had wanted a girl so badly that when Narain was born, she treated him as one. When he was a toddler she allowed him to keep his long hair loose and she took more time grooming him, wrapping his soft curls around her fingers and calling him her little darling. Narain knew this was true. There were photographs of Karam and Gurdev squinting at the camera, their hair neatly braided and piled on top of their heads in round buns, and then him, squatting next to them, long black tresses hanging past his shoulders. He had a hazy recollection of her disappointment the first time he told her he wanted to join his brothers playing football outside, although he had been just as relieved as she was to see him return in tears moments later with two fresh wounds on his kneecaps, bright declarations of his unsuitability for sports.

Childhood memories of his father always accompanied those of his mother, trailing like smoke from a lit mosquito coil. Father had always been brooding and impatient with her, injecting any silence between them with harsh criticism. Any longing that she expressed for having a different life angered him. "Accept your new country," he would say in disgust. Years after his arrival to Singapore, Father still reminded her that he had known nothing then. "No English, no experience, no money. Nothing. And I made something out of it. If you want to keep complaining, then just go. Just disappear." Nobody expected that this would happen, but one morning when Narain was six, he woke up to find that Mother was gone and that he had a new baby sister, Amrit.

In the long stretch of winter, the skies were the same clay colour each day. Narain didn't care to look out of his window at the warted tree branches clawing at the wind. It became more difficult for him to pull himself out of bed for his morning classes. Letters continued to arrive from home and he read them with the detached interest of somebody listening to music that drifted from another room. However, whenever Father wrote about politics, something stirred in Narain. Father was enthusiastic about developments in Singapore—he quoted from the Prime Minister's speeches: stricter laws, extensive housing projects, and more schools to build their fledgling nation. "Independence from Malaysia made us weep at first, but it is a good thing," Father wrote. "I hope you also have faith in our country because it is going to be important to the world."

Back home, Narain would not have contradicted Father, who read the newspapers from cover to cover every evening, stopping only to look up words in the *Oxford English Dictionary* that was displayed prominently on the dining table between meals. Now Narain dared to disagree. He did not think progress would arrive so swiftly, if at all. He had seen Singapore on a map pinned to his room-mate's wall and compared to most countries, it was a mere speck. His belief that Singapore did not deserve a longing of such magnitude helped to alleviate his homesickness. He fiercely reminded himself of what he did not miss: the sticky heat, the waft of stale fish skins that drifted through the open lanes beyond the Naval Base gates, and the stares and whispers of the Punjabi community.

In a reply to Father, Narain listed every sceptic's reasons for believing that Singapore would not manage to sustain itself. *No natural resources. Mass unemployment.* A lack of housing, land, sanitation. In his first genuine drive at scholarship since arriving at university, Narain pored over papers and books in the library and quoted experts whose opinions were not featured in *The Straits Times*. *We won't make it*, he wrote, forcing out the words as he convinced himself of a more fulfilling future in these blank Midwestern horizons.

Narain decided not to send the letter right away but he kept it in his room and read it often, proud of his own definitiveness. One day, as he was opening his post office box, a group of fraternity boys came barrelling through the hallway. The sheer wind of their entrance made Narain stumble back against the wall. Scattered around him on the floor were flyers for pizza delivery restaurants and credit card advertisements. He made a move to step around them delicately when he noticed that his left foot was pinning down a letter from Father. He picked it up, closed his eyes and brushed his lips against it. As he began to whisper an apology, he heard laughter and his eyes flew open. "Miss your mama?" one of the boys called out. The others chuckled. Narain responded with a blank stare, embarrassment stiffening his limbs.

That was the moment he decided to be less vigilant about where he stepped. Over the next few weeks, he became more aware of how he walked and paid less attention to where his feet landed. He practised making himself look wider and taller, gauging his progress by watching his dim shadow on stony November mornings. Scant sums of pocket money sent from home were spent on a new wardrobe—winter boots and bulky cable sweaters with smart V-neck collars. He took a campus job in the library and saved his wages to replace his thick frames with contact lenses. Reading passages from his textbook into a mirror, he practised deepening his voice. During lectures, he doodled in the corners of his notebooks and didn't bother completing assignments. He despised the other foreign students for their simplicity and eagerness. He strived to be their exact opposite—disinterested in his studies, witty and self-assured.

In the process of planning his transformation, Narain had to consider his hair. In Singapore, when passing another turbaned Sikh man, Narain would initiate a customary nod. His father had taught him and his brothers to do this because it represented religious solidarity. Despite teasing from Chinese and Malay children, Narain never once dared to think about cutting his hair. But now the turban felt bulky and awkward, making him stand out even more.

He focused on his face first. Hair had taken its time to sprout on Narain's cheeks and chin. It was such a delay, in fact, that Father accused him of shaving when he was fifteen. Narain had to convince him that he was just developing more slowly than the other boys, a fact that Father was willing to accept all too readily. At the time, Narain had been mortified, but now he saw advantages to having only a thin spread of beard. It didn't seem wrong to eliminate what was hardly there to begin with. He felt little remorse as he dragged the razor across his cheeks, even when he nicked his skin. However, the thought of his next task made his heart race.

Narain unravelled the fabric of his turban and loosened the pins and rubber bands that held together his fat knot of hair. It tumbled down his back in waves, releasing the light, flowery fragrance of Johnson's Baby Oil that he used to smooth it down after washing. He pictured his home in Singapore—a modest bungalow like the others that housed local officers for the British Police. In his imagination, it expanded to the proportions of an enormous old mansion with creaking corridors and hidden sections constructed for concealing secrets. He shut his eyes and manoeuvred his way around the house. Perhaps if he was careful, he could cut his hair to a shorter length and somehow conceal it from Father's view when he returned home for the summer.

As he searched for a pair of scissors, his enthusiasm quickly diminished. The weight of his hair and the daily routine of oiling, combing, braiding and wrapping were too familiar to eliminate so suddenly. Changes were necessary but a haircut would be too drastic, so he kept all of his hair but exchanged the turban for a baseball cap under which his braid sat coiled like a millipede in terrified defence.

At his first party, Narain was disappointed to find that nobody noticed the difference. He expected classmates to approach him with congratulatory smiles, warmth restored to their eyes. Deciding that going unnoticed meant that he blended in, he pushed through the crowds. Music throbbed through the walls of a three-storey brick house. Students leaned against the walls and nodded, sharing a familiar secret. Girls in tight skirts writhed and gyrated against boys they didn't know. He smiled at them and they smiled back, their dances a lazy trance to invite him into their world.

A blonde wearing heavy green eye shadow allowed him to put his hand up her skirt, then she led him up the stairs towards an empty room. Pausing at the threshold, Narain was struck with a profound and dizzying sense of despair—at that moment, he was sure of who he was, but this certainty brought back memories of the army and everything he meant to repair. Narain recalled the officers' grim faces as they explained to Father that Narain would have to undergo a psychiatric evaluation. As the girl shook off her clothes, Narain watched her and relied on the distant throbbing music to pump away his past. *Behaviour management. Removed from duties handling sensitive information.*

This is America. This convenient phrase, which came to him that night, obliterated his sins over the next few months. He began smoking cigarettes, but this was America. He wasn't studying, but this was America. He did not respond to Father's letters *because* this was America. The accumulations of all his misgivings—even for acts he was preparing to commit— occurred to him with an electric jolt.

The parties continued and the girl became Narain's first girlfriend. She was Jenny, a Philosophy major from Fairfield. She was near-sighted but hated wearing her glasses. Her parents had divorced each other and then remarried five years later. She had joined every activist group on campus and she confessed to spending more time at their meetings than in her classes. Her skin was so pale it sometimes turned blue in the eerie winter light.

Jenny was not ashamed to admit that she did not know where Singapore was. "Tell me more about it," she said to him one night, as they walked past a row of college bars. She backed herself against a brick wall in a narrow alley and drew him to her, pressing her thighs against his. "What's it like in Sing-a-pore?" she drawled, making the city's name sound like a scientific term. She planted a loud kiss against the side of his neck. The acrid mix of stale cigarettes and beer was wet on her skin.

"I'll show you," Narain said. He took her hand and led

her back to his dormitory. From his shelf, he retrieved his book of photographs. The first page contained pictures of decrepit kampongs flanked by the thick trunks of coconut trees and gnarled bushes. Children with legs like twigs stared into the camera, their expressions solemn. A pick-up truck was parked at an angle on a street corner and the driver stood nearby drinking juice from a clear plastic bag. Groups of women squatted among tall stalks of grass and grinned as they dunked their laundry in basins at a public standpipe. Narain felt a flash of panic. Nothing about this world would be familiar to Jenny. He hastily flipped to a picture of the modest city skyline.

"This is what it looks like at night," Narain said. "See how the buildings light up?" He traced his finger over the buildings and the calm river below. The city looked glamorous at night. Not a trace of the broken bottles and plastic bags that clogged the river could be seen in the shadows. Instead, lights melted across the water's surface.

"It's sort of like Chicago," Jenny said.

"Yes," Narain said, wishing he had the nerve to deny this. Singapore was nothing like Chicago. The air was sticky all year round and crickets filled the dusty kampongs with mournful songs after the rain destroyed their nests. There were people who slept on thin mattresses above the shops of their trades, their skin soaking in the smell of preserves and herbs. His favourite place to eat was not a restaurant or a diner but a street stall with only one dish listed on a handwritten sign. The facade of his local cinema betrayed its age with smears of soot and dust but nobody cared as long as the snack man was outside to serve sugar-coated nuts in paper cones. As Jenny shifted closer to turn the pages, Singapore came back to Narain in a rush of tangled telephone cables, houses with slanting tin roofs, vendors pushing wobbling trolleys, incense sticks glowing in the night like stars, men racing barefoot across coals to prove their faith to cheering crowds outside a Hindu temple.

Jenny smiled and pointed to a grainy photograph. "Here we are," she said. "That's how I pictured it." In grey and white, a bony Indian man wearing nothing but a loose piece of checkered cloth around his waist stood next to a lopsided rickshaw, gesturing to the camera, his mouth open wide, mid-speech. Behind him were the dark entrances to provision shops where bulging gunnysacks filled with rice, seeds and dried fruits leaned against each other. As Jenny tipped her head and cast him a dreamy gaze, Narain understood what they needed from each other. One day she would muse about her foreign boyfriend just as he would always remember the American he dated in college. Both would keep this relationship as a souvenir of the people they had once dared to be.

"Tell me more about where you're from. Tell me everything," Jenny said, lying across his bed. She was clumsy at being sexy, drawing a slow circle low on her tummy with the tips of her fingers.

That day, Narain showed Jenny Singapore's place on the map. He told her how families had crowded around their television screens the day Malaysia announced it wanted Singapore out of its union. Tears nearly sprang to his eyes when he described their fear at watching their own leader cry on the screen. He told her about the race riots, and the odd calm that descended over the island after curfews were imposed to keep the Chinese and Malays from clashing in the streets. Jenny responded with a mixture of sympathy and approval, encouraging him to continue. Then he accidentally mentioned the army.

"Wait. Start again," Jenny said. "You were in the army?" Betrayal flashed across her face. "You never told me that."

"No, no," Narain said. "I mean, yes, I was, but it's different over there. It's National Service. It's compulsory," he was quick to say. "I was in the country's very first cohort."

"I'm against the military," Jenny replied.

"I know," Narain said. One of the few times Jenny had interrupted one of his long stories about home, she went on a rant against the draft and the war in Vietnam, where her friend from high school had been so badly wounded he would never walk again. "What they're making our boys do over there is wrong—it's so fucking obvious," she said, slapping her hand against her head. "Why don't people see it, though? You know how long it took me just to get twenty signatures on my petition the other day? Nobody wants to believe the government's a bunch of lying bastards." Her forwardness was titillating. Back home, people had become more cautious about voicing such strong opinions.

On another occasion, Narain showed Jenny pictures of his family. She pointed out the strong resemblance his cousin Karam had to Father, and remarked that he was handsome. Narain laughed. "My brother Gurdev would not like to hear that." Jenny nodded and placed her fingers lightly on Gurdev's image, a gesture of consolation. A hint of his belly pressed through his shirt and his cheeks retained his baby fat even in his late twenties.

"You must be very close to Karam," Jenny said. "He's in all the pictures."

"He's close to the family," Narain said carefully. "His own parents died on their way to Singapore. There was a problem with the ship and it capsized but Karam was saved and brought over. He was raised by a distant aunt in Singapore—his father's cousin. She and her husband didn't have any children and they were happy to adopt Karam but I don't think they knew how to raise a child. They treated him like a guest. He started coming over to our house every day. He and my father had a special bond. By the time he was about ten or eleven, he was practically living with us."

Jenny cast a sad glance at Karam's picture. "It's like you have two brothers then."

"Not really. More like two fathers," Narain said. Jenny probably thought he was only referring to physical appearance.

Jenny commented that Narain's mother was pretty, with her pale skin, her sharp nose and those tiny, pursed lips that made her look even younger than her sixteen years in his only photo of her, balancing a baby Gurdev on her lap. "I bet she still looks like that," she said. Narain said nothing, but pointed out that daughters often resembled their mothers. He showed her Amrit. Jenny smiled. "The boys must be after this one."

"She's too young," he said, tersely.

"What, fifteen? I started dating around then," Jenny said, with a shrug.

For days afterwards, Narain found himself thinking about Amrit. Amrit dashing past his room. Amrit sprawled on their rattan furniture. Though he never admitted it out loud, he had always sought her approval more than anybody else's. For her age, Amrit had a surprisingly acute knowledge of relationships. He wondered what she would say if he told her he wanted to bring home this pale-skinned girl with her accent that widened every vowel. Would Amrit welcome the idea? Would she be disappointed? Would she explain that what he felt was not love? He could not see it any other way—Jenny was unwittingly helping him to become more like other men, and for this, he loved her. His love for her was so strong that it overrode those impulses that had led to his troubles in the army. Yet whenever he thought of asking Amrit about love, he imagined her leading him through an uncharted passageway in their house, laughing at him for not knowing it existed.

• • •

The morning Father called, Narain was still half asleep. Jenny's arm rested across his chest and she stirred slightly when he reached for the telephone. "Hello," he mumbled into the receiver.

"Narain? Please speak up," Father's voice gripped him. He sat up in bed and pulled the sheets over Jenny's bare shoulder, as if Father might be peering into his room.

"Sat sri akal, Father," Narain said.

"Sat sri akal. How are you?"

"I'm well."

"I said speak up."

"I'm doing fine," Narain said loudly. Jenny rolled lazily to her side.

"Have you read my letter?"

"I haven't received it yet," Narain lied, eyeing the envelopes scattered across the dresser.

"Well, what are you doing now?"

"Nothing. I mean, I was just waking up," he said. A soft moan escaped Jenny's lips. Her eyes blinked open. "Who is it?" she mumbled as he leaned away from her.

"Narain, I want to see copies of your exam results. You have no idea what this education is costing me."

"Results haven't come out yet," Narain said, keeping his panic from edging into the conversation. "I'll send them to you as soon as I get them."

"Yes, please do this," Father said. "Also, when is your summer vacation? You are coming back to Singapore."

Narain glanced at Jenny. "I'm not sure, Father. I might have some things to do here. Summer classes."

"No, you must come back," Father said.

"But it will save you a lot of money if I just stay here. I thought I could get a summer job as well."

"I am paying your school fees and transport. This was the arrangement so you could return home every year and see the family. Please do not argue," Father said sternly. "Your sister needs you."

There was a short silence. Narain found himself fighting the urge to listen to the noises in the background. On the phone with Father once, when the connection was poor, he had mistaken the static for Singapore noises—the buzz of midday traffic, sparrows chirping their uneven greetings, oil hissing on a hawker's wok.

Father told him to read his letter and with a curt goodbye,

he hung up. Narain reached for his dresser. There were four envelopes from home. He saw the most recently dated stamp and ripped the envelope open. After the usual formalities, Father's letters always contained a paragraph on latest developments in the country, followed by a few words of advice. This letter was different. It launched into a subject that Narain no longer felt equipped to handle from such a distance.

I must inform you about Amrit. She is out of control. Twice I have caught her outside chatting with boys near the shops. She wears very red lipstick and does not study anymore. One day, I could smell cigarettes on her clothes but when I asked Amrit about it, she said she had lunch at a coffee shop where people were smoking. You should know what to do in this situation— she needs to be disciplined. You are to return as soon as your term is over so you can monitor your sister. Remember, this is an important year. Her exams are coming up, and she must do well, as should you.

Narain re-read the letter as he paced the cramped quarters of his dormitory room. He glanced at Jenny and found it easier to dismiss Father's words. This was the problem? This was the reason he was being pressured to come home—just because his sister was *dating*? In his mind, he drafted a letter telling Father all the things he wished he had the courage to tell him. Father was overreacting. Father was distracting him from more important matters with these trivial complaints. But the letter was never scripted. Instead, Narain retrieved the other letter expressing his doubts about Singapore's progress and mailed it to Father that very afternoon. He hadn't mentioned Amrit.

The next day, Narain went to the library and applied for

extra shifts over the summer holidays. He began searching the newspapers for apartments available for rent. Jenny was planning on waiting tables all summer and he wanted to be close to her. Lately, he found himself wanting to spend every moment with Jenny. When they were together, he was always touching her—stroking her hair or grasping her hand, walking her to her classes—and he became unable to concentrate on his own work without her presence. At times, he felt as if he needed to be within Jenny, hidden away from the doubts that could spring without warning into his solitary moments.

A few weeks passed before another letter arrived from Father, reminding Narain to send his grades home once he got them. To Narain's surprise, there was no mention of his argumentative reply.

Narain pretended not to receive any more of Father's correspondence, wedging letters between a stack of unopened Engineering books. He decided to avoid telling his family that he was planning to stay in Iowa over summer until two weeks before he was due to come home. It would be too late then for Father to persuade him, and then maybe Father would realise that Amrit was not Narain's sole responsibility. He took it as a practice step. If he could disobey Father in small doses, perhaps one day he would muster the courage for a graver disagreement about his life choices.

The weather became warmer as spring finally took hold. Tiny buds appeared on trees and began to blossom, spreading colour through the university campus. There were more people walking about now, riding bicycles, lying on blankets on the front lawn. Jenny prepared a picnic and they lay sprawled on their bellies. They made plans to attend an anti-war protest that Jenny had helped put flyers up for around campus. The sun was bright and a light breeze rustled Jenny's hair, bringing strands into her mouth that Narain constantly had to pull away. "You're not listening," she complained after he tried to kiss her mid-sentence.

"The weather's too nice," Narain said.

"We have to go. There aren't enough people out there who are willing to fight for the truth anymore. It's important to show our support," she said.

"Of course," he told her. Evening was too far away for him to even consider. This was the happiest he'd been since arriving in Iowa. He said this to Jenny but she thought he was only talking about the weather.

"It's like this in California," Jenny said. "All the time. I went there one year for Christmas when my dad was living with this woman in San Diego. The weather was amazing."

"Let's move there," Narain joked. He laughed with surprise when she responded enthusiastically. Kisses suddenly rained on his cheeks and neck.

She asked him if he wanted to take a road trip to Los Angeles at the end of summer. "We'll save up and go see where all the movie stars live." She let out a delighted squeal and listed the celebrities they would see. "Okay?" she asked.

Narain closed his eyes for moment. "Of course we will," he replied. The farther away from home he was, the more things seemed possible.

• • •

Two days later, Amrit left the house in the middle of the

night and didn't return. Narain was the last to know because he had become so difficult to reach. It took a phone call from his father to the Dean, who sent a resident advisor to tell him in person.

"Come home right away," Father said gravely when Narain returned the call. His heart pounded. He could not think about refusing. Too many questions spun through his mind. Where was she? Was she safe? What was he expected to do?

As he packed his room for the return home, he pulled out the suitcase from under his bed. Thoughts of Amrit, her mangled body abandoned somewhere, flooded his mind and made it hard for him to focus. His hands shook as he struggled to open the suitcase. It contained items that he could throw out to make room for what he had acquired in America. Shot glasses. Photographs. Magazines that were banned back home. A clock radio.

Tears stung his eyes as he emptied the suitcase. He hadn't expected the smells of his home to remain so well preserved in this bag. Sandalwood and cardamom drifted into the air and tinted the skies a rich orange.

Narain spotted his thick-soled shoes. Amrit had done most of the last-minute packing. Probably out of mischief, she'd removed the shoes from his other suitcase and placed them in this one. He sat cross-legged on the floor and pressed his head into his hands. Fellow students peered anxiously from the doorway asking if he needed anything, but his crying only grew louder when he picked up the shoes and found them sitting flatly on a dictionary, a Holy Book and a popular novel.

Father

AFTER MAKING THE phone calls, Harbeer returned to his room, sat at his desk and waited for his wife. She would surely arrive soon, sensing the first signs of trouble with Amrit. Her secret visits had become so frequent lately that Harbeer became nervous the children would find out. He always kept his voice low and their conversations brief. Whenever she lingered and tried to offer advice, he reminded her bitterly that it was she who left. *If you know so much, why don't you come back to raise your children? Why don't you let them know you are here?* To this, she never had a reply.

On the corner of Harbeer's desk was a fresh stack of loose-leaf paper for his writing practice. Twenty-five years ago, during his first months in Singapore, he had practised writing in English, imitating the extensions and swoops of his British officers' penmanship. Graduating from single words, he focused on sentences and then paragraphs. Soon he was able to write lengthy letters without having to consult a dictionary. He still wrote letters often. These were different from the letters written to Narain in America or to his father in India. These letters remained unsent—they were not addressed to anybody in particular but somehow the format allowed him to articulate thoughts that he could not otherwise. Perhaps there was a worthy recipient out there to whom he would eventually send his musings, a person who would read them with sympathy as well as appreciation for his experiences and ideas. It was a far-fetched idea, of course. Harbeer could not imagine entrusting anybody with the contents of his mind, particularly his deepest disappointments. The letters sat in the bottom drawer.

When Harbeer first designated a place to store such letters, he was certain that just one drawer would be sufficient. There had been a promising future ahead. He and Dalveer had arrived in Singapore a few months before his sister, Rashpal, her husband and their toddler, Karam were due to follow. He had a dignified and respected post with the British Military Police so he had not arrived in Singapore as so many migrants did, as labourers and construction workers from China and India. His job was to protect the citizens, and there were opportunities for promotions to higher ranks in the coming years. He and Dalveer lived in a modest but comfortable bungalow on the British Naval Base in Sembawang.

The day Harbeer heard the dreadful news of Rashpal and her husband's deaths, he sat down to write a letter, intending to inform his officers that he had to take a leave of absence to tend to some family matters—the last rites in India, the question of what to do with young Karam. Instead, Harbeer began to write a list of questions. He asked his unknown recipient how Rashpal's ship could have capsized. He asked where her body was now and how to carry out a funeral with only a memory. He wanted to know how Papa, having only lost his wife two years before, would cope with his grief. He asked, pleadingly and with hope, if the fact that Karam had been saved by surviving passengers was a sign that goodness existed.

This letter was tucked away in the bottom of the drawer. Harbeer hoped to read it again one day and feel a sense of peace but over the years, more letters were piled on, burying those early regrets with more disappointments. His first son, Gurdev, born three years after Karam, was not athletic or confident; he pouted constantly and had outbursts of unnecessary emotion. His second son, Narain, was meek and always in tears. In his letters about these two, he speculated on the ways in which he might model another son to be more like him. When Dalveer was pregnant with a third child, Harbeer thought God himself might have been peering over his shoulders and reading his words as he wrote them. Then the child turned out to be a girl and no sooner had she arrived than Dalveer exited, leaving Harbeer with the baffling task of raising a girl. Letters overflowing with Harbeer's despair filled the drawer. Over the years he had to fold them into tiny squares to make room for more, determined that only one drawer was sufficient for all of his disappointments. He stopped writing for a brief period while he decided where to keep all of his old letters to make space for new ones. This period extended as Harbeer became busy with the task of raising the children on his own, and soon he had abandoned the letter writing altogether, considering it an indulgent pastime. There was plenty to be grateful for in this new country and he had allowed himself to succumb to the same melancholy that he had criticised his wife for.

Only two more events gave Harbeer reason to open that

drawer again and both occurred in the same year. It was 1967—the year Harbeer began studying for the written test to be promoted to Police Inspector, and the year Narain was conscripted into the army. Nothing turned out as expected. The British announced they would be withdrawing from the country, leaving Harbeer's aspirations suspended. He wrote furiously, scribbling out the practiced answers to the test, unloading them onto the paper until his mind was blank. Months afterwards, there came the phone call from an officer at Narain's base camp. Harbeer was called in for an interview—a standard procedure, they assured him, for identifying Narain's type of problem. They had sounded so confident, as if they had been handling these cases for years, but Narain was in the first cohort of National Servicemen in Singapore. He was supposed to make history in this country but instead he was probably the first case of…what did they call it? Sexual deviance. Evidence of effeminate behaviour. Homosexual tendencies. They had asked if any signs had existed when Narain was a child and Harbeer had said no. The officers must have thought the puzzlement and grave disappointment on his face were genuine signs that he had suspected nothing over the years. Actually, Harbeer wasn't entirely surprised but he was confused as to why Narain would admit to that filthy behaviour. Why hadn't Narain denied it? Why was he trying to destroy his family's reputation? There were Punjabis in all ranks of the army who would look at Harbeer now and know it was confirmed. His son was a homosexual.

After that meeting, Harbeer spent entire nights writing letters, recounting everything he had witnessed in Narain over the years: the left-handedness he had tried to correct by making the boy sit on his left hand while writing with the right; the nervousness; the posture; that girlish walk. The pages overflowed with regrets and so did the drawer. Only when Harbeer bade farewell to him at the airport did he feel his despair subsiding. America would change the boy, and four years away would buy some time for Harbeer to rebuild his reputation. "My son is studying to be an engineer," he would pointedly tell those Punjabis who had heard the rumours from their army friends. Surely this detail would be enough to appease them—no young boy went overseas unless he was serious about becoming a man.

Now Amrit was gone. Now more letters would have to be written. Harbeer cringed at the thought and reminded himself not to get carried away. She was probably playing an elaborate prank on the family, nothing worse. It was good that Narain was returning for his summer break—he would watch over Amrit and pass on some of the discipline he had learned in America.

The hinges of the back door creaked slightly—or was it a sound from outside? Harbeer strained to listen. Sometimes it was impossible to tell whether Dalveer was entering. Rain dripping on the roof could be mistaken for the patter of her feet. A gate opening, her languid sigh. A rustle in the trees, her fingers raking coconut oil through her hair until it was soaked. The only way to be sure was to see her. He waited until he caught her shadow, then her slight figure making its way through the corridors. Her questioning eyes darted at the doorways. Harbeer called out that nobody was home, just him. She entered the room and brought with her the hard scent of freshly-churned soil. Harbeer looked outside. Clouds were huddled in the sky. Somewhere on the island it had already begun to rain.

He informed her that Amrit had gone missing. "I checked her bed in the morning and she was gone," he said.

Dalveer let out a cry and tore through the house. Harbeer went after her, pleading for silence. The neighbours would hear her. Did she want that? Did she want the neighbours to come rushing over? She went through all of Amrit's things—her schoolbag, her clothes, her books. Harbeer sat and watched her. He had gone through these same actions this morning when he noticed the empty room. Amrit was nowhere to be found in those things.

Dalveer sat in a heap on the floor and wept softly into her hands. Harbeer crouched next to her. He waited for her breathing to slow, for the sobs to subside, and then he promised to find Amrit. He paused, and then softly told her that Karam and Gurdev were arriving soon. She understood what this meant and she picked herself up. She did not tell him when she would come back but he knew to expect her soon. He had stopped trying to follow her years ago, and so when she left, he went back to his desk and began to write.

• • •

The sharp rap of Karam's knuckles was familiar—he always made an announcement of his presence rather than a request to enter. Harbeer beamed when he saw the boy. He couldn't help it. People in the neighbourhood used to mistake Karam for his biological son, and if Harbeer had to correct them, he did so with great reluctance. Their surprise was not unusual—Karam's broad shoulders and confident stride mirrored Harbeer's, and his sharp features gave him a strong resemblance that Harbeer's own sons did not have. Somewhere in his letters of disappointments, Harbeer had written that Gurdev and Narain had taken after their mother.

"Any news?" Karam asked. "Have you heard anything?"

"I've only called you, Gurdev and Narain," Harbeer said. "I don't think it's a good idea to let anybody else know at this stage. It might just be mischief."

"You're right," Karam said, reassuringly. "I wouldn't worry."

"I've asked Narain to come back, though," Harbeer said. Karam looked a bit surprised at this. "I need him to be here to look after Amrit. The girl has no sense of right and wrong anymore because her older brother hasn't been around. This is their home and there are rules to be followed. They can't just run off like that. Both of them must learn this."

"Where do you think she might be?" Karam asked. "Does she have any friends that she might have gone off with?"

Harbeer could only recall the last time he lectured Amrit, after he spotted her in a coffee shop during his evening rounds. He had been with two fellow police officers, one of them a Punjabi man, and so he could not make a scene. By the time Amrit came home, his fury had subsided and he chose instead to appeal to the girl's sense of pride. "Amrit, you are the smartest girl in your class," he said. "If you want to keep that title, you should be studying after school instead of running around with those half-past-six characters." He had borrowed this term from a Chinese colleague who used it to describe boys with tobacco-stained teeth and dyed hair like burnt grass, who gathered in coffee shops. They were aimless with their days, unaware of the passing time, only interested in the crackling radio music to which they bobbed their heads and clapped. Amrit had cried, said she was sorry. Within days Harbeer saw her at the coffee shop again.

"No, no friends," Harbeer said quickly. Surely those coffee shop boys were not friends of Amrit's.

"Do you think she's gone to school for something? Should we check there?"

"The gates are always locked. She wouldn't be able to get in," Harbeer replied. "If she wanted something from school she would have told me. She was gone very early this morning, when it was dark. There's no reason for a girl to be out at those hours."

Karam gave Harbeer's shoulder a pat. "We'll find her," he said. They both fell into their usual comfortable small talk, the type of banter that Harbeer had never enjoyed with his other children. When he heard the creak of the gate opening outside, Harbeer felt a twinge of irritation that their conversation would be interrupted.

Gurdev arrived in his usual manner, huffing and puffing, wiping the sweat from his neck, his eyebrows furrowed in complaint. "I could have picked you up," Karam told him. "I drove over here."

"That's okay," Gurdev said. His tone contained more than the usual dose of coldness towards his cousin. He sneaked a glance at Harbeer. "It would have been too much trouble," Gurdev added more generously. Harbeer nodded approvingly. He had little tolerance for jealousy. It had no place between brothers. This was how he had always told Gurdev to regard

Karam—like a brother. *Learn from him*, Harbeer had always said, but Gurdev always insisted on continuing a petty rivalry that stemmed from their childhood.

Karam filled Gurdev in on the details concerning Amrit's disappearance. "We're not calling anyone," Karam said. "Once people start to hear that Amrit's gone missing, they'll just start gossiping."

Gurdev's eyebrows bunched together. "Not calling anyone?" He directed the question at Harbeer. "Not even the police?"

"This is not a matter for the police," Harbeer snapped, glaring at Gurdev. Imagine if he had left all of his problems in the hands of this boy—where would his reputation be? Harbeer was a policeman himself; if his colleagues found out that he had no control over his own daughter, he would be a laughing-stock. And with all the cutbacks happening in the force lately, with only a few years before he would be forced into retirement, did Gurdev want his last few years to be spent in disgrace?

"I doubt she's in any danger, Gurdev," Karam said. "We'll just hold on for now."

Gurdev looked back and forth between Harbeer and Karam as if he did not know who was who. "Hold on? This could be serious!"

Harbeer felt his anger mounting. "Gurdev," he said, warningly. "You're becoming too emotional."

Gurdev scrunched up his face and shook his head. He was overwhelmed now, Harbeer could see. "You're telling me that Amrit's gone missing and we're just going to sit and wait for her to return? What if she's been kidnapped, or worse?"

Harbeer's arms shot out. Only when Karam stepped between them did Harbeer realise that he meant to grab Gurdev by the shoulders and give him a firm shake. It used to steady Gurdev as a child when he became taken up by these sorts of theatrics. Kidnapping? Worse? Only Gurdev would voice such extreme possibilities. Not once had they crossed Harbeer's mind; he had exercised great restraint to keep such thoughts at bay. All he knew was that Amrit was not at home, where she was supposed to be. His imagination had stopped there because he was respectful to the superstitions about speculations becoming reality.

"You should know better than to say such things," Harbeer barked over Karam's shoulder. "Your wife." Karam gently steered him towards a chair into which he gladly sank, feeling the energy drain right out of him.

Gurdev's chest heaved unsteadily. He looked stricken. As Harbeer calmed down, he wanted to offer more soothing words, something to dull the sting of calling Gurdev's pregnant wife to mind. If Dalveer were in the room, she would chide him for not being gentler. She would go to Gurdev and calmly remind him that such thoughts invited misfortune during what was already a sensitive time for his wife. Anything an expectant parent speculated about somebody else's luck could impact their own child. This was what Harbeer meant but his words were always shards, his reminders turning quickly into insults. It was Dalveer's role to temper him but she was gone.

Gurdev

KARAM OFFERED TO drive Gurdev home in his new car and Gurdev declined quickly, saying that he would take the bus. "Nonsense," Karam scoffed. "I'll be passing your neighbourhood anyway." Gurdev insisted but somehow he ended up in the car anyway, listening to Karam's thinly veiled boasts about his new purchase. "It took a bite out of my salary," Karam said woefully. "But I just couldn't resist. There's nothing like being in control of where you're going."

"Yeah, must be nice," Gurdev said, vaguely. A pebble of jealousy over Karam's accomplishments had lodged itself in Gurdev's chest years ago. He concentrated on the view outside on the darkening island as they rolled out of the Naval Base—squat houses jammed together, patches of swampland, and the Chinese graveyard studded with plaques and flowers.

"The bus would have taken a very long time," Karam said. "How's your new place?"

"Good," Gurdev replied. "It's very orderly. The blocks are quite modern."

"Public housing," Karam pronounced, as if it were a novel term. He was able to afford a semi-detached house in Tiong Bahru, with a small garden. "It's a nice option in terms of pricing but I suppose everybody's flats will look the same."

"That won't happen," Gurdev said hastily. "We were assured there'd be plenty of renovation options. Banu and I have decorated the place. We've been looking at paint colours for the baby's room." Whenever he thought of Banu's pregnancy, the memory of his own mother's bulging belly—the tiniest version of Amrit curled inside—came to mind. Fifteen years ago: that was the last time he was near a woman in that state. He blinked away the thought, the sting of his earlier conflict with Father still fresh.

Outside, a man pushed a rickety cart down the street, his legs bowed. Patches of swampland shot past the windows as the car gained speed. These views did nothing to distract Gurdev, and soon the question was bursting from his lips. "Do you think somebody has taken Amrit?" Better to say it now than in the presence of his wife.

"I wouldn't worry," Karam said. "She's probably just gotten into some mischief. It can't be anything serious."

"I hope so," Gurdev said.

"She'll probably be back by tomorrow. Then when Narain returns, I'm going to give him a few days to settle in and then I'll have a talk with him," Karam said. "You know, remind him that he needs to protect his sister and set a good example while he's around."

"I could do that," Gurdev said, sitting up. "Don't trouble yourself."

"It's no trouble," Karam said.

"I think Narain needs to hear it from his own older brother," Gurdev said. "We're closer."

"That's the problem, though," Karam replied. "You aren't very assertive with him. Your father already asked me to sit him down, so I'm happy to do it."

"He asked you, did he? He made a special request that you discipline Narain and you couldn't help but say yes," Gurdev retorted.

Karam kept quiet until they arrived at a red light and then he turned to Gurdev. "You have to stop turning everything into a contest. Your father had Narain's and Amrit's best interests in mind when he approached me."

Best interests. Greater good. Karam had used these phrases when he proposed that Father send Narain off to America. Gurdev had been invited to the discussion as well but it had been a token gesture. None of his input seemed to count once Father was convinced that Narain could be reinvented.

Karam continued. "Some things should be reinforced. Narain's been taking advantage of his freedom over there. Your father showed me a letter that Narain sent home. It was full of opinions about how Singapore was never going to be successful. Very hurtful words, considering how hard we've all been working. Your father handed it to me and told me to give him a call, straighten him out. I had to think about what to say to Narain—it was disappointing, this letter. It showed he might be changing in all the wrong ways. Now Amrit's gone missing and he's been called back. He'll learn from this. I'll just have to remind him how hard his father is working to make sure he has a future."

Gurdev seethed silently, staring out the car window. Karam did not say anything until they pulled into the housing estate. A sprinkling of stars studded the night sky hidden behind the row of apartment blocks. "You sure you don't want to come in for a drink or anything?" Gurdev asked to be polite.

"No thanks," Karam replied. "I have an early morning tomorrow. I'm going in to the lab first thing."

"On a Sunday?"

"Scientific research doesn't just pause on the weekends, Gurdev."

"Right," Gurdev said. They said goodbye and Gurdev climbed out of the car. Conscious of his anger and the matching force he might use to shut the door behind him, Gurdev swung it gently—too gently. Rather than click, it thudded lightly, leaving their evening unfinished. Gurdev hastily opened the door and ducked his head in. "Sorry," he said.

"It's all right," Karam said with a smirk. "You're not used to having a car."

Gurdev gave the door a hard shove and walked quickly, hoping to abandon the implied insult floating on the kerb. As children they used to play-wrestle, a challenge in which Gurdev triumphed by instinctively knowing the exact combination of gentle pushes and harder shoves required to wear out his opponent. Then one day, Karam swiftly knocked him to the ground. Flat on his back, a stunned Gurdev realised that Karam must have studied his moves to anticipate them, proving that they were not nearly as complex as Gurdev had thought.

• • •

The next morning, a breeze passed through the open window and filled the limp curtains. Gurdev turned away from the sunlight to face his sleeping wife. A thin sheen of sweat

glistened on her cheeks and her breathing was a loud pronoun-
cement of the additional life she carried into her sleep.

Today was full of errands, all for the baby. Every
weekend had turned into a checklist. Gurdev wanted to
be prepared so that when the baby arrived, there would be
few surprises. It had already exerted so much control over
their lives. In the first months of Banu's pregnancy, he had
watched helplessly as nausea contorted her face and sent
her rushing to the toilet each morning. This was followed
by her refusal to eat laksa with him, claiming that the smell
of coconut had become sickeningly sweet, like wet rubbish.
There was also her constant tiredness, which led to a certain
unwillingness. Gurdev did not like to consider himself overly
demanding, but often when he tried to initiate something
in the bedroom—a stroking of her lower back, a kiss on
her shoulder—she heaved a sigh and turned away. In better
moods, she reminded Gurdev of the superstitions attached to
sex and pregnancy. "Our child could be born with all kinds
of problems," she said. "Do you want that?" She gave similar
warnings when he wanted to buy lottery tickets (tempting
fate at a vulnerable time) or eat pumpkin curry (making a
cut to a pumpkin would shorten a child's lifespan). As the
pregnancy continued, so did the list of superstitions. Every
simple consideration became governed by its potential for a
devastating consequence.

Gurdev swung his legs over the edge of the bed and
stepped out of the room. He rubbed the heaviness from his
eyes and flipped through the paint catalogues that Banu had
left on the dining table. Next to three squares of colour—
three shades of yellow almost indistinguishable from each

other—Banu had placed a check mark. He heard her house slippers swishing against the tiles as she approached. "Morning," she mumbled. "You want tea?"

Gurdev nodded. "The shop will open in about twenty minutes. I'll go and buy the paint for the baby's room. You're sure about these colours?"

Banu glanced at the catalogue. "Any one of those three."

"They're all very...yellow," he said. Their flat was a bursting testament to Banu's obsession with sunflowers. Over the short time they had been married, she had accumulated tablemats, framed paintings and ceramic replicas of bright bouquets.

"The man told me a bright colour would help to open up a small room," Banu said. "Really, Gurdev, does this have to be such a big deal? There are some more subdued yellows in the other catalogue but they're expensive."

"How expensive? This is our child's room. We'll have to face these walls every day. I'd rather pay a bit more..." He trailed off once he noticed the prices of the other palette squares. These colours were restrained and calm but three times the price.

The phone rang. Gurdev held onto the catalogue with one hand and picked up the receiver with the other. "Hello," he said absent-mindedly, as he did a series of calculations.

"Sat sri akal, Gurdev," Father said. Gurdev immediately dropped the catalogue on the table.

"Sat sri akal, Father. Any news?"

"Nothing," Father said. "I've informed some colleagues. They've been searching for Amrit since early this morning."

"The police?"

"Yes. Unfortunately, this is the only choice we have." His voice was heavy with reluctance. "If they find her, I'd rather she doesn't come home. Everybody in the community will know now."

"Please don't say that, Father," Gurdev said. "When they find her, we should be thankful she's home safe." Those ideas about Amrit's whereabouts danced in his consciousness: teenage boys with cigarettes; glasses clinking in coffee shops; a network of shadowy laneways where a girl could simply vanish. He shook them away, seeing Banu at the corner of his vision, placing two cups of tea on the dining table.

"I'm hoping Karam finds her first. If he does, at least my colleagues won't see the worst of Amrit. Who knows what she is up to? What if they find her with some boy?"

"Karam is looking for her as well?"

"Yes. I said so."

"No, actually you didn't." Gurdev saw the hostility in his voice reaching through the phone lines and twisting Father by the ear. Instantly, he wished he had not spoken this way.

"Am I supposed to feel bad for this?" Father demanded. "I forgot to mention it. You want me to say I'm sorry, is that it? There are enough problems going on in this house."

"I know. I understand," Gurdev said. He felt his face burning. "I'm very sorry."

Father continued. "This is the problem with you, Gurdev. Too emotional. You overreact to everything."

"I just thought that Karam was working this morning. Last night when he dropped me off at home, he said he had to go into the lab."

"Yes, well, he's taken time off from his work to help. God

knows I need someone in this family who can make my reputation a priority."

"I'm very sorry," Gurdev repeated. Banu gave him a questioning look. He turned away, showing her his back. Indignation gnawed at his insides. Father muttered that he would call with any further news and hung up before Gurdev had a chance to say goodbye.

"What was that about?" Banu asked. She rose from the table with difficulty as Gurdev marched past her to their bedroom. "Have they found Amrit?" she whispered. Gurdev pulled on a pair of trousers and grabbed his wallet. "I'm asking you a question," she called. He emerged from the bedroom to find her waddling towards the doorway, one palm resting on the mound of her enormous belly.

"I'm off to buy the paint."

"But your tea," she protested as he left. Father's taunts clawed through the doors of the lift and travelled along with Gurdev, despite his best attempts to dodge them.

The heartland neighbourhood woke lazily on Sundays, incongruous with his quick steps. He arrived at the entrance of the shop with ten minutes to spare. Next door, a stall-holder arranged cubes of watermelon, papaya and ice on a plate. He set it down on the counter and made a visor of his hand to block the sun's glare. Above this row of shops, an even stack of open corridors displayed the lives of Gurdev's many neighbours.

The paint shop owner arrived, tugging his singlet away from his chest. He was a thin Chinese man with greying hair. "So hot already," he lamented in Malay, looking up at the sky. Gurdev followed his gaze to a blazing sun and then stepped inside the shop where the air was just as stiff. The shopkeeper turned on a few small electric fans. From floor to ceiling, rows of shelves held cans of every colour.

"Okay, which one do you want?" the shopkeeper asked. "The yellow?"

"How do you know?"

The shopkeeper smiled. "Your wife came to get the catalogue. I've seen you walking together on some evenings."

"Can I see the catalogues again?" Gurdev asked. "We've changed our minds about the colours."

The shopkeeper obliged, bringing out copies of the catalogues Gurdev had pored through at home. Gurdev pushed away the familiar catalogues with newfound disdain for the gaudy, tasteless colours that lay inside them. "Here," he said to the shopkeeper. "The premium ones."

"Ah," the shopkeeper said, his face brightening. "Very nice." He disappeared behind the rows of shelves and emerged moments later with three cans. "Standard government flat room?" he asked. "You'll need three cans." Gurdev nodded and opened his wallet to pay quickly, before he changed his mind.

Leaving the shop with the cans of paint, Gurdev began to formulate his justification to Banu. *We should allow ourselves a small luxury*, he would say. *This is for our child*. He had already made the same case for the tall toy cupboard and the crib with the lacquer finish. He couldn't help wanting their child to be surrounded by wealth. The cans began to feel weightless as he headed home. He had decided years ago that he would excel at being a father when it came his turn— nothing would be out of reach for his children.

The sun beat against Gurdev's face. Beads of sweat sprouted

on his forehead and tickled his cheeks as they rolled down. He put the cans down and looked over his shoulder at the row of stalls in the distance, thinking about the cold fruits.

Then he saw her. Racing across the road, her loose rubber sandals slapping against the concrete. "Amrit," he said in disbelief. He squinted to track her movements. She was walking in the void deck of the government housing block across the road. An oversized red T-shirt hung from her slender frame and stretched to her knees. Gurdev kept his eyes fixed on her as he walked towards the road. The paint cans thumped against his knees. She stopped and looked around. Gurdev quickened his pace to catch up with her but then she headed off again, this time towards a courtyard. Panting and grunting, Gurdev followed. He pushed impatiently through a small crowd of boys gathered around a drain, taking turns to jab at something with a stick. She broke into a run and disappeared behind another block. "Amrit!" Gurdev yelled. The neighbourhood seemed to pause for a moment. Gurdev did not know if the burning in his cheeks was from the sun or from people's stares.

Gurdev slumped against a wall and shut his eyes. Specks of light danced against a blacked-out world. If asked to describe Amrit to the police, he would not know her actual dimensions. To him, she was small enough to fit in his pocket. Gurdev opened his eyes and looked in the direction of the blocks again but all he saw was blank pillars framing a white-hot day.

His heart still throbbing, he made his way back to the fruit vendor and ordered a plate. As he waited, the neighbourhood slowly came to life. Accordion doors rattled open and housewives struggled to haul the weight of their shopping trolleys.

"You again." Gurdev turned to see the paint shop owner waving. "Thought you went home already."

"Just having something to eat," Gurdev answered.

The shopkeeper glanced at the cans of paint at Gurdev's feet. "You're expecting a baby, right?"

Gurdev nodded. "Yeah," he said.

"You want a girl or a boy?"

"A boy," Gurdev said instantly.

The shopkeeper chuckled. "I asked your wife and she said, 'anything, as long as it's a healthy child'."

"She wants a boy as well," Gurdev said. 'She just doesn't think we should tell people what we prefer."

"Why?" the shopkeeper asked.

"It's tempting fate." An image of Amrit flashed into his mind. He turned to look over his shoulder, feeling an inexplicable tingle. When he turned back to face the shopkeeper, he was met with an apologetic look.

"I shouldn't have asked then," the shopkeeper said. "It's good not to talk too much. You have bad luck otherwise. The Chinese believe this, too."

"No, it's okay," Gurdev said. "We're just making sure we don't get ahead of ourselves."

The vendor arrived with Gurdev's plate. "I have a boy and a girl," the shopkeeper said. "Doesn't matter what the child is, you worry about them the same way. The night of the race riots—you remember that? I was very scared. My son spends so much time playing football in the sun that he has dark skin. People often think he's Malay. I thought, if this thing takes over our country, how do I convince anybody he's my child? The Chinese will attack him, thinking he's Malay. The Malays will attack him if he insists he is Chinese." The shopkeeper sighed and shook his head. Gurdev winced, recalling the riots. Father had worked overtime to help set up cordons. On the news, Gurdev had seen policemen lining the streets, their staunch expressions giving them an identical hardness.

The shopkeeper told Gurdev to enjoy his snack. He had to go back to work. "No rest, even on a Sunday," he said with a grin. "Good luck to you."

Gurdev thanked him. He finished eating his fruit and headed back to the flat, climbing against the intensifying heat of the day.

He noticed Banu pacing in the living room before he realised that the door and gate to the flat were wide open, as if to speed up his arrival. Banu looked up sharply and stopped walking when he entered. Her face was taut with pain.

"The baby," Gurdev said. "Banu, is it...is it time?" His mind was muddled. Didn't they have another month to go?

Banu shook her head. "Call your father. They've found Amrit." The words were spoken so quietly, Gurdev mistook them for something less newsworthy. "Call him," Banu repeated, this time with more force. Gurdev dropped the cans and made a beeline for the phone. As he waited for Father to pick up, Banu's grumbles faded in the background. "Why did you take so long? I got the call and then I had to wait here, worrying. I nearly went out to look for you—"

"Father, it's me. What happened? Is she okay? Where did you find her?" Gurdev was short of breath. In the background, he heard Karam scolding and Amrit crying.

"Somewhere in Khatib. A policeman found her and brought her straight here."

Khatib was on the other end of the island. That girl in the red shirt could not have been Amrit. "Has she explained what she was doing there?"

"I don't know," Father said. "I won't look at her. I will not speak to her." Gurdev remembered him saying the same thing about Narain. He glanced at Banu, who was looking at the paint cans curiously. A look of realisation crossed her face. She glared at him and stormed off into the bedroom.

"I'll come over," Gurdev said to Father.

Amrit

THERE WAS TOO much noise. Amrit felt it grinding into her bones. The normal level of noise in her home was acceptable—a low hum of electrical appliances, distant traffic, and thoughts. Yes, thoughts made noises too. Narain had pretended not to believe her when she told him, right before he left for America, that she could hear his thoughts. "What am I thinking right now?" he had asked.

"I can't actually hear each word you're thinking," she explained, "but I can hear something. Like a *zzzz* noise. And if it's loud it means you're thinking of something exciting." Narain had chuckled and told her she was full of rubbish. She knew he believed her, though.

Gurdev was here now, standing with his back to the wall. He kept on wincing and shifting his weight from one leg to another, as if he, too, were uncomfortable with the noise.

Amrit traced the source of the noise, following its invisible path until she reached Father. He was shouting and shaking his hands, gesturing to the ceiling and then down to the floor. She struggled to concentrate on what he was saying but his hands were so distracting. He struggled to be angry in English. She watched his mouth form the imperfect words and she heard the quaver in his voice before he gave up and began shouting in Punjabi. She still could not determine what he was saying. His face became blurry and out of focus and then, suddenly, it was painfully sharp in the late morning sun.

Amrit sat down on the sofa with her head in her hands. Everybody stood and watched, bewildered. She didn't know how to tell them to stop talking and let her think for just a moment. They wanted answers. Where had she been? With whom? What happened? Nothing she said would satisfy them. Her explanations didn't even seem plausible to her. They came to her as a whirlwind of nonsensical events, broken into pieces she didn't have the energy to re-assemble. There was school, the boys at the coffee shop, the street opera, a fire, a low ditch, and a mattress soaked in sweat. She remembered the burn of whiskey in her throat, and the hand that tipped the bottle gently towards her lips, then the sensation of her body adapting to things it had never experienced before. She felt a soreness in her arms and legs, and vaguely remembered running. "Wait, wait. I can explain," she heard herself saying. Her voice was still miles away.

· · ·

The boys liked to feel her ribs. They asked first, coyly reaching towards her torso with their long fingers and then asking, "Can?" And if she said, *yes, can,* then they shot forwards, tracing their hands along her T-shirt. She let out a giggle or a sigh as they felt the bump of each bone and pressed into the hollow spaces between them. Sometimes it made her wince because there were too many hands and she could not connect them to the boys. At other times, she wanted to lie back and let them slip their hands under her T-shirt and get closer and closer to her bones.

"What if your father saw us?" The boy with the tattoo whispered to her the first time she let him touch her under her shirt. He was Jaya, the first of four boys that she'd selected. *Yes, I choose you. I have a choice*, she'd said between fits of uncontrollable giggles. She couldn't stop her laughter even though she couldn't explain what was so funny. His fingers were cold as he spider-walked them across her belly. She felt a surge; she wanted all of the boys now, all of their cold spidery fingers. Jaya asked the question again and she shrugged him off.

"My father doesn't come here," she said, leaning against the wall. A protruding pipe dug into her back so she shifted before she closed her eyes. Satisfied with her answer, Jaya proceeded with his hands. His low breathing matched the guttural noise that rose from somewhere deep inside Amrit.

Her family probably believed she had run away just to be with boys. "She's impatient," they were thinking. The disgust in their thoughts produced a thick hum like flies around a clogged drain. "She just can't wait till she's married." Amrit could not fault them. The boys were the first thing that entered her mind as well. It was easiest to blame them and her temptation towards them. There were girls who could not wait. They were the stars of cautionary tales: pregnant-before-getting-married, seen-smoking-cigarettes, dancing-in-discos-in-short-skirts, giggling-with-boys-all-the-time. Itchy girls. Amrit's family knew she was one of them now. She could not escape their judgement;

she wanted everything she was not supposed to want, badly. She wanted to talk loudly when there was silence, to sob uncontrollably at the slightest grievance. How much of her life had Amrit already wasted on practising restraint? Too much, she decided. As the youngest child, there were so many rules that often became apparent only when they were broken. She would no longer be shushed and scolded for being wrong. As far as Amrit was concerned, there was nothing wrong with what she said and did. She heard a sudden and urgent calling to make up for those lost indulgences. She would devour all those grown-up novels she had not been allowed to read, and repeat all the dirty jokes she had been discouraged from hearing in the first place. She would stand in the sun and let it bake her fair skin; she would eat all the sugary, fattening cakes and sweets she wanted. She would not allow any more censorship in her life. It was an infinite task, to go back in time and collect these excesses, but she was confident she would manage.

It had not begun with the boys, though they looked culpable with their pierced ears and their stale cigarette breath. They were school dropouts who lingered on street corners and coffee shops and planned nothing for the long stretch of days ahead of them. They tried catching girls' attention by whistling or saying crude things. They'd been doing that to all the girls since they started secondary school, even though the pinafore tops the girls wore were tailored with stiff pleats to camouflage their growing breasts. No girl responded to those good-for-nothings unless she was desperate; their female teachers warned them against making eye contact. A few teachers made it a point to go outside and shoo the boys away as if they were flies swarming around a drain. Mr Rahman, Amrit's science teacher, was one of these teachers, and all the girls fell in love with him for being their protector. Amrit loved him too—she loved everyone, all the men, all the boys. It sickened and delighted her, this overwhelming love that brought her to shivers.

Narain would probably think this was all his fault. One night, he had seen her sneaking out to meet the boys, and he had kept it a secret. By that time, many things were happening that Amrit could not explain. The buzzing, as though her mind was a radio with its dial set between stations. She could go three days on very little sleep because other people's thoughts filled her mind. They had to be other people's thoughts—they were too complicated and far-fetched to be her own. Suddenly, she knew everything there was to know about the colour green because questions and theories and wild proclamations consumed her, and all of them had to do with greenness: green peas, green beans, electric green, lizard green, watercolour paint green, stale green. Then the same thing happened with crockery—Amrit had a sudden awareness of a range of dishware brands and she considered knocking on all the doors in her neighborhood, recommending better products to the housewives who used those outdated wooden spoons and shineless plates. Overhearing two classmates discussing a physics test one afternoon, Amrit wondered why on earth there was a subject studying wheels, and then for days, she could not stop seeing patterns of spinning wheels in her surroundings. The wheel patterns populated her vision, making her dizzy and breathless.

Exams approached but Amrit could commit no facts to memory. Every word that entered her mind produced a string of other thoughts so brilliant and distracting that it wasn't necessary to continue reading her textbooks. They were only slowing her down. She remembered the delirious way she befriended the boys; she was thrilled to sit with them in the coffee shops. They told jokes that made her sides ache from laughter, although she struggled to remember them immediately afterwards. As Amrit sat on their laps and sipped the beers they brought her, she was certain that this was what her life was supposed to be. Outside the confines of her house, she was not the protected youngest daughter. She was clever and articulate here—she told stories that captivated the boys, and when they teased her, she had the quickest retorts.

The excitement faded when the thoughts multiplied at too quick a rate for her to control. They branched off into hundreds of streams that burst through her mind. Wide awake and muttering to herself one night, Amrit was aware that something was not right. Too much schoolwork, she told herself. Too much schoolwork and too little sleep. But when she shut her eyes and forced herself to sleep, the thoughts shook her out of bed and forced her to pay attention. They became voices. She did not tell Father about this growing problem. He would panic and make her stay in bed, when this was the last thing she wanted. The house felt unbearably crowded with the cacophony of thoughts and ideas in Amrit's mind.

One day at school she locked herself in the toilets and stayed in the cubicle for two hours because she was certain that the other girls were talking about her. They were saying she was not the right height for their school, and she believed them—she was too lanky. She would die here. The thought made her shake so badly she looked like she was doing a dance. When she finally emerged and told the teacher she was ill and wanted to go home, her underpants felt slightly damp. She had wet herself and all the girls—even the ones who wanted her to die—were wide-eyed with sympathy. How could she explain this to her family? What would she tell them? They did not see her as somebody who could have problems beyond those they had already anticipated.

Another day she was sitting with the boys and she told them her idea for a business. "I can cut down all the trees— no, listen—I can take a parang, I can cut down all the trees in Singapore and I'll sell them to people who don't have trees in their countries. Everybody needs trees to survive. Look at the oxygen levels and you'll understand." She bit her lip to keep it from trembling with excitement. Something surged through her and made her want to leap on top of the table and dance. "If you help me, all of you will be millionaires. Think about it. All the windows and people will see the trees out of them and they will be able to make coffins and shoes and even car sellers will need to buy trees." The boys broke out in raucous laughter. They asked her how much beer she'd drunk. "Not that much, lah," she said, her eyes darting from one boy to the next. She was hungry for each of them. Another current ran through her, this one so powerful it straightened her spine and made her skin taut. She could have them all at the same time and it still wouldn't be enough. One night in the shower she had pressed the nozzle against her breasts. Her nipples grew hard; they swelled and screamed. She gasped and clutched her own skin, collapsing against the slippery walls. The next time, she brought the nozzle lower slowly, with more control, and she bit gently into her wrist. The boys' faces flickered and alternated in her mind until she was out of breath, and when she closed her eyes, she believed they must have been there with her. *Disgusting*, she chided herself. "Sick," she said aloud, trying to fill her body with remorse, but there was no space for anything else besides a tearing hunger for somebody—everybody—to touch her.

School became a dull pastime. She was there all day but all she could think about was the boys and the drinks they poured for her. During maths class one day, Ming Ni asked if she could borrow her ruler. Amrit passed it to her and then told her she could keep it. "I have millions of those. I could buy millions more," she bragged, whipping out her purse to reveal the money the boys had given her. Each boy had paid her a dollar. "For the pleasure of your company," one boy said. The others had laughed wildly. In another class, she was assigned to do a project with a group of students and she appointed herself leader. Their ideas were plain and boring and she told them so. "You're not seeing the real thing," she insisted, taking their bewildered faces as proof. She drew convoluted diagrams explaining her concepts. "Listen, I know this is right. You can trust me. If you all just put your minds to it, you'd get perfect scores like mine. Remember, I always get top scores because of what's up here," she said, tapping the forehead of the girl across from her, who flinched.

That night, ideas overwhelmed Amrit. She paced her room and jotted them down, her wrists hurting from the speed of her movements. *Go back. If you add the two together, you have another phase, and the quality is higher. For the project, mix two chemicals and test the point where they combust. Test all of the points, for all of the explosions, and then do it again.* Somewhere along the way, she realised she had not spoken to Narain, and although Father had warned her that overseas phone calls were very expensive and only for emergencies, she searched the family telephone directory for Narain's phone number in America and dialled. Waiting for the operator to connect her, Amrit flipped impatiently through the diary and stopped on the calendar page. January. It was winter in Iowa, and somewhere, Narain must be walking around in those thick-soled shoes she had placed in the other suitcase. He did not answer the phone but she stayed on until she could hear the buzzing of his thoughts, loud and persistent. Although there was a lot Amrit wanted to tell Narain, everything overlapped in her mind and she was speechless. After hanging up, she paced her room some more and finished her science workbook. *I'm too smart for this school, for this country. I could get all those bloody government scholarships, they're so easy*, she thought smugly as she scrawled answers in writing she later wouldn't recognise.

• • •

The day before she disappeared, Amrit skipped the Friday assembly at school and walked to the coffee shop. The boys nudged each other and whispered as she approached. "Saying what?" she challenged them.

"Nothing, nothing, sit," said the tall one with the gold

chain. He ordered her some breakfast and tea. A girl wearing a different school uniform sat on his friend's lap. Every now and then he tickled her and she squealed and twisted like a worm. Her laughter reminded Amrit of her own—loud and uninhibited. She watched the boy's hand disappearing into the pleats of the girl's skirt. An itch started somewhere in Amrit's belly and it spread like fire across her body as the boy buried his face into the girl's neck, making her giggle.

"I'm Seema," the girl said when she finally slipped off the boy's lap. "Amrit, right?"

"Yeah."

The girl took in Amrit's uniform. "I think you'll be late for school," she said. There was something unkind in her tone.

"Yeah, I'm late," Amrit said. She picked up her bag and made a hasty exit. Morning lights crept across the sky, making bold streaks of gold on top of the shop roofs. In the lane that Amrit used as a short cut, an old lady with a bent body threw a pail of water, washing lettuce leaves and hollow chicken bones into the shallow gutter.

Latecomers never had trouble sneaking into school since construction began at the back of the campus. Workers flowed freely through the open gates and said nothing if the occasional student did the same. Amrit felt the gazes of the men, warm against her bare limbs. She smiled coyly at them as she slipped into the school and walked around the ditch they were digging for a pond. It was a deep and wide crater in the middle of the ground, the borders protected by workers and their shovels. A strong vision shot into her mind. She was charging past the men and throwing herself inside. She was sinking far and dissolving into the soil. The vision was so clear she thought it was real, and for a moment she could taste the rich tangy earth in her mouth and feel her bones becoming pliant as they mixed with the rest of the earth.

"Amrit, did you just arrive?" She spun around to see Mr Rahman, her Science teacher.

"No," she lied, eyeing the open gate. "I was looking for something. I left something here."

Mr Rahman didn't look like he believed her. "Amrit, I must talk to you about something." He led her to a row of benches facing a copse of trees and shrubs. The decorated roof of a small Buddhist temple in the distance poked out behind the greenery. "You haven't been doing well lately," he said.

Amrit shook her head. "No, no, I'm fine."

"Your exam results, Amrit. I compared them with last semester's results. Shocking difference. I'm very surprised with your attitude. You used to be a top student."

"I'm still a top student," Amrit blurted. "Ask anybody."

"You failed everything," Mr Rahman said. He winced as he delivered the news, as though it hurt him more. "Every single subject. I checked with all of your other teachers and they all said the same thing. They don't know what's gotten into you."

"Nothing," Amrit insisted. "Check my exam results again. They're fine. I'm doing better than last year. Look." She unzipped her bag and produced her science workbook. "Just see, I did all of the work last night. I finished it ahead of time." Electricity surged through her. She wanted to burst out laughing. Which fool had miscalculated her exam results?

"There's something else I'd like to talk to you about." Mr Rahman said as he accepted her workbook. He hesitated. "Some of the teachers have seen you mixing with…bad company. Those guys who hang around coffee shops, they're not the types of people…" he faltered here, and changed tactics. "Amrit, you could go to university, do you know that? You have the brains. To see this kind of thing happening, it's very upsetting. There is time to meet boys later. Concentrate on your studies first." He opened the book and flipped through the pages as if they would hold the next part of his script. Amrit was thrilled. Nothing he said had bothered or embarrassed her. The sun glinted off the temple rooftop and the surrounding greenery, making all of it painfully bright to Amrit.

Mr Rahman handed the science workbook back to Amrit. "Buy a new one, and don't bother handing in your work to me until you're serious about it again," he told her curtly. "I'll see you in class this afternoon." He marched off. Amrit flipped through the pages. They were soaked with blue pen ink. Words overlapped each other, just as they had in her mind. They didn't make much sense but she couldn't recall what she had been thinking as she filled the entire book. She only remembered the emptiness of the night, and how, when she ran out of pages, she wanted to write across the walls, scrawl across the sidewalks and trees, and cover the blackboard sky.

After school that day, Amrit went straight to the coffee shop and told the boys about Mr Rahman. "He said, those boys are bad company. Concentrate on your studies. What a bastard."

The boys laughed. Seema did as well. She looked at Amrit admiringly as Amrit went on about how pointless everything in school was. "It's all so bloody boring, man. Who cares?"

As she talked, Jaya placed his hand on her knee. He was confident about it, raising it a few inches and then exploring under her skirt as she chatted. The other boys were amused. Even Seema saw what was going on. She rolled her eyes at the boys and got up to buy more cigarettes. When she was out of earshot, one of the boys leaned over and asked, "Does Amrit want to go behind?" Behind was the empty alley in the back of the coffee shop. She smiled and got up. "Come," she said simply. All five of them followed.

It was quicker than she imagined it would be. Against damp and rough concrete, Amrit leaned and did everything the boys wanted her to do. "Relax," each one whispered when it was his turn. The others watched and waited. One left and returned with a bottle of whiskey. "Give her this," he said. "She'll like the taste." She noticed vaguely that they spoke as if she wasn't there at all. She concentrated on the fire in her throat as the third boy pushed himself into her. The taste of sweat, the smell of whiskey, the searing pain of being split in half—she imagined all of it collecting in her throat so that she could scream it out later. She remembered the empty pond and how tangy and rich the earth had smelled; she imagined how the dirt would sink beneath her knees, how small sticks and rocks would lodge themselves in her hair. She pictured the workers standing on the edges and filling in the water while she was still at the very bottom.

• • •

This was where Amrit's mind began to go blank. She clearly remembered returning home and stuffing some clothes into her schoolbag. Then she had returned to the coffee shop to meet Jaya and that's where her memories became shards: pieces of conversation; a flood of light; his mother entering the room at dawn and staring at her, slack-jawed, before walking out to make tea. She remembered the repetitive croons of birds and wondering if they ever tired of singing the same song. She remembered the pounding in her head and the strange appearance of her flattened clothes on the floor, as if she had melted and dissolved into the floorboards, leaving a shell of thin fabric. She remembered growing frustrated with Jaya when he refused to wake up, and him picking her up and pushing her down on the bed again after she tried to scare him by threatening to call the police. "My father is a policeman. I'll tell him you kidnapped me," she said desperately.

"Shut up, shut up," he said roughly, before rising and leaving the room. He returned with water and a kind smile. "How do you feel, Amrit?" he asked, tracing her lips with his fingers. She waited for him to tell her he still loved her— wasn't that the point of all of this? He said nothing, and she ran out of his house.

Afterwards, she wandered. She walked through Singapore, hiding her face in her hands when she saw other Punjabis. She slipped into underground pedestrian tunnels and emerged on the other side of the street. She lingered at a night market, squatting with the vendors and admiring their goods. There were rows of shallow wooden trays filled with plugs, toy telephones, assorted batteries, nail clippers, rubber balls and wooden clothes pegs. She wandered away from the stalls when the vendors grew suspicious of her. The sweet, smoky smell of roasted chestnuts clung to her hair as she walked through darkened neighbourhoods. The only lights visible were in the small, square windows. She could not stop walking, even when she was hungry; she had to keep going. She breathed in the island air, fresh and thick with dampness. Had it rained just moments ago? Was it raining now? She didn't know. She stopped when one vendor called out to her. "Pretty girl. You can wear pretty jewellery," he said. She crouched at the velvet mat on which hundreds of little gemstones shimmered in the waning daylight. He pointed to each stone and explained its particular promise: "This one will make you strong. This one will help you in business." When she opened her mouth to haggle, muddled numbers and made-up currencies came out. They tumbled into the space between them, bewildering the vendor, who quickly began to search for other customers.

She walked into a crowd standing near a makeshift stage on an open field. A travelling Chinese opera troupe was performing. The actors' faces were painted white, their features ghastly and exaggerated—long chins, severe cheekbones, eyebrows drawn to sharp peaks. Their long robes brushed the stage as they made their sweeping gestures and wailed along with the plucking music. She wanted to join them. She opened her mouth and sang, but her song matched theirs so perfectly, nobody heard.

Amrit did not think about going home. Home was miles and miles away now, after what she had done. *I am different now.* They would see it on her face; they would smell it on her. She bought food and vomited later, when she remembered how she had afforded it. She lay in the hollow cavity of a drain when it became dark, amazed that time was passing so quickly. Her thoughts began to speed up again, invading her body and making it difficult to be coherent. The occasional passersby asked her what she was doing sitting in a drain and where she was from but her responses left them confused and they edged away nervously.

"Don't you know how worried your family is?" the policeman who eventually found her had scolded as he roughly led her into his car. She did not want to think about her family.

She wanted to make her family disappear now, too. They were staring, waiting for an answer that she could not provide. Father moved towards her, then shook his head and retreated to his bedroom. In a small voice, Amrit heard herself ask for a glass of water. Nobody moved, then Gurdev went into the kitchen and brought one out for her. She placed the tip of the glass on her parched lips, letting the water soothe them. She decided that they could keep on waiting. She could sip the water slowly while the seconds and minutes and hours shed away.

PART II
1977

Father

NOTICE OF his father's condition came by telephone one evening. Harbeer heard the strained voice of Rabinder, a distant cousin in Punjab, mumbling the details of Papa's weakening heart. He knew that any matter necessitating a long-distance phone call was grave. Rabinder made every effort to use euphemisms in describing Papa's illness and the doctor's diagnosis but Harbeer knew that his father would die soon.

He thanked Rabinder and returned to his bedroom to retrieve two pillows and a sheet. The next telephone call from India might come at an odd hour and he couldn't miss it so he set up the rattan sofa as a bed. Each night as he tried to fall asleep, he felt the immovable weight of his father's impending death, as if time was also running out for him. He ached to speak to Papa but how was that possible? Even if Papa was conscious, it would be disrespectful to a dying man to hold a phone to his ear and compel him to speak. Harbeer had always known such a time would come. It was the migrant's sacrifice—a distance so vast it seemed immeasurable. For comfort, he sought the image that had always soothed him—his father's lush farmland in Punjab. Instantly, his square eighteenth-storey flat was transformed, with wild stalks of green grass, and cattle roaming between clouds of golden dust.

One night as he tried to sleep, Dalveer came in for a secret visit. When he, Amrit and Narain had first moved into this flat two years ago, he thought it would be the end of Dalveer's appearances. She would not favour the tall concrete building, and discreet entrances would be impossible without a back door. These government housing blocks were built to prevent secrets. At dusk, the fluorescent lamps in the hallways blinked on and stairwells and corridors were exposed. Yet Dalveer's visits continued. She entered through the front door late at night, knowing that Harbeer did not lock it in case Amrit returned without her key.

When Dalveer sat down next to him, the stench of dirt and sweat that clung to her clothes drifted through the flat. She must have been searching for cures for Amrit again. This had become Dalveer's mission since it had occurred to her that Amrit was possessed by a stubborn and tenacious spirit. He pretended to share her faith in the supernatural only because he had run out of explanations for Amrit's behaviour. On those evenings, Dalveer had blended an old-fashioned potion—turmeric, fennel seeds, mashed red dates and holy water from the temple. Then she instructed Harbeer to visit Amrit while she was sleeping, stand over her and chant a prayer, sprinkling the liquid over her mattress. She had collected Amrit's hair from the bathroom sink and wrapped it in a small package with seeds and sticks, which she handed to Harbeer. Together, they had said prayers before going outside during a rainstorm. He had twisted the package into the earth, feeling Amrit's curse lifting as his fingers sank. Once, Dalveer was even bold enough to go to Amrit's door while she slept, and listen to her unsteady breathing. Afterwards, she had mixed holy water and mint leaves into her morning tea and left Harbeer with detailed instructions. That day, Amrit did not wake till noon, and while Harbeer was in his room, writing his letters, she left the flat and did not come back for three days. After that day, Harbeer ordered Dalveer to stop with her cures, but, of course, she defied him and searched for them in secret.

Now, Harbeer waited for Dalveer to settle into the flat and then he told her that his father was dying. Her face softened with sympathy and she reached out to stroke his hand. At her touch, he began to weep. Within moments, he was wiping the tears away, embarrassed at his grief. Dalveer stayed at his side until he finished crying and then she let herself out of the flat as swiftly as she had entered. He remembered how, when they were first married, she would trace the rungs of his spine with her fingers as he fell asleep. He always thought this was something she had learned to do, some soothing massage her mother had passed down to her, until he turned to her one night and saw on her moonlit face an expression of pure wonder. He had realised only then that he was married to a child; he was just eighteen and she, fifteen.

The phone rang the following night when Harbeer was fast asleep.

"He has passed," Rabinder told him. A respectful pause, and then, "You will receive the land papers in the mail. He left everything to you."

Long distance phone calls, Harbeer had to remember, were still expensive in the village. Telephone connections from India were poor, so any news or information had to be crammed into one conversation. Had there been an upcoming wedding in the family, it would have been announced in the same breath as the death. Nevertheless, both announcements arriving at once gave Harbeer the sensation of his limbs being pulled in opposite directions—the grief of his father's passing and the joy of his new wealth. He cleared the living room methodically, picking up the pillows and folding the sheets before he changed his mind and decided to strip them all and put them in the wash. A plump moon dangled low in the window like a pendant. Harbeer settled at his desk with a pad and a pen. He wrote the estimated amount of the land's worth at the top of the page and then listed his children's names in a column on the left: Gurdev, Narain, Amrit, and then he wrote Karam's name. Wasn't it only fair that Karam received some of the money as well? He would receive the same amount as Gurdev, Harbeer decided.

He stared at Narain's name. The boy had yet to pay him back for the years of tuition spent on that university education in Iowa—and for what? He had graduated three years ago and he had a job as a civil engineer with a private company, but Harbeer suspected his habits had not changed. Lately, he had been coming home late in the evenings, stinking of sweat, with no apologies or explanations as to his whereabouts. Sometimes Harbeer wanted to ask Narain whether his stay in America had done him any good—had the independence of living in a new country turned him into a man? But somehow Harbeer knew Narain's answer and he couldn't bear to hear it. Harbeer expected a bigger payback than just the tuition money: Narain's job was to protect the family's reputation by making sure that Amrit stayed on the right path. Six years had passed now since Amrit's first disappearance and Narain had failed in these responsibilities as well. Amrit drank whiskey with strange, classless men. She had no qualifications. She was not able to hold down a job.

Harbeer decided he would give Narain a token amount and no more. He looked over the figures again and, dissatisfied, crossed them out and started over, applying a more benevolent logic this time. Perhaps Narain should get a higher amount as an incentive? Maybe Gurdev deserved all the money because he had two small children? Harbeer grumbled softly to himself and pictured his father's land scarred and chopped into uneven pieces. He divided the sum again, this time in equal parts for all of his children. The numbers still didn't look satisfactory. Why should Gurdev get as much as Karam? Why should Amrit get any at all? He flung the pen across the room with a frustrated cry.

Outside, he heard Amrit's bedroom door creak open and her footsteps shuffling across the tiles. She must have returned while he was asleep, just before the phone call. She stopped at his door. "Are you okay?" she asked. Harbeer recalled an incident a couple of years ago when Amrit came home late, stinking of beer, and passed out on her bed. He had towered over her limp body and slipped off his belt in a rage, ready to teach her a lesson and set her straight. He raised his arm high above his head but when he brought it down, the belt buckle clanged against the bedpost, missing Amrit's body and waking her with a start. She stared at him, frightened, only enraging him further. He tried to hit her again but the belt slipped from his grip and wiggled to the floor like a fish.

"It's nothing," he called back when he saw the doorknob turning. "No need to come in here." He stared down at the sheet, at the numbers. Next to Amrit's name, there was a blank. What portion did the girl deserve? Any amount would look like a reward when all she brought him was grief. Things were being said about Amrit. At every turn, Harbeer heard jokes about his name and reputation. The early evening breeze carried the neighbours' collective disapproval into his thoughts. The announcer on the neighbour's radio seemed to broadcast Amrit's latest crime and the unfit parenting that prompted her to it. The whole world was talking about Amrit.

"Can I bring you something? A hot drink?" Amrit asked from outside his door. Harbeer shut his eyes to banish her voice. Why did she show her concern in gestures like this but then did so much to shame him? He did not answer and eventually she wandered away, her shadow clearing in the gap beneath the door.

Harbeer could only think of one possibility for Amrit's future. The idea had been brewing for some years now but each time he brought it up with Dalveer, she refused and begged him to let her try more remedies first. He knew why she was so opposed to an arranged marriage for Amrit—he saw the faint disgust in her eyes, recalling that tearing, piggish thing that men enjoyed and women tolerated. Years after they were married, Dalveer told him that her own mother had prepared her for marriage only by alluding to this act, which was a necessary routine to drive the silliness out of a girl and turn her into a wife. Marriage was a proven cure. For a particular type of girl, it showed her that there was no joy in the act, only a routine consideration of her husband's needs. Harbeer considered the changes in his own temperament after he got married. "If you had stayed," he once told Dalveer, "I might have become an even better man."

Dalveer was not here to oppose his decision now. He looked at the pad and sprang from his seat to pace the room, allowing his idea to gain momentum. Yes, yes, yes, he thought excitedly. He searched the floor for his pen and brought it to his lips for luck before letting it touch the pad. Next to Amrit's name, he fiercely scribbled the names that came to mind.

Gurdev

AT FIVE O'CLOCK, Gurdev completed his ritual of rearranging the items on his desk. On a piece of paper, he had written down the name of the bar Karam had wanted to meet in. The last time they caught up, Karam had just been shortlisted for a position with the Ministry of Health's committee for the eradication of malaria. "They say that one of the defining elements of a developed country is an absence of infectious diseases like malaria. I'd be making history," Karam had boasted. Today, Karam wanted to introduce Gurdev to his new fiancée.

The bar in the city was crowded when Gurdev arrived. He pushed through the throngs of office workers holding glasses in their hands. Chatter rose and shot through the smoky air. A firm hand clapped him on the shoulder. Gurdev turned to see Karam grinning. They patted each other on the back, their greeting restricted by space. "Sona, this is my cousin, Gurdev." Karam said, gesturing to a fair-skinned woman with her hair pulled back, revealing a long, slender neck.

"Very nice to finally meet you."

"Yes, you too," Sona said.

"I'm going to go order drinks at the bar," Karam said. "Is Tiger beer okay with you?"

"Yeah, that's fine," Gurdev said.

"Glass of white wine," Sona said. Gurdev looked at her in surprise. Although the bar was packed with customers of both sexes, he had never seen a Punjabi woman order a drink.

Karam chuckled. "Relax, Gurdev. I told you, this girl is different. She's a connoisseur."

Gurdev did not know what that word meant but he laughed along.

"You're trying something different this time," Karam told Sona before heading to the bar.

"So, congratulations on the engagement," Gurdev said.

"Thank you," she said. "It's all happening so quickly now."

"Chaos," Gurdev said, settling into his seat. "That's what I remember. There was so much chaos leading up to it. The day itself is a total blur. I look back at the photographs now and I wonder, did all of this really happen?"

Sona's laughter was delicate. "I've heard it's like that. You should at least remember what the bride looked like, though. That's the most important thing."

"Of course." He recalled Banu's profile, obscured behind the jewelled hem of her red dubatta, the intricate swirls on her hennaed hand containing a code to decipher. In the evening, he had found his name woven into the patterns. The searching had given them an excuse to touch.

"Karam says you have your hands full with your kids," she said.

"Yes," Gurdev said. "Two girls. Kiran is six and Simran is five." He pulled out his wallet to show her their photos.

Karam arrived back at the table. "Ah, the girls." He placed the drinks down. "How's the school thing going?" Karam turned to Sona. "Gurdev's trying to get his daughters into

Sacred Heart Primary. They just opened a branch of the school in his neighbourhood."

"My girls go to a neighbourhood school now," Gurdev explained. "Of course, I'd rather send them to a mission school, like Sacred Heart. The Prime Minister's wife went there."

"Those mission schools have strong standards," Sona agreed. "The girls will speak better English."

"Exactly," Gurdev said. "But it's nearly impossible to transfer them. We've tried everything. We've gone through the appeals process, we've shown them documentation to show how close we live to the school. The waiting list is full."

"They might just let the girls in based on your desperation," Karam joked.

Gurdev felt his muscles tense but before he could come up with a retort, Sona interjected. "I wouldn't call it desperation—it's perseverance."

"Gurdev will need some financial help. What are the fees like?" Karam asked.

"They're not terribly expensive compared to the government schools," Gurdev replied.

"Yes, but think about all the other costs," Karam said. "Ballet lessons, tuition, third language classes. It adds up. Those schools don't just want to churn out smart children. They want to make sure they can do everything."

"Those things are not compulsory," Sona said.

"No, but think about it. Every other kid at the school will be doing those things."

"We can figure it out," Gurdev said dismissively, but in truth, he had started to panic over these additional costs already.

Sona smiled sympathetically. "My brother and his wife are thinking about migrating to Australia. Their kids will have a better chance in a bigger country."

"I don't buy into that mentality," Karam declared. "It's cowardly." Gurdev noticed the indignation on Sona's face. "What is he teaching his children by quitting and moving to a new place because he doesn't want them to experience some rigour and healthy competition?"

"He's not quitting," Sona said stiffly. "He'd just rather see them in a school system where they are allowed to make mistakes. Singapore is tiny. Our schools are unforgiving of errors."

"It's the best way to weed out the weaker ones," Karam argued. "As you said, we're a small nation. We can't afford errors."

Amrit barrelled into Gurdev's consciousness, bringing her past several years' worth of unforgivable mistakes. She had stopped going to school after failing her exams twice. Father sent her to secretarial school but she skipped classes to linger in coffee shops and back lanes with strange men. Gurdev wished Karam were wrong about errors, but Amrit's failures had begun to trail her. Every potential employer wanted to know her exam results, even for the most menial jobs. When she produced her scant portfolio of certificates, they turned her away. For the past month, she had been working as a receptionist in an office building nearby but Gurdev suspected that this too would be short-lived, as she often called in sick or showed up late, as she had with all of her jobs, leaving her bosses and colleagues frustrated with her inconsistent work.

"Hey, how's your father doing?" Karam asked.

"He's all right. You know him—he won't talk about his father's death," Gurdev said. "I'm supposed to go over there one of these days."

"Has he spoken to you about the land money? He's going to have a chat with each of us about it."

Gurdev nearly choked on his beer. "With you too?"

"Well, it's my grandfather's property, isn't it? Why not?" Karam demanded. Sona shifted uncomfortably and gave Karam's sleeve a tug. "No," Karam said, shaking her away. "I don't care if this isn't the place for it." He turned back to Gurdev. "I'm entitled to my share of whatever land money was left behind."

It felt as if all the noise from the bar evaporated in an instant. Gurdev could see nothing but his cousin's determined face. "Karam, I have a family to raise. You just said it yourself; I have added costs to bear. I thought you were getting some big position with the Ministry of Health—is that not enough of a payrise for you?"

A taut silence fell over the table. Karam cleared his throat. "Sona, did you want a glass of water? You're not enjoying that wine, I know."

"Yes, please," she said. Karam nodded and headed towards the bar again. Gurdev watched small groups of people part naturally to let him through.

"He's very sensitive about it," Sona informed Gurdev, drawing his attention back to her. "He didn't get the job."

"What happened?" Gurdev couldn't help the tone of glee creeping into his voice.

"The other scientist was from London. Benjamin Polley.

He's not nearly as qualified as Karam but he's British. That's the mindset these days. The government didn't just want a leading scientist—they wanted a poster boy. An Indian man with a turban wasn't going to do it for them. Better to have somebody with yellow hair and blue eyes, just like our founders themselves. It becomes more convincing to the rest of the world that we're on the fast track to civilisation. It's for the prestige."

Gurdev noticed the way she said that last word, softly stretching out the *zhhh* sound. "You went to a mission school yourself, didn't you?"

Sona blushed. "Yes."

"It's your pronunciation," he said.

The redness in her cheeks spread. "I did a lot of reading when I was growing up. It was the ultimate escape. Singapore was so unstable then. One day it was part of Malaysia, the next day we were on our own. It felt like the ground was always shaky. I found a lot of comfort in the classics. They were set in well-established places and they had survived over the centuries and been reprinted." She paused and smiled. "I guess I've encouraged this fascination with the British as much as anyone else."

"I don't see why Karam's making such a big deal out of it," Gurdev said. "He's accomplished so much in his career already. He'll have a second chance."

"That's exactly what I said to him." Sona tossed a look over her shoulder. Karam was still standing at the bar. She turned back to Gurdev and leaned closer, dropping her voice. "He was just shattered. He wouldn't even talk to me about it."

"You're telling me, though," Gurdev pointed out. "Won't

he be upset with you?"

Sona pulled back her shoulders and gave a shrug. "People come to know eventually. I keep trying to tell Karam this. When your father first found out about his father's death, Karam wanted to go over to his place to see how he was doing, but he was afraid your father would ask him about the position. Karam just couldn't face him."

Moments later, Karam returned with a glass of water. He placed it in front of Sona and whispered something in her ear; a small, secret smile blossomed on her face. Karam turned to Gurdev and extended his hand. "I haven't been myself lately," he said. "I must apologise."

"That's okay," Gurdev said, shaking Karam's hand. He glanced at Sona but her gaze darted away as if their conversation hadn't happened.

•   •   •

Making his way up the stairs of his building, Gurdev heard the girls before he saw them. The door of the flat was open and their giggles and eruptions of chatter burst through the corridor. Reaching the threshold, he felt the echoes of their voices ricocheting across the walls. "Daddy's home!" Simran's unmistakeable pitch, followed by scrambling, and knees and elbows squeaking across the tiled floor. At the gate, they presented themselves to him like dolls whose parts had been crudely re-assembled—rumpled clothes, wiry halos of loose hair.

Banu greeted him with a wave from the end of the kitchen. She balanced a stack of plates and called out for the girls to help her with the cutlery. Dinner was fish curry, fried long beans and a steaming portion of white rice.

"What did you do in school today?" Gurdev asked the girls.

"We played 'What's the Time Mr Wolf'," Kiran said.

"I won it," Simran said, through a mouthful of rice.

"You're lying," Kiran accused. "You can't win that game. There's no such thing."

"I did," Simran whispered. She shot a grin at Gurdev.

"Good girls," Gurdev said. Banu looked distracted. "If the two of you finish up your dinner quietly, you can have popsicles." Any rivalry between the girls dissipated immediately. They bent towards their plates and chewed in silence.

"What's wrong?" Gurdev asked Banu quietly. She looked as if she might cry.

"It's Amrit," Banu whispered.

Gurdev glanced at the girls. Kiran pierced pairs of long beans with her fork and chewed them quickly with her eyes screwed shut. Simran used her butter knife to cut hers into tiny portions, and popped them into her mouth. The strangest things made him ache for them as if they were not sitting right in front of him.

"Just wait for them to finish their vegetables first," Gurdev said. Banu nodded. They sat in silence while the girls painstakingly chewed their way through the tough beans. "That's all right, Kiran, Simran. Well done," Gurdev said. "Go get your popsicles. One each."

The girls tumbled into the kitchen. With one blink, Banu's tears splashed down her round cheeks. "I was at the shops this afternoon, buying some milk. The girls were with me," Banu said. "I ran into Avtar Kaur. You remember her—she was my neighbour back in Sembawang. She told me Father's been asking around for boys for Amrit but all of the families know her reputation and don't want her. It's so embarrassing."

The girls were returning from the kitchen as Banu began to choke on her tears. They froze and stared at their mother. Simran's face crumpled, sympathetic to her mother's despair. Kiran took Simran's hand and led her to the table. "It's nothing, Simran," Gurdev said cheerily. "Just take a seat. Mummy and I are going to have a talk." Gurdev gave Banu's shoulder a feeble squeeze and led her to the couch, while the girls obediently took their seats at the table.

"I just don't know what to do when people tell me things like that. When I have the girls with me, it's even worse. People don't say it, but I know they're thinking that this sort of thing runs in the family. How do I convince them that our daughters aren't like that? What if one day Kiran and Simran get rejected because parents don't want their sons marrying into our family?"

"That's a long time from now," Gurdev said. "We don't have to worry about that yet."

"Gurdev, before you go to see Father tomorrow, I need to make something very clear to you," Banu said. "If Amrit gets any share of that inheritance money, she's going to waste it all away. She goes on shopping sprees. She buys the same pair of shoes in four different colours. Every pay cheque she receives is wasted on rubbish."

At the table, the girls were applying the popsicles to their lips and pouting. Kiran puckered at Simran.

"You need to talk to your father. Tell him what Amrit will

do with that money."

"I'm sure he's aware of it," Gurdev said. "He has a plan."

"Kissy kissy," Kiran sang to Simran between giggles. "Like a fashion model."

"That's the other thing I heard from Avtar," Banu said. "She told me that your father's plan is to offer a dowry—a dowry, like they do in India!—to the family of a cousin of hers. A bribe, essentially to get them to take Amrit off his hands. Anyone who wants to marry Amrit now is just going to go for the money. They'll see her as one big bundle of cash. You think Amrit won't see right through that? She won't put up with it. Marriages based on that type of thing don't last. She'll be back in Father's home within weeks of her wedding. Divorced."

The word made Gurdev wince. Why did Banu have to speak like this in front of the girls?

Banu continued, oblivious to Gurdev's tension. "The only solution, Gurdev, is to be frank with your father. Tell him that giving any of that money to Amrit is as good as flushing it down the toilet. Just convince him to think twice about it."

Kiran gave her lips an exaggerated lick. Simran mimicked her. "Daddy, look," Simran called out. "We're fashion models."

"Enough," Gurdev snapped. Banu and the girls froze; nobody seemed to know who Gurdev was directing his anger at. "I've had enough of this silliness," he declared. "The two of you are finished with those popsicle sticks. You can throw the rest into the rubbish. Go on. Now." The girls slipped away from the table, shooting reproachful looks at

Banu, whose wide eyes were fixed on Gurdev. "And you," he said to Banu. "Enough with the complaints. This is all I hear about from you these days—more rumours about Amrit. Those rumours continue only because people like you listen to them."

Banu stood up and began stacking the plates before marching off to the kitchen. The girls were instructed to go to the bathroom for their evening wash. When Banu returned, her face was still flushed with anger. "Don't you defend her," she warned.

"There are things we can't change," he said. "How do we stop people from talking? How do I stop Amrit when I'm at work all day and trying to spend time with you and the girls in the evenings? Cutting off her portion of the inheritance money is not going to solve all of our problems."

"That's the problem with you, Gurdev. You're so afraid of your father that you won't even try. When have we asked your father for money? We don't owe him years of tuition like Narain does. We're not living in his home and squandering our wages like Amrit is. Why can't we claim a bigger share? It's just going to go towards our daughters' education anyway. I know exactly what will happen when you go to see your father. He'll tell you how much you are entitled to and you will say yes, that's fine, thank you. You won't try to reason with him or show him how much you need it because he'll start comparing your income to Karam's, and you can't handle that. I'm just asking you to put aside your pride and do this for our girls."

"It's not that simple," Gurdev argued, but Banu had already stepped out of his view.

• • •

A new routine was born. Gurdev came back from the office later than usual, and Banu and the girls ate early. His dinner was left on the table. After dinner, he sat in the living room and pored over the papers, reading about the government's latest initiatives towards developing Singapore: land reclamation projects, the clean-up of the river. Gurdev scoffed at the latter. The river was clogged with rubbish and silt. On walks through the city, its stench filled the air like a string of vulgarities. It would never be a tourist site.

He and Banu only spoke when necessary; the girls had a chance to greet him in the mornings, and say goodnight at bedtime. As in all of their misunderstandings, it was tacitly understood that this arrangement would last until Gurdev fixed something. A week passed. Gurdev delayed meeting with Father, explaining that he had mountains of paperwork to get through in an unexpectedly busy week. Gurdev thought of Karam's smug face, the false crispness of his words in Sona's presence. How had Sona said that word? Prestige—she had made it sound exotic. It came to him then, unexpected yet obvious, like the answer to a riddle: what to do with Amrit. He bolted from the office and took a taxi straight to Father's flat, his heart drumming so loudly that he placed his hand over his chest to silence it.

The flat was dark behind Father when he opened the door to let Gurdev in. He flipped the appropriate switches as they made their way through each segment of the flat: living room, dining room, hallway, bathroom, kitchen and bedrooms. The fluorescent lamps flickered, as if waking. Everything was cast in their stinging, white glare.

They sat down at Father's desk in his room. Father reached into a desk drawer and pulled out some papers. "Gurdev, I have something to discuss with you."

"Before you do," Gurdev said, "I want to talk to you about Amrit."

Father dropped the papers on the desk. "I did not call you over to discuss Amrit."

"I actually have a plan for Amrit," Gurdev said.

"You have a plan?" Father asked, mockingly. "Tell me, Gurdev, when have you made plans for Amrit?"

"I think you should look overseas for a husband for Amrit."

This caught Father's attention. He stared at Gurdev, who continued. "There are plenty of eligible men in the Sikh communities in Toronto or London. I'll help you look into it. We'll throw a wedding for Amrit—something lavish, a big send-off. Use her portion of the money for it. It's a worthwhile investment. It will make more sense to spend the money this way than to offer it to her or to her future husband."

Father picked up a pen and began writing on the pad he always kept at the corner of his desk. Gurdev kept a respectful distance, knowing how Father hated having his privacy compromised when he was writing.

Gurdev continued. "While I've been thinking about Amrit's future, I've also been thinking about my daughters'. This country is getting more competitive. The girls have to do exams every six months and there's no guarantee that they'll get into university here, even if they work hard. Once Amrit is abroad and established, I can think about moving my family there as well."

Father looked up. "I didn't know you were considering migration."

"We weren't," Gurdev said, "but everything here is so uncertain. The girls will have a wider range of opportunities abroad. Our community here is very small. Amrit's reputation might tarnish the reputations of our girls." He had not actually considered moving the family abroad, but Father was sure to appreciate the pressures to leave home for the sake of his children's futures.

"So Amrit's portion will be taken care of by the wedding," Father said slowly to himself.

"Yes," Gurdev said. "Here is the other issue, though." For this, he leaned closer to Father, as he had seen Karam do, closing the gap between them. "Father, for the sake of my daughters' futures, I need a bigger portion of the inheritance money."

"You don't even know what I'm going to give you," Father argued.

"The cost of living is rising, Father. Everything is going to get more expensive. I can't keep promising the girls a better life if I can't pay for it. You know my girls—they're bright. I want to keep them from going down the wrong path."

"It's unfair, Gurdev," Father said, with a sigh. "He was Karam's grandfather, too." He turned back to his pad and read his scribbles.

"Have you spoken to Karam lately?" Gurdev asked.

Father's eyes did not leave the pad. "He's been very busy

with his work. I called him about the land money. I told him I'd confirm a time to meet with him after I discussed the money with you. I wanted to speak to my own son first."

This gave Gurdev a boost of confidence. "When you do have a chance to speak with Karam, don't mention that Ministry of Health position."

Father looked up. "Why?"

"He didn't get it," Gurdev said. "They just didn't think he was a strong enough candidate."

Father looked crestfallen. He stared at Gurdev for a moment, as if not believing his words. "Really? He was so certain," he said. He looked at the pad again. His brow was furrowed, as if a thought had just occurred to him. "This is why he has been avoiding me?"

"Oh, I don't know about that," Gurdev said. "I feel sorry for him, actually. He's been taking it quite badly."

Father threw him a suspicious look. "How do you know all of this?"

"I met with him recently. He told me everything. We speak quite often about these things. I caught up with him and asked him for tips on getting the girls into Sacred Heart—connections he might have, things like that."

"Did he help you?" Father asked.

Gurdev sighed. 'I don't know. He didn't really have any answers."

"You can't expect answers, Gurdev, but he must have had some advice," Father urged.

Gurdev shook his head. "Honestly, Father, he didn't know. It seems as if he's lost all of his confidence. He's become quite shy since this rejection."

"Becoming shy?" Now Father looked disturbed. "No wonder I haven't heard from him. He thinks he can hide this from me?"

"I wouldn't blame him completely," Gurdev said. "I don't think it's all his fault." He paused, revelling in Father's full attention. "It's the girl he's marrying. You probably haven't had a chance to speak with her yet, but I met her the other day and I can tell you this: she's very independent. An individual."

Those words did not agree with Father. What, surely, flashed into his mind was Mother: her surprising passion; her stubborn refusal to learn English; and her ability to dismiss his most cutting words. He would attempt to stir her up by saying she was illiterate and too traditional. Simple, a venomous insult in his vocabulary. Without batting an eye, Mother would continue to do things her way. Father had no patience for that type of woman. He picked up the pad and began to scribble again. The room filled with Father's mutterings and the sounds of frantic scratching of pen on paper. "All right then," he kept saying as Gurdev waited by his side. "All right, all right."

Amrit

EVERY EVENING, HE called. Father always picked up the phone, but Amrit was right by his side, expecting the call. He and Father exchanged pleasantries and then Father handed the receiver over to Amrit. Father was courteous enough to leave her alone in the living room while she spoke to her future husband.

On the first phone call, there were many awkward silences, which were then hastily filled with polite questions confirming the biographical sketches they had been provided. She knew his name was Jaspal and that he worked for an insurance company in Toronto. He had a younger brother. On weekends, he went to the movies with friends, and he was helping his family renovate their home in a suburb of Toronto. His voice was deep and gentle and his accent curled around his words like somebody from a television show.

What he knew about her: aged twenty-three; born on 18 August; completed secondary school exams; learnt some skills at secretarial school; pursued work afterwards. Even those facts were padded. She did not so much complete her exams as scrape through with two passes, which did not grant her admission into any pre-university program. Secretarial school had been the only option. On some days at secretarial school, she had felt that the world was hers; there was nothing she could learn that she didn't already know. Thoughts shot through her mind, convincing her that she was too clever, tearing her away from dull routine. Then, when she sank, the last place she wanted to be was at a desk, learning the proper typing hand placements and how to address letters. She wanted to be in bed or trapped inside it somehow, woven into the thick linings of her sheets.

When Father had informed her of the arrangement, he made it very clear that she was to give Jaspal the best impression of herself, so she pretended that everything he knew about her was accurate. This was her only chance to change.

In their second conversation, he asked her tentatively if she liked to cook. "I do actually," she said. "Curries and things."

There was a laugh of relief on the other end. "You never know if you can ask that question nowadays," Jaspal said. "Some girls get offended."

"You don't expect me to cook for you, do you?" she asked. A pause, and then she added, "I'm joking."

He laughed again. "That's cheeky of you," he said, and she smiled to herself, warm in that recognition. Father had not told him that she had a sense of humour. It occurred to her that Father knew little about her beyond her behaviour and failed accomplishments. During the conversation she cracked a few more jokes, noticing with triumph the laughter that tumbled down the line. The next day she spent an entire afternoon daydreaming about her new life in Canada. Jaspal featured infrequently in her fantasies but she told herself this was because she had not met him yet. She had only seen a photograph; he was pleasant-looking, with light skin and greyish-brown eyes.

"Does it snow a lot?" she asked, during their third conversation. "Is it very cold?"

"You'll get used to it," he said. "Driving on icy roads can be dangerous, though. Can you drive?"

"No," she said.

"You'll have to learn. Once you have a licence, you'll be able to go anywhere on your own."

"That's nice," she said, picturing herself behind the wheel of a car, surrounded by white landscapes. "I've always wanted to see what snow looks like. I know it's actually quite troublesome, but there's a bit of novelty to seeing it for the first time. It sounds like a nice change. It's always so hot here."

"I'll get to see it for myself soon," he reminded her. "We'll be in Singapore on the 7th."

"Yes," she said. It's all happening so quickly, she wanted to say, but she didn't know if this would make her sound reluctant. She wanted to marry him. Marriage was exactly what she needed. Nobody had explained it to her; nobody had to. They wanted her to be expunged of this tendency towards recklessness. She did, too. She was tired of who she had become. Marrying Jaspal was a start to something new and she was in dire need of a change. Everywhere she looked, it seemed as though Singapore was hurtling forwards into the future, with a new order that made people more straight-backed and tight-lipped. The air was still and humid, a constant heavy breath on her skin. Yet Amrit remained unsettled, her mind overtaken by uncontrollable bursts of brilliance for days and weeks before the helplessness crept in. One morning a few months ago, she opened her eyes to realise that she had wet the bed in a drunken stupor. The stench of urine had filled the room and travelled into the hallway. Yet she could not fathom getting up and cleaning herself. It took an effort to make the smallest movement, and mysterious aches shifted and intensified in waves.

During their fourth conversation, Jaspal mentioned that she wouldn't have trouble finding a job in Toronto. "You speak English pretty well," he said.

Amrit was indignant. "I was the best speaker in my class," she informed him. In fact, on the merits of her excellent English, Mr Lau had hired her to answer phones at the advertising agency. She had originally applied for a copywriting job but had no experience or prior employers to vouch for her. Mr Lau had told her that she could answer phones for six months; in the meantime, she could learn the inner workings of the company. Last week, when she returned to work after three consecutive sick days, she had avoided Mr Lau, the guilt burning into her.

Jaspal's laughter was empty. "You're funny," he said.

"I wasn't joking," Amrit replied. "Or boasting. My English results were the best in the school. I'd like to work in advertising."

"Do you want children?" he asked.

"Of course I do," Amrit said. "I want two. Two girls." She thought about Simran and Kiran, their soft hands and feet when they were babies, their gentle smiles and the way they clutched Gurdev's pant leg and hid behind him shyly. "I want to work and raise children as well. I know it's hard, but people manage."

"That's nice," Jaspal said vaguely. "It's very modern of you." The distance between them did not hide his disappointment at her mention of working. Amrit racked her brains to think of lighter subjects, but besides their shared future, what would they have together?

• • •

A few days later, Amrit woke to the sound of her alarm. It fell with a crash from the edge of her mattress to the floor, but it continued a jerky ringing until she pressed the button. She lay in bed, the sheets heavy and moist with sweat, and knew that she would not go to work today or tomorrow. She had taken another three days off and claimed a flu, unverified by a medical certificate. "I was so sick I couldn't see a doctor," she'd told Mr Lau over the phone. "It's my back. And my stomach. Everything is painful," she said, knowing that no doctor would take her seriously. It wasn't pain or fatigue exactly. There was no precise way to talk about it. She had tried to go to the clinic several times but a succinct way to describe her symptoms eluded her and she ended up leaving.

She blamed herself. Somewhere there must be the terminology for the way thoughts sped through her mind, tricking her into thinking the world was illuminated solely by her ideas. There was a name for what would inevitably follow: a plummeting sense that she should not exist. Amrit's regrets were endless. If she had finished school and gone on to university, she was certain she would have the words. Education was the way out of any state of uncertainty or misery. The government was always saying that Singaporeans had to compete with each other; Amrit could compete with nobody. With her limited words, all she could say was that it felt like hell.

The phone rang at 8.45am. She heard a door open somewhere in the flat and, moments later, a light tap on her door. "Phone call for you." Narain's voice was muffled through the door.

"Come in," she called to Narain. She had not spoken to him in ages. He was rarely around when she got home, and in the mornings, she was still asleep when he got ready for work.

The door opened. In the doorframe, Narain looked larger than he was. He tucked in his shirt as he spoke to her, avoiding looking at the room. She assessed it through his eyes. Worn and unwashed clothes lay strewn across the floor; a pair of underpants dangled from the corner of the ironing board. The dressing table was crowded with make-up and accessories still wrapped in their packages. Glasses lined with Ribena and crusty Milo stains littered the floor next to her bed. The dust on the floor was thick and visible, even though only a tiny sliver of light entered through a space between her curtains. Before going to sleep last night, she had used clothes pegs to bind them together, but the draught through the open windows must have caused them to snap off.

"I'm not going in today," Amrit said.

"You have to work. You're not going to get anywhere with this career that you want if you don't put in the work."

Amrit sat up. "You know what they make me do the whole day in that bloody office? Smile. Smile when clients come in, smile when I show them to the conference room, smile even when I'm on the fucking telephone."

"And what's so hard about that?" Narain asked.

Amrit stared at him. Smug, that was the word for him. Self-satisfied, just because he had a degree from America. "I'm smarter than that. I could write better ads than half the people in that office. Mr Lau just doesn't want me to succeed."

"Grow up, Amrit," Narain said. He shut the door, shielding himself from the insults she would hurl if she didn't feel so drained. She felt something low in her stomach, a plummeting sensation that was not pain—but what was it then? What doctor could cure disappointment that grew into a pile of stones within her, or elation that made her skin tingle with pleasure?

There was only one consolation today—she could still recognise the emotions stirring within her. It was better than the days to come, when she would feel nothing at all.

· · ·

Two days passed. Amrit woke one evening to find the room engulfed in shadows. While she was sleeping, somebody had come inside and parted the curtains in a bid to rouse her. Weak light from the opposite block of flats only succeeded in casting her surroundings in different shades of grey. She rubbed her eyes with the back of her hand and caught a whiff of vomit on her pillow. A vague memory: she had called her office, finally, to say she could not come in, and Mr Lau had said, "You're fired."

She had hung up and walked to the coffee shop where the usual customers let her share their whiskey. "Promise I'll pay you back," she'd said after a few drinks, and then she left with one of them. In a damp patch of wet grass, she crouched and threw up, and he rubbed her back, saying soothing things. He led her to the park, where he unzipped his pants and pushed up her skirt. They were frantic and flustered as their bodies slammed together, as if this was all that was necessary. Before placing her in a taxi, he gave her a five-dollar note and wrote down his phone number on an old supermarket receipt. "I can't call you," she told him. "I'm getting married."

"To who?" he asked.

"A graduate from overseas," she said. She hoped this would impress him and scare him off. She placed the paper in her purse anyway. His name was Hakim.

Amrit's bedroom door opened with a nearly inaudible creak. In the old Naval Base house, things had announced their presence, even if everybody was still. Floorboards creaked from invisible pressures, windows drilled at the slightest breeze. This flat felt like an airtight box in comparison.

Father stepped inside and flipped the light switch. It blinked, bringing flashes of diluted light into the room before flooding it completely. Amrit groaned and sank against her mattress. Father began talking loudly, then shouting. "Getting married in two months and you still can't behave like a lady. Taking advantage of my kindness. One fine day, I'll lock you out. I'll make sure you don't have a way to enter my house again."

But it isn't your house, Amrit thought, through the haze of her hangover. It would baffle him and then incite more anger, but wasn't it true? Sure, he had paid the mortgage and signed the paperwork, but this flat had been designed to be identical to thousands of other government properties on the island. Again, Amrit struggled with words. She wanted to reassure Father that he didn't have to feign pride in this place. What they once had—the Naval Base bungalow with jungle vines masking the concrete—had been his house. What he had before she existed—a fertile spread of Punjab farmland passed down through generations—had been his house. Living was messy. These uniform flats, stacked on top of each other, were tidy solutions. Nothing about this square room or the sturdy cement tiles or the high-rise view of the estate from the window sufficed as a house.

"You hear?" Father was saying. He thrust his thumb behind his shoulder, gesturing to the unlit passageway behind him. "Listen, you hear it?"

Amrit shook her head and shut her eyes. The light penetrated and produced a string of dancing shapes through her skull.

"Outside. Your mother is crying. She is sitting and crying and wondering: why, why, does my daughter behave this way? When so many other daughters are so good, why does mine shame me? When will I ever rest?"

Amrit stared at Father, amazed. It had been so long since he had used Mother to evoke guilt that the moment would be nostalgic if it weren't laced with absurdity. As a little girl, his mere mention of Mother's disappointment made her wary of causing mischief. That first time Amrit ran away and returned, Father thought he could prevent further incidents by describing how Mother's cries filled the room at night. He told her he could not sleep because Mother did not sleep.

"I don't hear anything," Amrit said.

Father lunged into the room and grabbed Amrit's arm. "Then come. You hear it for yourself." His fingers dug hard into her skin.

She shouted: "If Mother isn't happy, she can talk to me herself. Tell her to come to me and say something!"

Father looked as if he might lunge at her, his feet separated at an awkward stance. Then the padlock to the main gate clanged faintly like a bell, announcing Narain's arrival. A distraction. Satisfied, Amrit flipped to her side and tossed the sheet over her head. The light seeped through the worn cotton and made her entire body throb with pain. Later, Father came in again to tell her Gurdev and Banu were on the phone. They were going to Malaysia for the weekend and wanted to know if she needed anything from there. Amrit pulled back the sheet and told Father she wanted nothing from anybody. The door slammed, and then Father moved about the house, yelling, banging more things. She drifted back to sleep and had dreams of the walls splitting like eggshells.

•   •   •

Mr Lau was not there when she went to collect her last pay cheque, but the other people at the office conveyed his resentment. The women in the payroll department shrugged when she asked them if her cheque was ready and then they deliberately took a long time to locate it. The marketing manager, who had always made it a point to say hello to her, regarded her coldly. He said something in Chinese to the man sitting next to him, who looked up at Amrit.

"When the receptionist isn't around, you know how many things are out of place?" one of the payroll girls asked angrily when she returned. Amrit could tell she relished the opportunity to scold somebody, in Mr Lau's absence. She shook the envelope at Amrit. "Mailings were not mailed. We all had to take time from our lunch hour to answer your calls. You know that or not?" She tossed the cheque at Amrit. It slid off the desk and floated onto the floor. Everything fell quiet. Too proud to pick it up, but too broke to leave without her money, Amrit crossed her arms over her chest and tried to look as if calmness was her only plan. Somebody finally came along and picked up the envelope. It was the marketing manager, whose name she was having trouble remembering. She didn't know any of their names; she started this job knowing she didn't have to remember because she would not be here long enough. He shot the payroll girl a disapproving look and told Amrit she needed to go.

She clutched the envelope to her chest. On her way out, someone loudly remarked, "I told him: next time, don't hire these kinds of people."

Jealous, Amrit thought triumphantly. They had seen her engagement ring—she might even have mentioned it on the phone to the payroll girls when she called to say she would be picking up her cheque.

Today the sun beat furiously against the windows of a nearby building. On either side of it, construction cranes stooped towards the complex bamboo scaffolding that shrouded the buildings-in-progress. The city was being built before Amrit's very eyes. There were times when she sensed it was important to acknowledge this but the urgency didn't overwhelm her today. The buzzing traffic and the drilling and clanging of construction failed to excite her. She remembered she was supposed to leave Singapore. The point of the marriage was to make her disappear. A heavy wave of shame washed over her, momentarily dissolving her surroundings. When she tried to count her misfortunes, none were detached from her own foolishness.

A bus honked, jolting Amrit from her thoughts, but she couldn't figure out where she was in relation to the bus. She was too close to the kerb; she was standing on the road. A man caught her sleeve and jerked her back. "See where you're going. The light is still green," he scolded. She turned to see a small crowd watching, and a young woman she vaguely recognised coming towards her. No, Amrit pleaded silently. Although she had long forgotten their names, her former secondary school classmates were always similarly dressed—tailored jackets and high heels, briefcases swinging at their sides.

"Amrit from Stanford Girls' School, right? I knew you right away," the woman called. "It's me, Gail." The crowd behind her looked reluctant to disperse until Amrit waved back. Then their interests waned.

"How are you?" Gail asked. Her voice had not changed since she was sixteen. It was high and breathy, easy to mimic. It was the only thing Amrit remembered about her.

"I'm well, thanks."

"What happened just now? It looked like you were going to jump out in front of that bus," Gail asked, laughing lightly.

Amrit forced herself to laugh as well. "I wasn't looking."

"So what are you up to these days? I haven't seen you

in ages." Her words were clipped in a faint British accent, a remnant of their diction classes at Stanford Girls. Amrit had not spoken like that for years. Everything that spilled from her mouth was tainted in Singlish, that foul dialect of common Singaporeans. If she spoke, she would not convince anyone that she had once been a Stanford girl.

"I'm getting married," Amrit said.

"Congrats," Gail said, nodding. "That's good news. So I suppose you work around here?" She glanced uncertainly at Amrit's denim slacks.

"No, not today," Amrit replied, offering no further explanation, though Gail waited. "I'm...I just left my job. I'm getting married and we're moving to Canada."

"Oh, congratulations. Canada is very nice," Gail said, brightly.

"We're really looking forward to it. It will be nice to get out of here," Amrit said pointedly.

Gail offered a tight smile. "Won't you miss your family? That's why I didn't want to study abroad. I was afraid I'd miss my mum's cooking too much."

"Well, my fiancé's family is there. I can adjust easily to a new place."

"You're in love!" Gail said, blissfully.

Amrit feigned the same joy. She loved the change he could bring to her life, the escape route he offered. She loved what a husband represented. As Jaspal's name lingered in her mind, his face appeared and became Hakim's, the man she had gone to the park with. She pressed her fingers to the piece of paper with his phone number on it that she kept in her purse.

After she and Gail parted with promises to stay in touch, Amrit boarded a bus home. Her seat at the back was hot from the engine. A gash in the upholstery poked the back of her thigh. As she shifted, her purse slipped from her hands and coins scattered across the seat, some falling into the exposed stuffing. She stared helplessly at the coins, and a stream of tears poured down her face. More passengers got on and stared before finding seats away from her. The conductor finally came bobbing along with the vehicle's jerky rhythm. "Going where?" he asked, snapping his ticket puncher at his side. He was taken aback when he noticed her crying. Amrit fumbled for her ticket and passed it to him.

"You still must tell me where you're going," the conductor said.

Amrit shook her head and looked away. Straight rows of evenly spaced trees shot by the windows. Outside a church, two workers were struggling to keep a banner tied to a fence, as a strong gust of wind made ripples through the fabric. At the next stop, she pushed past the conductor and stumbled off the steps. She walked briskly until she found a pay phone, and then she opened her purse and pulled out the piece of paper. Hakim. She felt her heart thumping as she dumped out all of her ten-cent coins. She could talk to him all day.

Narain

AFTER WORK, NARAIN went to Bee Bee's Food and Beverage, and bought three packets of nasi goreng for the family. He entered the flat sensing that Amrit was not there, but if he only bought two packets, Father might be offended by the presumption. Eating out of the brown paper packets reminded Father that his dinner had been cooked by strangers so Narain placed the packets on the kitchen counter and began taking out the plates and cutlery.

Father shuffled out to the table when he was told dinner was ready. As he ate, he seemed lost in thought. He scooped the rice with his spoon and fork, and his gaze followed the release of steam. Suddenly, he asked Narain, "Did you learn anything in America?"

Narain was taken aback by the question. It seemed like something that would arrive in the middle of an argument. "What do you mean?" he asked.

"Did it benefit you? All those years away, all of that money…" Father's voice trailed off.

Narain looked down at his plate and noticed that the fried rice was oilier than usual. He pushed away his plate. "Of course it benefited me," he said. "I got a degree."

"Yes," Father said, "a degree. But that wasn't the only reason you were sent to America."

Narain felt his face burning. Not now, he thought. Not that he could ever think of an appropriate time to have such a conversation. Father began to talk about his own father, his dreams for all of his grandchildren. When he brought up the topic of the land money, Narain relaxed a bit. I don't care about the money, he wanted to say, but Father would surely find this offensive. Instead, he just listened and waited for Father to tell him, in the manner of a judge reading a verdict, that he would not get any portion of the land money. "I paid so much in university tuition fees, Narain. And flights, and books, clothes—so many expenses to help you become a man," Father explained. "Honestly, I don't know if it was worth it."

Narain wished he weren't so afraid of standing up to Father. *How much does it cost to hire a full-time caretaker for Amrit? Because I've been doing that for free at the expense of my social life.* Instead, Narain finished his dinner and excused himself, saying he wanted to take a walk.

Outside, as a weak sun descended below the shophouse rooftops, Narain caught a glimpse of himself in a shop window. He brought a hand to his face and touched his thin spread of beard and felt the full weight of his turban as if it was crushing his skull. He remembered keeping track of his shadow on those frosty Iowa mornings, and those thrilling prospects for change. How disappointing it had been then to return that summer and apologise—for writing those letters, for not studying hard enough, for inadvertently causing Amrit's disappearance. On the plane back to Iowa at the end of that summer, he had felt the guilt building and pushing his first year off his shoulders like an old cloak—

Jenny, the parties, the protests. When he returned, he abandoned his ideas to study politics and began to distance himself from Jenny. They broke up within weeks. In his second year of university, Narain declared his major in Engineering and attended an information night with many of the foreign students he had initially ignored. They looked eager and earnest, their faces scrubbed and their postures tilting forwards, wanting to please. Narain could not feign such an interest in Engineering but he accepted that he was not in America to discover himself. As his remaining years of study passed and he gained more distance from that first year, Narain began to omit it completely from his memory. By the time he graduated, that Narain had become so unrecognisable that on the morning of the graduation ceremony, when somebody tacked to his door a photograph of a man with his arm around Jenny, it took a while for him to recognise himself. The photograph, filled from end to end with Narain's and Jenny's grins, had been taken at a protest outside the Dean's office. Narain flipped over the picture and found a note scrawled on the back. "Keep believing," Jenny had written in her distinct cursive. Narain sat down and studied the photo more carefully. He shut his eyes and concentrated on picturing Jenny. After her, there had been no more girls. There had been anonymous encounters in the shadows of parking lots and parks, but they had been with men. He opened his eyes and looked at the words again, searching for meaning in her simple message. Perhaps she had known about Narain all along, and like him, she knew he would not change.

Narain had returned to Singapore with a suitcase lighter

than the one he had brought to America. Father watched him unpack and reached eagerly into his suitcase for the diploma, which he unrolled and flattened against the dinner table, like a map. He had it framed immediately, and it was one of the first items to be mounted on their new living room wall. Looking around the flat for the first time, Narain was glad he was not sentimental for any items from his past. This new home was compact, allowing only for symbols to be displayed. Potted plants lined the entrance like miniatures of the palm trees of the Naval Base. The sun spilled tentatively into their small balcony, whereas it used to drench their entire home, stretching each passing hour until each day felt endless. Father exalted the public housing initiative; he praised the structure of the buildings, a sign that their country was moving forward. Narain heard the hope in his voice and knew that Father thought their problems with Amrit would be reduced in scale as well.

For years since arriving home, Narain had worked each day and then gone home to deal with Amrit's antics. He took her side in arguments against Father. He kept track of her departures and arrivals. He noticed that she could be present in their home, flipping through a magazine or dusting the carpets, but not there at all. "She's gone again," he would tell Father, when she was like that. In between those moments, anonymous encounters with men divided Narain's days. He found them in similar locations to those in America: in thick, unkempt bushes or narrow alleyways that reeked of drain water and rot. They never spoke to each other and they understood, without being told, that they were not to let their gazes linger on each other's faces. What they did was purely for release.

Sometimes Narain caught sight of a man's wedding band or he heard in his own breath the sound of pleading, and he wondered if he would spend his whole life in disguise. Recently, since Amrit's engagement, this question had begun to play on his mind. After Amrit, it would be his turn. The community would begin parading their most eligible girls for him and Father would happily entertain their requests, hoping that marriage would be successful in fixing Narain. Father would advertise him as the perfect potential husband: a son with a degree from America; an engineer from a good family. Punjabi parents would be satisfied to hand their daughters over, based on these credentials alone.

Now, Narain walked until he came to a familiar place to rest his feet; Bee Bee's Food and Beverage. This coffee shop was a modest establishment but it burst with activity. Mandarin songs crackled from the radio while spoons and forks chimed an accompanying tune. Ashes from cigarettes melted into tiles covered in oil and sweat. There was no entrance to the coffee shop; it was a string of food stalls with boundaries only made known by the furthest table. Close to this table was a tall wooden stand. Narain assumed that its previous incarnation might have been a television console or a low bookcase. Nails jutted crudely from the sides. One shelf held an outdated Yellow Pages directory. Another shelf was on the verge of collapse, its edges eaten through. The payphone was bound to the topmost shelf by rows of strings and padlocked chains. There was rope, raffia string, fishing line, a delicate necklace bearing a jade Buddha. Who would steal a telephone? Narain wondered each time he saw it, until he realised that fear of theft was not the owners' concern. They liked the authority; they enjoyed knowing that theirs was the only discreet payphone in the area, that its patrons could pull the cord to a shadowy corner and become invisible as they arranged rendezvous with their mistresses or lied to their mothers. They were not securing it; they were ensuring that the customers were aware who was responsible for making their little escapes possible.

Narain felt his own secrets bursting in his chest but somehow he could not utter them, not with this turban and beard reflecting the Sikh values that Father had instilled in him. He made the decision there: he would cut off all his hair. He would be able to reveal that he had not changed since the army, and when Father replied "You are no longer my son," it would already be true. They would already have nothing left in common.

• • •

The next afternoon, Narain left work after lunch. In his mind, he had played out every scenario and rehearsed every response. Before leaving the office, Narain unwound his turban and replaced it with a cap.

These days, the afternoon heat radiated from every surface: car windows glared; smoke billowed from the stoves cramped into hawker stalls; the warmth of concrete soaked through the soles of his sneakers. Looking for shade, Narain quickly entered the empty deck of a block of flats. The walls were pockmarked and dusty with handprints. A bow-legged man wearing black shorts and a white singlet stood facing the rows of metal letterboxes. His hand shot swiftly in and out of the flaps, depositing a flier into each box. As he worked, sweat slid down the back of his neck and the wide armhole in his singlet shifted to one side, exposing his pinkish chest.

Narain knew the name of the shop he was looking for: Hassan's Haircutters. He had looked up barbers in the Yellow Pages and picked out the first one he could find in a neighbourhood on the other side of the island. He assumed it would be visible once he arrived in the neighbourhood, but he found himself in a maze of clothing shops, hawker centres and newsstands. The sun glared from above the concrete towers of flats. There was more shade under the canvas awnings of shops, expansive like large wings. They did not only block out the heat but also the light, so as Narain entered, he felt like he was walking through a dark corridor. Display shelves crammed with loaves of Gardenia bread and pandan rolls flanked the entrances to the stores. Triangles of bright red, blue and green agar-agar sat on plates in display cases. Narain stopped to buy one piece and felt the shock of cold as his teeth sank into the firm jelly.

A set of bells made a hollow and rusty announcement as Narain arrived in the barber shop. It was empty.

"Hello, hello," a male voice sang from the back room. "Sit down, please." Narain looked around. The seats looked too firm. The radio at the front desk blared so loudly it was possible that the barber would not hear his instructions. Narain took off his cap and waited.

"I'm Hassan," the barber called from the back room. "You want a cut? Hold on, ah. I got moustache dye on my fingers, lah. Must clean properly otherwise next time fingers become all funny colours." He was still chuckling when he emerged but when he set his eyes on Narain, the joy faded from his face.

"I'll pay you double," Narain said. He had expected some reluctance—there was, after all, an entire lifetime of hair growth to tackle. He pulled out his wallet. Hassan shook his head. "Cannot," he said. "Please go."

Narain turned around and left the shop. It was only a minor setback, he told himself. There were plenty of barbers who would be happy for business. He crossed a playground and passed a community centre before noticing another barber shop. When he entered, the Chinese barber was busy with a client. He caught a glimpse of Narain in the mirror reflection. "What do you want?" he asked in Malay.

"Haircut," Narain said, removing the cap. The ponytail spilled out eagerly and danced down his back. The barber's eyes widened.

"So much hair? So much?" he kept asking. "Why have you grown so much hair?" Narain's answers did not seem to satisfy. "So much hair!" he exclaimed, circling Narain, but reluctant to touch him. "How often do you wash it? How can a man have so much hair?" Other customers in the shop looked up and tried to hide their amusement. Frustrated and humiliated, Narain hastily tucked his hair back into his cap and left. He wandered again through the neighbourhood until he found a single shop wedged between a dental clinic and an abandoned clothing store where naked mannequins lay scattered like corpses across the floor. This man was also Chinese, with an oblong face. Even before Narain confronted him with the heavy task, he looked worried.

"Cannot," he said apologetically. His eyes followed the rope of hair.

"I'll pay double. Triple." Narain offered. He was beginning to understand, however, that money was not the issue.

He left the shop feeling dejected but still willing to try a few more. In the next housing estate, he saw an opportunity in a small shop. The barber had left a sign with a drawing of a clock indicating what time he would return. In the ten minutes that Narain waited, he couldn't take his eyes off the altar in the corner of the entrance. Rows of pudgy, grinning Buddhas were crammed into the lopsided shelf of a bookcase. Tall candles—some new, some half-melted—formed a semi-circle around a pair of oranges and a plate of sticky rice. When the barber returned, he was all smiles. "Welcome," he said, jovially. His tone quickly changed when he saw the task Narain laid out for him.

"Your God hate me!" he exclaimed. "Cannot! I cut your hair, your God curse me!" he shooed Narain away as if Narain were the smiting God himself.

Narain stormed out of the shop feeling the weight of his hair—years of growing, tending, tying, washing, neatening, oiling—pressing down on his scalp, like a cancerous lump. He passed a stationery shop and had a passing thought to buy a pair of scissors, find a spot and simply cut it all off himself. But this had to be done properly. He re-traced his steps and returned to the first shop, where Hassan was reading the paper.

"Who will cut my hair?" he demanded. "If not you, if not any barber, how am I supposed to do this? I just want to get rid of it."

"It's not the length, son," Hassan said.

"Yes, I know," Narain said impatiently. He recounted for Hassan the incident with the barber who was afraid of being punished by his God. "It's the religion, I understand it, but what am I supposed to do?"

Hassan shook his head. "It's not just the religion. It's your community. If one person sees a Sikh man sitting in a barber shop window getting his hair cut by a Malay or Chinese barber and word gets around, there goes that barber's reputation. That barber has helped to get rid of your hair. Do you see what I'm saying?"

"But Sikh people don't go to barbers, so what's the big deal if they think you're bad?"

"When one shop has a bad reputation, all the other shops in the same row suffer," Hassan said. "People might stop going to buy desserts from the bakery next door. They might avoid getting their lottery tickets from the provision shop on the other side. I don't want to cause that kind of trouble for this row. Shops are being stacked together now, joined by walls. It's no longer individual kiosks and carts; we have to think about each other."

Narain put his head in his hands. A haircut could be so complicated; the absurdity of it! Hassan sat down next to him. "What's your name?"

"Narain," he said.

"Narain, what will your family do when they see you with short hair?" he asked. When Narain didn't reply, Hassan sighed and said, "Okay." Narain looked up.

"No, not me. I won't cut your hair," Hassan said. "But I know a few places where you might find someone to do it."

"Where?" Narain asked eagerly.

Hassan drew out a simple map of intersecting junctions. Narain's hopes fell. "I was just there," he said. "I went to all those places."

Hassan shook his head. "Not the row of shops. The alleyways behind them. There are a few back lane barbers there."

"I didn't know they still had those," Narain said. "I thought they were being cleared out and made to license their businesses."

"Mostly," Hassan said. "But they crop up here and there. I've got a friend who does it. He was saving up to rent a shop but then the government caught him doing the back lane trade and he was fined. Now he's started all over again. If you get caught, you'll be fined as well."

Narain was willing to take that risk. He thanked Hassan and left the store.

•   •   •

As per Hassan's directions, there was a service lane between two coffee shops. It was so narrow that Narain had to press his arms to his sides to avoid scraping them against the walls. He emerged into an alleyway and was relieved to find that Hassan had not been merely trying to chase him out of his shop. A varied network of makeshift businesses seemed to thrive here. There was a row of small tents, some with tin sheets for roofs, strewn along the narrow path. Inside each tent, an upturned fruit crate draped in cloth made a table for the barber's tools: scissors, razors, combs and powders arranged in order of size. The men inside the tents worked quickly, glancing occasionally at the mirrors their customers were instructed to hold up.

Narain went to the closest barber, a stout, tired-looking man who was gazing up at the sky and lamenting in Hokkien. When he made eye contact with Narain, he called out for somebody. A young man appeared from behind the tent. "I'll take you," he said. "My uncle has had enough for the day." He smiled and Narain felt a distinct tingle. This was going to happen. It would be this easy.

Inside the tent, Narain warned the young barber about his circumstances. "I've got very long hair," he said, before removing his cap.

The barber looked at him thoughtfully and quoted his price. "Twelve dollars," he said. It was four times as much as a normal haircut but Narain was happy to pay it up-front.

"I'm Adam," the barber said. "What's your name?"

"Narain," he replied. Adam raked his fingers through Narain's hair, sometimes touching Narain's back as he separated the long locks. Narain felt another tingle, this one more electric. He took in a sharp breath.

"You okay?" Adam asked.

"I'm fine," Narain said. "This is just a big deal. It took me a long time to find a barber who would do this."

"You came to the right place. We can't afford to turn down customers back here." He handed Narain a mirror.

"I didn't even know this existed," Narain said. "Another barber told me about it."

Adam picked up a pair of scissors. There was the sound of crunching, and then Narain felt the hair grazing his back as it fell away. He shut his eyes and placed the mirror in his lap.

Adam chattered as he worked.

"I help my uncle with this business. I'm saving up for my studies. I think I might go abroad," he said. "Perth probably."

"I studied abroad," Narain said. "In America."

"What did you do?"

"Engineering. If I could do it all over again, though, I might have chosen a different course."

"Why did you do Engineering?"

"My father wanted that," Narain said. He opened his eyes. He could feel Adam's stare on his back, urging him to move beyond the small talk. "I had to do what he wanted." This was all Narain could manage. His stomach was twisting into knots now; as more hair fell away and clustered around his feet, his head felt lighter.

"What will your father do when he sees you with your hair cut?" Adam asked.

"He'll probably ask me to leave the house," Narain said. He had not spoken the consequence aloud until then. Adam paused for a moment and then resumed the cutting.

"There are lots of rental rooms," Adam said casually, "around the area. People leave home all the time. It's not such a big deal anymore."

"True," Narain said.

"If that happens, come back here. Anyone who works in a back lane will know how to find you a cheap place to live."

"Thanks." His heart had begun to drum in his chest. He brought the mirror up to find a crude hair style of uneven lengths. But it was short. Most of it was gone. As Adam picked up a razor and began to shape it, Narain closed his eyes again.

"Remember the long hair ban?" Adam asked. "You would have been exempt from that."

"Yeah," Narain said. "Sikhs didn't have to cut their hair but everyone else did."

"Good times for barbers," Adam said, laughing. "I had some friends who were caught with long hair and they were made to go to the police station to get their hair cut. One of my friends dared to ask why all of a sudden the government had banned citizens from growing long hair. The policemen didn't really know the reason. One said it was to eliminate hippie culture infiltrating from the West. Another one said long hair was unkempt and dirty—citizens have to look respectable and clean, he said."

Narain smiled. As Adam continued to tell him stories, he felt himself relaxing into the chair. For some reason, he felt like telling Adam about Amrit. "My sister is getting married overseas," he said.

"You're close?" Adam asked.

"Yeah," Narain said, wishing it weren't so.

Adam dusted the hair off his shoulders and tipped his head back for the shave. Within minutes, it was complete. "Ready to look?" Adam asked, excitedly. "Bring up the mirror." He tapped Narain's wrist. His fingers, light and playful, lingered for a moment and Narain knew what was happening. Over the years he had had moments like these with men—the familiar anxiety, the anticipation, and the subtle passing of signals. They usually occurred out of sight, in places like these. He had never brought it beyond these tentative touches; the turban and beard had prevented him from acting upon his impulses.

"Twelve dollars?" Narain mumbled. He reached for his wallet and paid Adam. "Thank you," he said, stumbling away and only catching a glimpse of himself in the mirror. It was all too much for now. He needed to go home first.

• • •

It was early evening by the time he arrived home. The sun had begun to set, bathing the concrete apartment towers in amber light. He only hesitated for a moment before pushing his key into the padlock and popping it open. The gate swung back and bounced against his shoulder. As he picked the door key from his wallet ring, he noticed something strange. The door to their apartment was ajar. A familiar anxiety filled his chest. Had somebody spotted him and called Father, before he had a chance to explain himself? This means nothing, he told himself, but it did not erase an image of Father sitting in the living room, forewarned and waiting.

The sharp squeak of hinges made him jump back. Gurdev poked his head out. "You're home finally. Where—" his gaze travelled to Narain's head. His eyes became wide and round. "Have you gone mad? There's so much trouble in the house already," he hissed, stepping out and shutting the door behind him.

"What are you doing here?" Narain asked. "What happened?"

"Amrit," Gurdev said. He took in Narain's appearance again and shook his head. "They're about to call off the wedding."

"What? Why?"

"They know. Her in-laws. They know what she's like. People have been talking. Param's brother—you know, that man who works in the civil defence?—he saw her in a bar yesterday. Not even ten o'clock yet, and she was so drunk she couldn't tell the bartender where she lived. Then her purse fell and all kinds of rubbish fell out. Underpants. Cigarettes." He looked around and lowered his voice to a whisper. "Condoms also. The guy told his cousin, who told his wife, who happens to be the sister of somebody married into Amrit's in-laws' family. It's over. They don't want her. They're inside right now telling Father he deceived them, calling him all kinds of names. That's why he called me over. He was looking for you as well. So this is what you were doing?"

Narain straightened his shoulders at the hint of anger in Gurdev's question. "This has nothing to do with you. It's my choice."

Gurdev snorted. "Try, lah. Tell Father that. Maybe he'll slap you in front of everyone also."

"He slapped Amrit? In front of them?"

"What did you want him to do? Sing her a song?"

Narain didn't say anything. Gurdev located his shoes on the rack and brushed past him, pushing his feet into them as he walked lopsidedly towards the lift. "I have to go. Simran has an ear infection. I can't sit inside there listening to them anymore. They've been blaming Father for deceiving them." He lowered his voice. "They said, 'we should have known something was wrong with a girl who didn't have proper guidance from her mother.' Father lost his temper then."

This information made Narain feel a bit dizzy. His

mouth went dry. Panic made his heartbeat seem audible as he realised he could not walk through that door looking like this. Any day but today. He fished in his back pocket for the cap and threw it on. Gurdev waved grimly at him as he stepped into the lift.

The figures in the flat were shrouded in shadows when Narain entered. The curtains were drawn, allowing only a sliver of weak light into the room. Father must have done this as soon as he received the call, attempting to drown his shame in darkness. Narain reached to switch on the light but a movement caught his attention. Amrit's father-in-law-to-be, a small-boned man in comparison to Father, had stood up and crossed his arms over his chest. His wife turned away, the pain in her face unmistakeable even in the bluish dark.

"I'm sorry we cannot go through with this," the father-in-law said. "We cannot have this girl in our family."

"You're mistaken," Father said pleadingly. "It wasn't her." The family had begun to walk out. Father trailed after them, making excuses. Narain lowered his head but when Father passed him, he sensed him staring. Narain looked up to face him. Father's eyes flickered and Narain felt his heart stop, knowing in that instant that Father had noticed the shaven face and figured out what he had done. After a moment that seemed to last for days, Father was the first to speak. "Get out," he said softly.

• • •

Narain raced blindly to the road and hailed a taxi, but when the driver asked him where he wanted to go, he didn't know the street name. "I'll show you," he said, as he shut the door. He led the driver through the streets and landmarks, squinting to recognise the shops as they were closing, the streets as the lamps cast shadows on them. The taxi went as far into the back streets as it could go. "This is fine," he said, passing the fare money to the driver. "Thank you." He leaped out of the taxi and ran, his feet thumping against the ground, his heart thumping not from exhaustion but from the excitement of what he was about to do. In the distance, he saw Adam, alone in a corner, packing up his tent. He pushed past the other vendors. Conversations broke and then resumed again. Adam looked up as Narain approached and touched his wrist. They stepped into the shadows of the narrow service lane. There it was, that shot of pleasure, one he had been waiting to feel for such a long time, as he pressed his lips, and then his chest, his limbs, his thighs, to Adam's.

PART III
1984–1985

Gurdev

IN THE HALLWAY, Banu called out another reminder to the girls to button up their cardigans. Their protests came bouncing back.

"You knew these dresses were sleeveless when you bought them, Ma," Simran whined.

"We've worn them before anyway," said Kiran. Both of them appeared in the doorway of Banu and Gurdev's bedroom. They stood tall in their defiance, their cardigans hanging limp in the crooks of their folded arms.

"You haven't worn them in front of the Punjabi community. It's different," Banu replied. "I don't want my daughters walking across a stage to receive their honours and people only focusing on their bare arms. This is like going to the temple."

"It's the Hilton," Kiran corrected.

"Yes, Kiran Sandhu, I know very well where we're going, thanks," Banu said. "Now put on that cardigan or you're not going anywhere."

With matching scowls, the girls reluctantly put on their cardigans. Banu turned to Gurdev with a sigh. "The same battle every day. They're shameless. You should see what they do with the Sacred Heart uniforms—how they tighten those belts and roll the waists of their skirts." She shook her head.

"Do you think this is too much?" she asked. She held up a pair of glittery earrings. "I don't want people to think I'm showing off."

"You look very nice," Gurdev said. He stole a quick peck on her cheek. She gave him a playful shove in the chest. "Chee. In front of the girls!" The girls were nowhere to be seen. "Rani!" Banu called. "Rani, what are you doing in the toilet?"

Rani's tiny voice came as an echo. "Just finishing."

Moments later, the sound of the toilet flushing, the tap running, and Rani appeared in the doorway in her puffy pink dress. "This is my baby," Banu cooed. "This little baby doesn't want to look silly, hmm?" Rani giggled and buried her face in the pleats of Banu's sari. "Go sit in the living room and wait for us, okay?"

"Kay," Rani said.

Banu turned back to Gurdev. "So? Earrings or no earrings?"

"They look fine," he said. "They match your sari."

Banu held the earrings up and turned her head at an angle. She slipped them on and then turned again. She frowned. "It's okay for me to be wearing a sari, right?"

"Why wouldn't it be?"

"I don't know, I overheard some temple ladies, the younger set, saying they might wear evening gowns."

"Evening gowns?" Gurdev repeated.

"It is a hotel function, not a temple thing," Banu said nervously. "But it's a Sikh Association dinner. Oh, I don't know. I'm sure I won't be the only one in traditional dress." She went to the doorway and called out for the girls to finish getting ready. Gurdev held out his wrists in a silent request for Banu to fasten his cufflinks.

"He'll be there," she said quietly to Gurdev. "Your favourite brother."

"Cousin," Gurdev corrected. "I'm not afraid of him. We saw him last year at Surtaj Singh's son's wedding. He was fine. He's over it."

Banu shook her head. "Gurdev, where money is concerned, things don't just become water under the bridge. I've been telling you for years now, call him, have a talk and sort this out. Explain why we did it."

"He would have brought it up by now," Gurdev said. "I don't know why he hasn't. Maybe he realised he was being greedy. Maybe he knows it's going to a worthy cause. Look at what our girls have achieved. A Sikh Association Award recognising them for the highest primary school exam results in the community. Karam and Sona don't even have kids."

Banu stared at him and pulled away. "I certainly hope you don't bring that up!" she exclaimed. According to temple gossip, Karam and Sona had tried unsuccessfully for the past few years. Sona wanted to adopt but Karam didn't and the resulting rift explained why they were rarely seen together. Rumour had it they were separated.

After a bit more primping, Gurdev and his family left for the Hilton. Orchard Road glittered with Christmas lights and displays. The girls stared out of the taxi windows in awe of the looming buildings. Gurdev recalled none of this spectacle when he was growing up. "There was only one department store: CK Tang," he told the girls. It was still there but the original building, an Imperial Palace replica, had been demolished two years ago to make way for a new, sleek Tang complex.

As they set foot in the cavernous hotel ballroom, Gurdev felt his pride swell. All of these tables, all of these members of the community, would see his daughters honoured for their academic achievements. He searched the room for Karam but did not see him. *Even better*, he thought.

An usher showed them to their table and pulled out the chairs for Banu and the girls. Kiran and Simran chatted excitedly, ignoring their younger sister. "How's my Rani-Pani?" Gurdev asked.

"Fine, thank you," Rani said, with a grin.

A woman passed their table. Banu and Gurdev both turned to watch her. Dressed in a deep green evening gown with a bare back, she sauntered to a table where another woman sat in a similar outfit. Gurdev shared a look with Banu. She looked down at her sari and smoothed out the pleats. "Shameless," she whispered to him. There were other women wearing saris and salwar kameezes as well, but they were clearly in the minority. Gurdev was reminded of the wedding he had attended a year ago when he saw the twin boys of Vickram Singh, an old classmate of his, with their hair completely shorn off. It certainly seemed more common these days but it did not make it right. He glanced over at Kiran and Simran and noticed—though it might have been a trick of the dimmed lights—that their cardigan buttons had come undone. Simran turned to catch his eye and quickly whispered something to Kiran. They hastily buttoned up their cardigans.

Banu found a friend and began chatting with her. Rani looked bored. Gurdev picked up a programme from the table and showed it to her. "Read the header for me, Rani," he said. Rani frowned and looked away. "Come on," he coaxed. "Just show Daddy you're a smarty-pants like your sisters." Rani had taken longer to learn to read than any of the other children in her class. Gurdev and Banu practised with her at home each night, but she struggled to form the words.

"Welcome to," he began, "the…"

"An… annu…" Rani read.

"Annual," Gurdev completed. Rani looked away.

The lights dimmed further and the celebrations began. Tablas thumped loudly as a bhangra group danced. Three course meals were served. The Minister for Education gave a speech. Gurdev had highlighted this feature of the evening's programme to Father when he tried to convince him to come along. Father did not leave the flat often these days and only went to the temple on weekday mornings, when fewer people were likely to see him.

An usher came to tell the girls to sit up at the front. "Go on," Banu said, waving at Kiran and Simran. They smiled shyly and followed the usher, walking close together. Once they were seated, Kiran turned back to look at Gurdev and whispered something to Simran. Casually, they both slipped out of their cardigans and left them hanging on their chairs.

Staring at the girls in the hope of getting their attention, Gurdev vaguely noticed somebody pulling up a chair next to him, as the president of the Sikh Association was called to the stage to give his remarks. When the applause died down, a familiar voice asked, "How are things going, brother?"

Gurdev turned to face Karam. "Hey," he said with a quick cough to hide his surprise. "I didn't think you were here."

"I arrived a bit late. That Christmas traffic is madness,"

Karam said. He nodded at the president. "I'm on the Board."

"I didn't know that."

"I knew you'd be here tonight." As Karam spoke, Gurdev caught a whiff of whiskey. He searched the room quickly for Sona, but she wasn't there. "You must be very proud of your girls," Karam said. There wasn't a trace of pleasantness in his voice.

Banu returned to the table. She and Karam greeted each other. Rani tugged at her sari. "I need to take Rani to the rest room. I'll be right back," she said, shooting another look at Gurdev.

"How is work?" Gurdev asked.

"Good," Karam said. "Great, actually. I got a grant to spend my sabbatical year in Malaysia doing some research there."

"That's nice. Congratulations."

"Thanks." Karam took a sip from his glass. "How's the family? How's your father?"

"He's all right."

"I haven't seen him lately."

"He doesn't go out much," Gurdev shrugged.

"And Narain?" Karam asked.

"He's all right," Gurdev said. "I haven't seen a lot of him recently but he's still living with Father."

"No plans to marry?" Karam asked.

Gurdev felt his face flush. "Karam, why do you do this?" he asked.

Karam held up his hands as if to surrender. "I'm just asking," he said.

"Let him be," Gurdev said. "He's never done anything to harm you."

"I wouldn't say that," Karam replied. "I've seen him around the university lately, causing trouble."

"Narain causing trouble? You've got the wrong person."

"It's definitely Narain. Your little brother. Handing out leaflets and talking about staging a demonstration. He mixes with a certain crowd—postgraduate sociology and political science students. They get so caught up in all their questioning and case studies that they forget where they are."

"You must have mistaken another man for Narain. With that short hair—"

"Oh, I know his face very well. I'll have no problem describing it to the authorities," Karam said calmly, turning towards the stage. "Your girls are about to receive their awards," he told Gurdev. An announcer was on the stage, reading out the list of accomplishments. Kiran and Simran sat up, their shoulders taut.

"Don't you dare, Karam," Gurdev said. "Narain could be locked away." This was all he knew of what happened to dissidents nowadays. Detained in a dark cell, somewhere in a corner of the island. The newspapers didn't mention it; nor did they mention the agencies that kept track of citizens' movements, placing them on blacklists for disrespecting the government. Everybody just knew they existed.

"You know what I can't stand about people like Narain?" Karam continued. "The lack of gratitude. Look at how far the country has come. He goes out and complains because he doesn't want to work to fit in with the rest of us. He just wants to carry on with his bapok ways."

The word, implying that Narain was a transvestite, gave Gurdev a chill. "You don't know anything," he told Karam.

"This is none of your business."

Karam turned to face him. "It's every bit my business. I'm a citizen. I have the privilege of knowing that my country won't be wrecked by the instabilities that have brought down so many other nations. If I need to report your brother, I will. I would think you'd be on my side on this. It's bad enough that people are always talking about Amrit. What has she done with herself? Never married, never even able to get engaged again after that last time. Living in bars and wasting her life away. You know her latest, don't you? Cleaning toilets at Singapore General Hospital. I'll be surprised if she holds down that job."

Gurdev clenched his fists into tight balls. Over the announcer's voice, he could hear his own quick breathing, like steam escaping from a pressure cooker. Karam seemed unaffected by his anger. The announcer called out, "Kiran Kaur Sandhu." Kiran walked across the stage, smiling radiantly.

Gurdev's heart began to pound as Karam leaned towards him. "Don't," he began to say. It came out like a plea. *Don't ruin this moment for me.*

"Simran Kaur Sandhu," the announcer called. Simran stepped out onto the stage, her smile less confident, her eyes squeezed against the brightness of the lights.

"Amrit was good at her schoolwork as well," Karam said. "What is she doing with all her big talents now?"

Gurdev saw nothing but darkness. He grabbed Karam by the collar with one arm and swung back the other. When a woman across the room gasped, Gurdev realised that his fist had connected with Karam's jaw, the first in a succession of punches. Expletives flew from his lips.

Two firm arms clamped tightly around his chest, pulling him up and away. The house lights were turned on and the evening suddenly washed in brightness, stripping away its glamour. There were several people talking to him at once, and a firm voice telling him to sit.

· · ·

In the morning, he woke to find himself alone in bed. Weak threads of sunlight streamed through the windows, giving the faintest glow to the cupboards and the bathroom door. He turned to his side, then turned back again. It was time to face Banu.

She was sitting on the living room couch with a cup of tea. When she shifted to place the tea on the table, the rattan creaked to protest her movements. Gurdev knew from the way she stiffened that she was aware of his presence. The flat was entirely silent. He strained his ears to hear the girls' voices.

"They're not here," Banu said. She had a way of anticipating his questions. "I sent them out to the shops to buy a few things." As she spoke, Gurdev saw faint lines spreading on her face. She had not taken off her make-up. The glittering earrings from the night before had been tossed onto the coffee table. In all of their years of marriage, they had always slept in the same bed. "Banu," he started, feeling a lump rising in his throat.

"You can't say anything to justify it," she said. "He angered you, I'm sure. I don't want to know who said what or who threw the first punch." She turned to Gurdev. "You fought, Gurdev. A grown man getting into a brawl with his cousin in front of all those people."

"He was telling lies about Amrit," said Gurdev. He ignored the hand that Banu held up to silence him. "He was saying that our daughters would be just like her, that she works as a cleaner."

"He wasn't lying," Banu said. "I heard about it last night, too. Now they'll go around saying you're a violent drunkard as well."

"How can Amrit be cleaning toilets?"

"Go over to your father's flat today," Banu said. "Bring Amrit back here."

"For what?" Gurdev asked.

"She'll stay here. I will have her help me around the house. Cooking, cleaning, laundry."

"That doesn't make any sense," Gurdev said. "She'll be fine for a few days and then she'll just take advantage of the situation. That's what she does, Banu. Worse yet, our girls will be exposed to all of it."

"She won't have a chance to misbehave," Banu said. "All she needs is discipline. What do you expect from a girl who was only brought up by men? She's been rebelling like a teenager for years now, going wild because nobody ever taught her about moderation."

Gurdev folded his hands over his chest. "This is ridiculous. You're just inviting trouble. Do you know what type of company she keeps? You want those men to come knocking around here?"

"They won't," Banu replied. "Amrit won't be given a house key and we'll tell her that if we get so much as a phone call from any man—"

"What makes you think she will agree to it? She's not a child."

"You let me handle that," Banu said. "I will talk to her very frankly about where her life is going to go if she continues like this. Over here, she has three meals a day, a clean room and a job. I will pay her. She is already doing such work. She might as well do it in the privacy of our home rather than in public. No telephone, no going out at night. If she wants to be entertained, we are here. If she makes one wrong move, if she tries to sneak out, if she uses the phone to call any of her friends, she's out and she won't have a second chance."

Gurdev opened his mouth to say more but he was met with Banu's steely stare. "You keep protesting and you can be the one who sleeps on the couch from now on. What you did yesterday, Gurdev—I don't know if our daughters will ever forget that humiliation. It will take a long time for things to get back to normal in this home."

Gurdev took in a sharp breath and looked away from Banu. He could hear his heartbeat; it felt as if it had not stopped this rapid, insistent beating since his fight with Karam the night before. "I'll call Karam to apologise," he offered weakly.

"Oh, yes, you'll do that too," Banu said with false cheer. "Don't think I've left that out. You will tell him that you were wrong, cowardly and plain stupid. You will also have that conversation that you've been avoiding for years about the damn inheritance money." She looked around and sighed. "If I had known, Gurdev, that it would cause so much trouble for us—"

"You would have pressured me to take it anyway," Gurdev cut in. "Let's not pretend that our daughters' education was not worth that. If anything, I did my father a favour taking that money from Karam. Karam was always after the money."

"He was always after winning," Banu said. "Yesterday, you allowed it to happen." With that, she picked herself up off the couch and left Gurdev in the living room, his heart pounding to the sound of this fresh truth.

• • •

When Narain opened the door, Gurdev was greeted with a familiar odour. The flat was musty, the living room carpets faded, the coffee table surface stripped of its sheen. "Is Amrit here?" Gurdev asked. He wished Banu were here to see the state of this place. *And you expect her to clean our house*, he would retort.

"No," said Narain. He nodded towards the master bedroom door. "Father's inside but I think he's taking a shower."

"That's all right," Gurdev said. "I can wait." He stood awkwardly towards the hallway. "Where do you think Amrit might be?"

"The usual," Narain said. Gurdev took a careful look at Narain and noticed the tension with which he carried himself. His arms didn't just fall at his sides; they were rigid like rifles.

"How are you these days? How's work?" Gurdev asked.

Narain shrugged and muttered that he was doing fine.

To fill the silence, Gurdev launched into an update about the girls. Their antics never failed to bring a smile to Narain's face. He told Narain about how Rani had thought that the bus interchange was where money came from. "Those change machines. She saw all of those coins and thought that dollar notes were some sort of coupon that you exchange for real money. You should have seen her face—so confused when Kiran and Simran explained that coins were worth less than dollars. She said, "but coins are heavier." If you think about it, children have the right logic."

It worked somewhat, although Narain's smile was distant. He made a vague motion at Father's door. "He should be out in a bit." He wandered into his room and looked surprised when Gurdev followed him in.

"What do you want, Gurdev?" Narain asked sharply.

"I just want to check up on you," Gurdev said.

"Why?" Narain squinted, as if searching out Gurdev's intentions.

"We haven't spoken in a while," Gurdev said. "How are you?"

"I'm just fine, Gurdev. When I'm not at work, I'm busy making sure Amrit stays out of trouble. I only catch a break when she's gone or when nobody is at home. When I'm not doing either of those duties, I have to keep Father company because he's at home all the time now. I run his errands for him, and when Amrit isn't around I cook and clean. I attend all the weddings and prayer sessions that he is too embarrassed to go to, like I'm some kind of representative of his. I try to leave quickly, yet somehow people manage to stop me to ask about our family. They ask about you and Banu and the girls, and I always tell them that you're all doing very well, even though you hardly ever drop by."

Gurdev flinched at the accusation and wanted to say something in his defence but Narain was intent on continuing.

"Then they ask about Father. Why haven't they seen him

lately? How long has it been? I tell them that Father has been feeling a bit unwell. They nod sympathetically and say, of course. I've been giving them this excuse for years now and they have been accepting it. You know what they do next, Gurdev? They ask me why I'm not married. They say, 'why haven't you settled down with a nice girl?' As if they don't know what I am—they want me to say it. Do you know why they feel as if they can twist some sort of confession out of me?"

"Narain—"

Narain's voice rose. "Because they haven't asked about Amrit. They think they've done us a favour by not talking about her, as if she's dead to us. They think this means they're on my side."

Gurdev's eyes roamed across the room. A pair of jeans and a shirt were strewn across the ironing board and a few open bills lay on the bedside table. These were all the things Narain owned. By the time Gurdev was his age, he had two daughters and a home filled with furniture. He had a wife who cooked his favourite meals and ironed his clothes.

"We have a plan for Amrit," Gurdev said. "We want her to stay at our place for a while."

Narain looked at him with suspicion. "What kind of plan is that?"

"Just leave it to us," Gurdev said. "You can have a bit more time to yourself then." A question burned in him and he wished he could just ask Narain—was he? Was he gay? But each time the word reached the tip of his tongue, Gurdev could not bring himself to say it, as if the word itself was as difficult to pronounce as its meaning was to understand. "Narain, have you been at the university campus lately?" he asked quickly.

Narain stared at him as if he didn't understand the question. Gurdev felt a tickle of irritation. "Leaflets, anti-government things. I heard that you've been passing them out and talking about organising some sort of demonstration. Is this true?"

"We live in a democracy," Narain finally said. There was only a hint of sarcasm in his voice.

"That's what you'll say if they throw you behind bars?" Gurdev shot back. "You're being stupid. You're jeopardising all of our lives."

"How am I doing that?" Narain asked. "You think some mysterious officers, some henchmen, are going to slip into your flat in the middle of the night and haul your family off to a jail cell because I've handed out some fliers?"

"That's what they've been doing," Gurdev insisted. He noticed the sneer on Narain's face, telling him how naive he was to believe in such things. "This isn't a joke."

"How do you *know* this?" Narain asked. "How do you know those aren't just rumours? Has it been in the papers? Have the ministers gone on television and threatened to do this?"

"No, but, listen Narain you don't want to challenge—"

"It doesn't happen, Gurdev. These are scare tactics. They've been spreading them for years to keep us in order. I'm not breaking any law by speaking up against the government. A democracy should allow for conversation."

"So that's what you plan on telling them if they arrest you," Gurdev demanded. "You could lose everything if it turns out that you're wrong."

"Everything," Narain repeated. "Tell them to come and take it then." He stormed out of the room, leaving Gurdev standing there, bewildered. Gurdev looked around, unsure of what to do. He picked up a few of Narain's things, absent-mindedly clearing the mess, as if he could make sense of his brother if he just reduced this clutter. He picked up a pair of Narain's jeans and noticed that the back pockets were padded with paper. He reached in and pulled out a folded square of yellow paper. A flier with bold-printed words shouted:

Do you want to fight for your rights?
Are you tired of being told that
your opinions don't matter?
NO MORE NANNY STATE

Below those headlines were details of the meeting of a collective. *Join Us For An Open Discussion*, encouraged the welcoming print. Gurdev scrunched the flier into a ball and tore through the room, looking for others. He found them in the pockets of pants, in a satchel, in drawers. He collected all of them and bolted from the flat without saying goodbye.

Father

SHAME HAD A blinding effect on Harbeer. Leaving the flat one morning, he opened the main door to discover Amrit sleeping near the potted plants, a set of house keys dangling from her pocket. He stepped around her like a thief, and hurried away as she began to stir. Shame fuelled his walk to the coffee shop.

The next day, the newspaper ran an article about a collision that had occurred on the corner of their street at 8.30am, between a bread truck and a motorcycle. Witnesses to the scene were encouraged to call the listed number with any information. Harbeer recognised the location but he could not recall noticing an accident scene. Surely police officers and flashing lights would have captured his attention. He searched his mind, but he realised that his inner turmoil had transported him to some pitch-black road, where all of his worst thoughts nested.

When empty, the temple was Harbeer's daily refuge from the thoughts that crowded his brain. It was the only place he ventured to, besides the shops. Every day at the crack of dawn, the chill of morning bristling the hairs on his arms, he took the bus and then walked into the narrow lanes. How different the world was when the day was just beginning. School children slumped like sacks of rice on the low plastic bus stop seats. The sky displayed an ever-changing palette of pink, blue, orange, and sometimes fiercely red, streaks. He could not adjust his ears to this absence of noise. Taxis and buses sailed along the roads at intervals instead of as one gushing torrent. The typical chatter of children was replaced with a collective mournful sigh, the sound his granddaughters emitted when told they had to finish all their vegetables.

The temple was vacant on weekday mornings, save for a few elderly retirees and the granthi, whose warbling voice filtered out of the gates and broke like dew among the morning murmurs. Harbeer always took time washing his hands after removing his shoes. It disgusted him to see people walking shamelessly into the temple without cleaning their hands first. After touching the dirt of the earth, how could they enter a place of worship and press their palms to the carpet as they bowed before their Holy Book? And how could they use those filthy fingers to offer their coins to the temple before rising and finding a spot on the carpet to sit? Witnessing such atrocities brought to mind a list of grievances. The strip of red carpet on which people walked when they entered and bowed—when was the last time it had been vacuumed or at least beaten with a straw sapu? It was so littered with lint and thread and hair that it had turned into a dusty red, the colour of crumbling brick walls. The constant chatter during services bothered him as well. It came mostly from the women's side of the temple, where covered heads huddled together and exchanged the latest gossip. He did not like the poor ventilation or the slow-running fan that didn't stir the air so much as weakly shift and toss the occasional string of dust onto the floor. There were issues with the cutlery in the dining hall. Several times he had picked up a spoon to see a faint half-circle of dried yoghurt mirroring his frown. There were problems with the splintering benches, the dented aluminium table tipping his cup of tea at a dangerous angle, the winding food queues that looped around so that there was no way of knowing where they began or ended.

During prayers, Harbeer caught sight of Bhajanjit Singh, the President of the Sikh Association. Retired from the armed forces, Bhajanjit Singh was in the temple on most weekdays but he did not stay long in the prayer hall. He had his own office on the second level of the temple, where he ran committee meetings. Harbeer had long given up trying to join the committee; as Amrit's father, he was not welcome in those circles. However, looking at his surroundings, Harbeer felt confident enough to catch up with Bhajanjit in the langar hall afterwards. He told Bhajanjit that the temple needed to change.

"Yes," Bhajanjit said, "very good. Unfortunately, our committee is full."

"I'm not asking to be on any committee," Harbeer said. "I just want to know if these things are on the agenda."

"They're not a priority," Bhajanjit replied. "I see your point, but as you know, the government is tearing down the property. It's become too old. We will be moving into a building in the east. We hope to avoid all of those issues in the new place."

"Tearing it down?" Harbeer asked, incredulously.

"Yes," Bhajanjit said. "It's been in the newspapers." Harbeer didn't tell him that he'd largely stopped reading the newspapers lately. The government's new tactic to curb littering and rule-breaking was to publish photos beside full names and job titles of culprits, and he discovered that he could not face the shame of strangers any more than he could handle his own.

Bhajanjit continued: "The new location is different. It won't be a temple on its own. There are other religious organisations in this building, so there's one large room for each. There's a Buddhist prayer centre, a Taoist room, and classroom spaces for lessons. And then we have the gurudwara in one room and a langar hall in another. There's a lift…"

As Bhajanjit continued, Harbeer looked out of the window and decided that from now, it would be better to follow his own instructions. If he had to pray to God in a soulless concrete room that was stacked with other religions, then he might as well worship from home. One of his former police colleagues who had moved to London, Surinder Singh, did this. He told Harbeer that his bones could not handle the chill of the walk to the temple, even though it was well within walking distance, so his children had arranged to convert his spare bedroom into a prayer room.

Back at home, the portrait of Guru Nanak was already on the wall in the corner of the flat where Harbeer had his afternoon tea. Guru Nanak had the kindly eyes of a holy man who had been through his own troubles defending the truth. Harbeer brought out his Holy Books and stacked them carefully on the coffee table. On their threadbare covers, some of the gold printed letters had faded into oblivion, leaving gaps that reminded Harbeer of his granddaughters' smiles in the days when their first few teeth had emerged. He cleared the unimportant items from the vicinity of the Guru's portrait until all that was left was this tower of books, a cassette player for playing prayer tapes, and a potted plant. He sat on the floor, crossed his legs, and began to pray. He hadn't missed the temple until today: New Year's Eve.

• • •

Harbeer had gone to the temple every year on 31 December, praying solemnly with the rest of the congregation, as white balloons spiralled and tumbled towards the dome ceiling at the stroke of midnight. He had been planning to go this year but while bringing out a shirt to iron for the evening, when he passed Amrit's room he thought he saw her gazing into her mirror. He paused and blinked. The room was empty; Amrit had been gone since yesterday. His mind was simply playing tricks on him. This Amrit pressed a cotton-tipped brush into a vial of dark green powder and brushed it across her eyelids. Instantly, her face became fierce. Harbeer swallowed a few times but the dryness in his throat remained.

Harbeer left the flat and headed to the nearby 7-Eleven. He picked up a bottle of Jack Daniels and passed it to the cashier, who smiled. "Happy New Year, Uncle! You're celebrating tonight, ah?"

Harbeer responded with a tight smile. "Happy New Year," he murmured as he descended the single step and turned back towards the street. Back at the flat, his heart leapt when he saw the padlock dangling from the gate. She was back.

In the living room, he made a show of pouring the drink over piles of ice in two of his fine crystal glasses. The tart smell stung the air. "Amrit," he called. He assumed that the shuffling footsteps and the faint shadow that fell over the table were hers, so he continued. "Amrit, I'll make a deal with you." He picked up a glass and turned his head, only to see Narain looking at the glass.

"Is your name Amrit?" Harbeer snapped.

Narain walked back into his room. Harbeer put the glass down on the table and sighed. "What are you doing tonight?" he called.

There was a long pause before Narain finally poked his head out of his room and replied. "Going into town."

"Amrit?" Harbeer called out again.

Again, Narain appeared. "She's not here," he said to his father.

Harbeer looked in the direction of the front door. He noticed Narain watching him. "Do you want a drink?" he asked.

Narain hesitated before taking a seat across from him. "I don't like it with ice," he said. Harbeer ignored the comment and pushed the glass towards him. Narain took a quick sip and then put the glass down and looked away. Harbeer also turned his head towards the balcony, hoping that the view would present something neutral to discuss. The glow of city lights drowned the presence of stars. Later, Harbeer hoped, the sound of fireworks would crush this silence as well.

Narain picked up the glass and took another sip. This one was more drawn out, and when he placed the glass back down on the table, Harbeer noticed that half the drink was gone. Narain grimaced, sucked in his lips and then appeared to relax.

"Some more?" Harbeer asked.

"Why are you doing this?" Narain asked.

"It's New Year's Eve," Harbeer said.

"This glass was for Amrit, wasn't it?"

"Yes."

"Why?"

"We already knew she'd be drinking tonight. There was no way to stop this. I thought we could have an agreement. If she had a few drinks here, maybe we could convince her to stay at home for a change. She can be as stupid as she wants but still be under this roof." Harbeer searched for the right word. "Contained," he said, gulping down the remains of his drink and pouring another glass.

Narain shook his head. "She would just drink here and then drink more once she got out. And then after this, she'd think the rules were relaxed. Don't you know anything about Amrit?" He looked disgusted as he rose from the table. "And then you know what happens?" he continued. "I have to go pick her up or bail her out and bring her home. That's what I have to look forward to in the new year—more worries with Amrit."

Harbeer set down his drink. "Who the hell do you think you are?" he shouted. "Calling me stupid. You better watch your mouth. Remember whose house you're living in, who paid so much money to send you to America, who gave you a future after you nearly ruined yours. One drunken daughter and one useless son I have."

Narain dismissed his tirade with a wave and walked away.

Harbeer felt the heat in his face and his lips curling into a snarl as he continued to list all of Narain's failures. "Couldn't play a single sport, couldn't spend one day in primary school without crying, couldn't pack your own bloody bags to go to university."

The bedroom door slammed shut behind Narain. This was what he had become lately, sullen and angry all the time. "Does he think it's easy for me?" Harbeer asked aloud. They were trapped in this flat because of Amrit, reduced to catering to her whims.

Harbeer felt a twist in his chest and took a long sip of whiskey to recover from it. He cleared both glasses from the table and put the bottle in his cabinet, which was now secured by a heavy padlock. He sat back on the couch and stared at the sky. He should have been seething. He should have been pacing the house, preparing a response for a follow-up confrontation. He would have been doing just that if not for the crippling sense of shame that flooded his body and drowned his surroundings in its large black tide. Narain was right. In his desperation to save face, he had thrown away his common sense. What was he thinking, buying whiskey for his daughter?

He put his head in his hands for a long time and only looked up when he noticed that Dalveer had entered the flat. Even she seemed to tower over him now. He shot up angrily from his chair. "What are you doing here?" he whispered urgently. She had begun to appear unexpectedly, taking him by surprise. Narain was inside his room getting ready to go out; what if he emerged from his room and saw Harbeer talking to her? Harbeer waved her away. "Come back later," he insisted. "Just go away now." As usual, she paid no attention to his demands. She disappeared into his room and returned, holding out his shirt towards him. He was not aware of the evening breeze until it rippled through the fabric. There was a distant rumbling outside.

"I'll celebrate quietly here," he told her dimly. "The temple is always too crowded on New Year's Eve." He had to raise his voice slightly. Some early fireworks had begun. They shot up in single arrows above the buildings and then blossomed into brilliant flowers. As she turned towards the kitchen, he considered asking her to sit with him here and watch the display, even though he knew she would refuse. She never enjoyed a spectacle.

Narain

HE RUSHED TO get dressed, ignoring Father's silence. In his own mind, his own raging thoughts were a whirlwind. What was Father thinking, buying whiskey for Amrit? The mere idea of it made Narain want to storm back into the living room and give Father another piece of his mind. He glanced at his watch and realised he was already running late for his dinner plans. A pair of jeans lay slung over the ironing board. These and a button-down shirt would have to do.

In the taxi on the way into the city, Narain created a few excuses for his lateness. He would need to tell Dennis that something had occurred that was out of his control—a traffic accident, a plumbing problem in the flat. "Acts of God," his friend Wei Yi used to say, having discovered the term in the fine print of an insurance booklet. Narain found himself constantly creating acts of God to explain his tardiness and absences. Months ago, they were enough to convince Dennis, but Narain failed to maintain their veracity, so that a few days later when he was asked about his fictitious burst pipe, one blank stare betrayed his dishonesty.

The city lights glittered as the taxi inched across the highway. Narain tapped impatiently on every surface he could find—the seats, the door handle, the window—until the taxi driver glanced at him in the rearview mirror and politely told him to stop. The taxi's interior smelled overwhelmingly of the pandan leaves used to ward off cockroaches. "Do you have plans for New Year's?" Narain asked the driver, hoping to be distracted by conversation.

"No," the driver said, sullenly. "Just working only."

When he finally arrived, he saw Dennis standing at the entrance to the restaurant. "Forty minutes," Dennis said. "I didn't even go in because I didn't want to be waiting alone." His mouth was set in a grim line.

"I'm so sorry," Narain said. Out here in the open, he couldn't draw Dennis closer and apologise more tenderly. Except for in Dennis's condominium, they had to present themselves as business associates or family friends. They could also pass as cousins, with Dennis's Portuguese Eurasian ancestry giving him the same skin tone as Narain. Maintaining the stance of a teacher seeking an explanation, Dennis always prolonged these awkward moments. Narain immediately became the wayward student, shifting his weight from one foot to the other. "I didn't actually leave that late. The traffic is building up. I had this unpleasant taxi driver." Dennis sighed and walked ahead of him into the restaurant.

"So what was it this time?" Dennis asked when they were seated and their drink orders had been taken.

Sensing that he could not get away with a lie tonight, Narain opted for the truth. "It was Amrit. My father went out and bought her drinks tonight so she wouldn't be tempted to go out and find a party."

Dennis's face softened. "That's terrible," he said.

"I can't believe he would do that," Narain said. "It's just encouraging her. He must be going mad, staying at home all the time as he does. He honestly thinks this is the right thing to do."

"On the other hand, I can see the logic behind it," Dennis pondered aloud, "as strange as it seems."

"Let's not talk about her any more," Narain said. "I've said it—there, it's out. I don't want to drag my problems with Amrit into the new year." His face brightened. "Did you write your resolutions? I've got mine. I suppose I've already told you my first one: stop getting mixed up in Amrit's problems." This resolution was written nowhere. It had only occurred to him now. "I shouldn't have lingered to argue with my father tonight. I had plans with you. Next time I'll just give him my input and leave before it turns into a debate."

There was a pause, an expression registering on Dennis's face. It was a look that, over the years, Narain had come to recognise on these men in his life. It was the same mix of weariness and gentleness that appeared when adults were left with no choice but to explain to children the facts of their world. "Narain," Dennis said, "as long as you're living there, she's going to be your problem. You'll be involved wholeheartedly."

Narain looked away. From the window, the city shone like a jewel. Revellers sauntered past in gathering crowds. "I can't just pack up and leave home," he said.

"You've done it before," Dennis said. This, too, was familiar to Narain. Men always thought they could motivate Narain by citing his previous brushes with rebellion. They appealed to his history and told his tales as if they had been there themselves. Before Dennis, Narain had been with Alex, a German expatriate who ridiculed Narain for believing he could maintain this double life. Alex had taken every opportunity to remind Narain of his first affair, Adam. Narain did little to protest such taunts from Alex because they made him nostalgic for those days—fleeing from his home as Amrit's engagement dissolved, rushing into that maze of back lanes as if he already knew its turns and corners, pressing his lips to Adam's as the smoggy air swelled to greet the monsoon. Each time he got a haircut now he remembered every titillating sensation of that evening: Adam's warm chest, the pelts of rain surprising the nape of his neck. He had sneaked into the flat later that night to collect a few of his things and returned to the back lane to rent a cheap room, opening his door only for visits from Adam. For six weeks, not a word from his family. His chest had housed a hard ache during the first days, as he pictured the shadows on Father's face darkening at the knowledge of another betrayal. He thought often about what was going on in the flat in his absence, watching the details of Amrit's broken engagement play out like a muted movie. The family would return the rings, cancel the invitation orders, haggle over the return of the venue deposit. Narain had expected that such stories would always occupy his mind, whether he ever heard from his family again or not, but soon his daily life began to take on a routine that did not include them. In their absence, there was Adam and the bustle of the back lane to fill his days. "I have never been so happy," he had told Adam. Recalling that he had said these words to Jenny years before on that lawn in Iowa, Narain had been struck by how pale that old happiness seemed in comparison.

Then one day Amrit showed up at the flat. "I followed

you from your work," she had said, her flitting eyes and matted hair giving the words a more sinister meaning than the simple affection she meant to convey.

"Go home," Narain had said nervously, feeling exposed. He had pushed her away, roughly. Watching her stumble out onto the back lane, a knot of guilt tightened in Narain's stomach. He had packed his bags to leave the following day, explaining to Adam that he would only be gone for a few days. "I just need to make sure she's okay. I have no idea what's going on over there." Adam had eyed the bags, filled with everything Narain owned, and did not say a word. Father was similarly quiet when Narain returned. Whenever he remembered his time with Adam, Narain thought about how silence had bookended both his departure and return.

"I know what will happen," Narain said to Dennis, now. "I can't just leave her. Look at what nearly happened tonight. If I hadn't been there to talk some sense into my father, he and Amrit would be getting drunk together now."

The waiter arrived to take their orders. Narain scanned the menu and pointed to an item. He had lost his appetite anyway. He waited for the waiter to leave before he leaned closer to Dennis. "I'll figure something out. Something will change."

"You've been saying that for years," Dennis reminded him.

"I've known you for five months," Narain said.

"You know what I mean, Narain," Dennis said. "You've never been in a serious relationship."

After Adam, there was Jai, a married colleague with teenage children. They met in hotels and had rendezvous in Thailand and Indonesia. Business trips, they told their families. Then there was the baby-faced Michael, whose blissfully senile mother never questioned Narain's evening visits. Alex came next. His status as a visitor to Singapore was a relief to Narain because it made the relationship temporary. In between, there had been brief flings and one night stands that had originated in secret bars like the one they were going to tonight.

"That's not true," Narain joked. "There was a girl in America."

"This isn't funny," Dennis said. "If you want to be with me, with anyone, you have to be able to give up something. Your family knows you're gay. You just haven't acknowledged it to them. You're trapping yourself in that flat and you're using your sister as an excuse—but really, you just don't want to leave. It's comfortable there."

Narain's throat felt dry. "Why are we talking about this?" he asked, after taking a sip of water. "It's New Year's Eve. We should be celebrating."

"That's exactly why we're talking about it," Dennis said. He sighed. "You were forty minutes late tonight, Narain. I don't want to sit here and pretend it didn't bother me. I'm not starting off a year with lies."

"That's why I told you the truth about Amrit tonight."

"This is the problem. You've become so used to living a false life that you think you should be commended for telling the truth."

"Look at us," Narain said. "What difference does another lie make? Everything we do is packaged in lies. We can't hold hands, we can't kiss, we're speaking in whispers right now because we're so afraid that we'll be heard." He felt a stab as he listed each of his limitations. Somewhere tonight, Amrit was doing all of these things with no fear of legal consequences.

"Now you're using the government as an excuse," Dennis said. "It's because of them that we can't live together, right? That's rubbish, Narain. If neighbours ask, we can say we're flatmates. Some young people are starting to do that; they want a taste of independence so they rent apartments now. That's a lie I'm willing to tell because it's also true—we will be flatmates. What we do in the bedroom is nobody's business. The police are only going around arresting gays who flaunt it in public. Mocking family values, they're calling it."

"I can't," Narain said quietly, knowing that everything Dennis said was true. "I'm sorry, Dennis, I just can't." How many times had he come to the same conversation and with how many different men? He looked pleadingly at Dennis, hoping that this time, there would be a different conclusion.

"Then I can't either," Dennis said. He looked mildly surprised at his decision, as if it had just come to him.

They agreed to be amicable. Their plan was to attend the celebrations with their friends that evening, and then go their separate ways. They walked through the city, too conscious of the space that had to be kept between them. The streets were beginning to fill with people. Narain allowed the current of the crowds to carry him along.

He filled the silence between them by talking about Gurdev's visit. "It was strange. He showed up at the flat and asked me whether I had been spending any time at the university."

"How did he know about that?" Dennis asked.

Narain shrugged. "Somebody must have mentioned it. I have a cousin who works in the Science faculty. My brother started going on about blacklists and consequences.

I couldn't listen to any of it. All of that fear. He thinks I'll lose my job—or worse: have my picture on the news."

"Imagine what my work would do to me if they knew," Dennis said. He was a researcher for one of the news radio stations. "That would be the end."

"But it hasn't stopped you," Narain pointed out. He and Dennis had met through a small underground group, mostly postgraduate students who were dissatisfied with the government. Alex's friend, Wei Yi, had invited him into the group. The group used to meet on weekends, in Alex's apartment, Alex being unafraid of consequences because of his diplomatic immunity. After Alex was posted to London, Narain urged the group to stay together. He found other locations for them to meet and plan—they had picnics in parks, study groups in libraries where they passed extensive notes to each other, and long drives across the country. They dubbed these last ones the Forty Minute Meetings because that's how long it took to cross the length of Singapore by car. There were members of the group who only showed up to the occasional meeting, and few of its original members still remained. Many had been scared off by the prospect of being caught, but to Narain, the small possibility of such consequences was motivating. They renewed his enthusiasm for this struggle against the government's increasing oppression tactics. Of course he didn't want to be caught, but he also doubted that he was being watched in the way that Gurdev had warned him about. Rumours about punishments for dissidents were a government tactic, a bogeyman to keep people in line. This knowledge fired him up even more. In the past few years, the monotony of his days at work and his nights at home had become unbearable. He looked forward to these meetings; they made him feel as if he was truly living, not merely existing.

"Nothing has to change between us," Narain said unconvincingly, as they approached the end of the empty street. There were two side lanes to pass through and then they would be inside the club.

Dennis said nothing and glanced at his watch. "About an hour and a half till midnight," he said. He looked at Narain and sighed. "Don't look at me like that, Narain. It isn't easy for me either. We'll remain friends."

They looked in both directions before they slipped through two black double doors at the end of the lane. The entrance was pitch black, but the beat of music and the murmur of conversation wrapped snugly around Narain. He squinted, waiting for his eyes to adjust to the dark as he stepped cautiously towards a sliver of light at the end of the hallway. His foot caught on something—a vent or a jutting floorboard—and he reached out to Dennis for support, but his arms drifted through the air. Narain called out Dennis's name and realised he was gone.

Knowing that his voice was drowned by the music, Narain vented loudly at Dennis, shouting out the truth behind all of the excuses he had created over their short relationship. He stopped when his voice became hoarse. He made his way towards the bar to get a drink of water.

"You made it," called a familiar voice. It was Wei Yi. She took his hand and guided him through the cramped space.

"He promised we'd at least spend New Year's together," he told Wei Yi when they settled at the bar. In the faint bluish glow, Wei Yi's pageboy haircut gleamed. She gave him a sympathetic kiss on the cheek.

"Tell me everything," she said. Narain appreciated that she asked to hear the story, even though it sounded exactly like every relationship he had been in. After he finished, she simply reached over the bar and picked up a bottle of whiskey. "Have you tried it with green tea?" she asked. "Jasmine green tea—the bottled kind."

Narain made a face. Wei Yi gave him a very stern look. "You don't know that you won't like it. Just try." She waved to get the bartender's attention and made her order in Chinese. A few more of their friends entered—Jay, Fadi, Luke. Along with Wei Yi, these were the only people who knew Narain for who he was. They had formed the collective together, starting at Alex's house and then boldly moving their meetings to public places. Their boldest initiative was handing out fliers at the university, a move suggested by Jay and Fadi after they were threatened by a police officer who found them sitting and holding hands on a park bench one night. Luke, Wei Yi's twin brother, had been the one to introduce Narain to a string of underground bars like this one—shophouses converted at night for a particular clientele.

Wei Yi handed Narain a glass and asked the others for their orders. Narain took a sip of the whiskey and green tea combination expecting not to like it, but it didn't taste too bad. He gave Wei Yi a thumbs-up. She grinned back at him. Music pulsed through the room and warm bodies pushed past each other, crammed into every space.

"Resolutions?" asked Fadi. He gave Luke a nudge. "You go first."

"Save more money," Luke said.

There was a collective groan from the group. "Typical," Wei Yi said.

"Hey, things are expensive and my stingy company doesn't believe in end-of-year bonuses."

"You'll get something at Chinese New Year,' Narain pointed out. "That's only a month away."

Fadi pointed at Narain. "You. Resolutions?"

Narain shrugged. A look crossed between his friends; Wei Yi must have mentioned Dennis to them. "Aiyoh," Wei Yi said. "Oh well. Who cares about resolutions? Nobody bothers keeping them past January anyway. Every year I aim to eat healthier and exercise every day. Do fifty sit-ups, twenty-five jumping jacks, twenty-five push-ups. It doesn't even last a week." She stepped close to Narain and linked arms with him. "To aimlessness!" she cheered, raising her glass. Everybody laughed. Wei Yi's breath was damp against Narain's ear as she leaned in and whispered, "Kiss me again at midnight, okay?" Narain did not remember ever kissing her. He put his arm around her and gave her shoulder a friendly squeeze. Dennis had never liked Wei Yi; he thought she only hung around gay men on the chance she might convert them.

The rest drifted off to chat with other people, leaving Narain and Wei Yi sitting at the bar. She pointed at a television screen above the counter. "That's my favourite show," she said. It was a local Chinese drama with no subtitles. Two women wearing stylish clothes chatted casually in a cafe that Narain recognised as being local. "It's a re-run; I've seen this episode before."

"What's going on?" Narain asked. "What are they talking about?"

"They're rich young housewives and they're talking about their husbands being too busy to pay attention to them. It seems as if they're complaining but it becomes obvious that they're actually boasting and competing to show that their husbands have important jobs. The one in the blue dress isn't over her first love but her family wouldn't let them marry."

"Why not?"

"Family politics. He was the son of a rival business owner. In the episode after this one, she'll run into him and they'll start sneaking around together."

"Scandalous," Narain said.

Wei Yi nodded gravely. "The thing is, she's going to find out that he's actually only wooing her to find out some secrets about her father's business."

Narain feigned a look of horror. Wei Yi gave him a jab in the ribs. "Don't make fun."

"I can't believe you take these shows seriously. You're usually such a rebel."

"Nothing says a rebel can't enjoy a good story," Wei Yi replied. She took a gulp of her beer. A shadow fell over her face. "Narain, what I said just now about the kiss...I didn't mean it."

Narain smiled and planted a kiss on Wei Yi's cheek. "It's forgotten," he said.

She giggled and tipped his chin towards the screen. "Okay, here's the best character, the brother." A thin young man wearing a hospital gown chatted casually with a doctor.

"He's a doctor himself, but now he's got some rare disease. This is the episode where he's told his case is terminal."

Narain couldn't help chuckling. "Your Chinese shows are just like Hindi movies. So much melodrama."

"Yeah, but our shows don't waste time with all that singing and dancing. I can't keep up with your movies, even the subtitled ones. They're too unrealistic," Wei Yi said, never taking her eyes off the screen.

"And this is more realistic?" Narain asked. "Let me guess. Does this guy have a secret twin who donates organs to him at the last minute to help him live?"

Wei Yi burst into giggles. Narain placed his hands over her eyes. "No more rubbish TV for you," he said, laughing as well.

"Stop," she squealed, twisting away from his hands.

In the near distance, a crashing sound made them both freeze. Wei Yi whirled around, her eyes wide with fear. House lights flooded on and the music stopped abruptly. Panic washed over the room. Narain grabbed Wei Yi's wrist and dove for the back door. "Don't move!" a police officer shouted, but he was too far away. Narain felt the cool night air whip his face as they left.

Wei Yi's hand grasped his tightly. She kicked off her high heels to keep up with him. "We can stop," she panted, but their momentum easily propelled them through the maze of side lanes. Eventually there was a dead end. They collapsed in a heap against the wall. Narain felt as if his lungs might explode. His mind could not catch up with what had just happened. Seconds ago, he had been watching a Chinese drama with his friend at an underground club; now here he was, having escaped a real police raid. "Oh my God," Wei Yi kept on saying. "Oh my God." She brought Narain's attention to a gash in her foot. She must have stepped on a piece of broken glass.

"You'll be fine," Narain said. "We just need to hide here a bit longer." His heart slammed in his chest.

Wei Yi began to cry. "Where are the others? Have they been caught?"

"They're fine," Narain said, feeling the panic rise in his chest. "Don't worry."

A few minutes passed before Narain decided to step out of the lane to check on the others. He asked Wei Yi if she would come with him but she began to cry again, holding on to her foot. "You stay here then. I'll get you something for your wound," he said. She nodded. Narain walked out, feeling the humid island breath on his skin again before he caught sight of the flashing blue and red lights. A line of men crouched on the ground, their heads hung low. Officers surrounded them, barking orders. Narain dodged back into the lane, pressing himself against the wall. Moments later, he slowly leaned out again to look at the men. In the dark it was impossible to distinguish any of his friends, but a growing sense of dread told Narain that most of the men from the club had been caught. The line stretched along the sidewalk.

One of the officers jerked his head up suddenly, meeting Narain's stare. He let out a shout and pointed. Narain raced back into the lane, feeling the men advance on him. The ground rushed up to meet his head. The officers grabbed him roughly by the shoulders and propped him against the wall. Narain winced as a jut of stone scraped against his back. The ringing in his ears was so loud that he didn't hear what the officers were saying at first. "Pardon?" he asked weakly, squinting at them. He remembered Father teaching him to take note of what police officers looked like when he was a young boy. "They always remember your face. If you ever offend one on the street, you make sure you never do it again to the same one." The officer who was addressing him was lanky; the other one looked Malay and had grey specks in his hair.

"What are you running from?" the Malay officer shouted. He leaned close to Narain as if he might attempt to press the truth out of him.

"Nothing," Narain murmured. "I was just going out to celebrate New Year's."

"Where?"

"Just Orchard Road," Narain replied. Wei Yi flashed into his mind. "I was with my girlfriend and she stepped on some glass, so I was looking for a convenience shop to buy her some plasters. I got lost."

They exchanged glances. The lanky one leaned in so close to Narain that their noses practically touched. He glared at Narain, then turned and whispered something to his colleague. "Please," Narain said. "She's really hurt."

"Show us where she is," the Malay officer challenged. "Where's your girlfriend?"

Narain gestured weakly towards the lane. There was nothing within sight but a mossy darkness. He attempted to give the officers directions to where Wei Yi was waiting for him, but his voice wobbled.

The officers had a brief discussion in low tones. They

looked at Narain again, assessing him. He felt his skin prickle as their eyes bore into his, seeking out his lie. The Malay officer whispered to his colleague, who nodded. "My girlfriend," Narain attempted again weakly.

"Quiet," the Malay officer commanded.

They made Narain turn around to face the wall. "Spread your arms and legs." Narain pressed his palms to the wall and shut his eyes in terror, knowing what they would find and wishing he had not worn these jeans. They patted him on the insides of his thighs and arms. One officer received a call on his radio and turned away to respond to it. The other continued patting Narain down, and then he dug his hands deep into Narain's pockets. This was the same pair of jeans he had worn to his last visit to the university; some of his fliers were folded into those pockets. Possible excuses flooded Narain's mind. *They don't belong to me*, he thought. *Somebody handed them to me just now and I was going to throw them away.*

Then, as suddenly as that, they let him go, with just a warning. "Don't run from the police again," they said. "You do that, you'll look suspicious." He was free to go. After they left, he checked his pockets and found them empty. The fliers must have been removed somehow. He thought back to Gurdev's visit, and remembered his questions. Had he looked through Narain's clothes?

He walked slowly, panting hard, as if he had been running for miles. When he finally got to the end of the lane, he expected that Wei Yi might be gone, but she was still sitting there, crying softly. "Did you find them?" she asked, her face tear-streaked. Narain shook his head and sat next to her. Outside, an explosion of fireworks rocked the island, drowning out the sound of Wei Yi's sobs.

•   •   •

Daylight sparkled against the rows of apartment blocks. Narain peered outside in search of the dancing girl he'd seen through a window in the opposite block but the thick cables that held the painters' lift cut off his view. The painters had already passed his flat and now they were working on the one directly above. Their lifts swayed and tipped to each movement, rattling him awake in the mornings.

Yesterday, he had called work to say he was sick, and dragged himself to the polyclinic for a medical certificate. He had told the doctor he had a splitting headache and a sore throat; he coughed feebly to show it was true. The doctor nodded and wrote his certificate. Valid Until 3 January, the certificate said. Two days off. He had gone straight back to the flat and stayed in bed for the entire day. He told himself he would return to work today despite having a medical certificate—it was better to stay busy after all. But it was past nine o'clock now and he had made no effort to get up.

Father was at the door now. "Narain, you are not working again today?"

"No," Narain called back. "Still sick." He stared at the ceiling.

There was a prolonged silence and then Father asked, "What is wrong? Just the flu?"

"Yes," Narain said. "I need some rest."

The smell of paint fumes, strong and plasticky, wafted into the flat. Narain looked outside and searched again for the window girl. He had first noticed her a few months ago, on a rostered day off, as he watched the painters. From her flat in the opposite building, she peeled off her clothes in slow, cat-like movements and danced in the window. The distance was too great for Narain to catch her facial features. He could only see the tan of her flesh, her round breasts, and the dark patch between her legs as she spread them and lowered herself to the floor. If he recognised her outside, he might tell her she was wasting her time trying to seduce him, but he enjoyed her show nonetheless. Her languid rhythm served one purpose: it defied every ordered brush stroke on this city's landscape.

Narain spent the remainder of the afternoon drifting in and out of sleep. He stretched out across the mattress as the afternoon sunlight poured into the flat, soaking the room in its warmth. Dreams came to him in fragments, quick scenes, and voices strung together, incomprehensible. Whenever he woke, he was dazed and tired. He sank back into the mattress and slept again, only to be confronted with the puzzling dreams again.

When he got out of bed it was four o'clock in the afternoon. His stomach rumbled but the cabinets and fridge shelves were empty. He headed back to his room to get his wallet. Passing Father's shut door, Narain heard talking, Father's voice rising. Narain squinted in an attempt to make out Father's words, and he leaned closer to the door. As if sensing his presence, Father's voice was reduced to whispers. Narain wondered for a moment if there was someone in the room with him. He shook the thought from his mind— Father was simply transcribing a letter to himself or reading the newspaper aloud.

On his way to the shops was a traditional Chinese clinic with its strong herbal smell, and a daycare centre with bright blue gates. His old route to the shops did not use to take this long but it was blocked off now for construction so he had chosen a different way. Rows of decrepit shophouses and the site of a wet market had been razed to make way for a new shopping centre with gleaming fluorescent lights, air conditioning and escalators.

Narain stopped at a provisions shop to buy a newspaper. Yesterday, he had done the same thing and found no mention of the raid. His stomach began to twist as he searched the pages and he felt a cool wash of relief when his search came up empty again. Perhaps the police had let them off. Perhaps it had just been a scare. He was about to pay for the paper when he spotted something on the front page of a Chinese tabloid. He asked the shopkeeper for a copy of that paper as well. "This one is in Chinese," the shopkeeper said.

"I know," Narain said. He dumped the coins in the man's hand and did not bother waiting for his change. Clutching the papers close to his chest, he walked briskly until he found a quiet corner. The Chinese characters made no sense but the picture was unmistakably of the raid. At the bottom of the page, there was an indicator that the story continued on page 8. He turned to that page and found individual mug shots of Dennis and Fadi. Numbness seeped through Narain's stomach and legs. He sat down, staring at the pictures. There were numbers in the article: 10, 4. He made his way back to the shop and presented the article at the shopkeeper.

"I told you already it's in Chinese. No money back," the man protested before Narain could make his request.

"I don't want a refund," Narain said. "Just tell me what the article says. Here. And here." He pointed to the numbers.

The shopkeeper squinted at him suspiciously. "For what?"

"Please," Narain said. He was aware of the tears forming in his eyes.

The shopkeeper's face softened. He pointed to the headline and ran his finger along each word as he translated it. "Sixteen arrested in nightclub raid." He paused to read the article to himself. Redness crept to his cheeks. "For dancing with other men," he said simply.

Narain tapped at the numbers. "What about this?"

The shopkeeper looked up at him. "Why you want to know?" he asked.

Tears spilled down Narain's cheeks. "Just tell me what it says," he said, with gritted teeth. "Please."

The shopkeeper looked very reluctant. He let out a sigh. "Up to ten years jail," he said. "Four strokes of the cane."

•   •   •

Narain went straight to Father's room and knocked loudly on the door. "I need to talk to you." He knew he was shouting louder than necessary but he had to drown out the sound of his own doubts.

Father appeared. "What is it?" he asked.

Narain looked over his shoulders and saw that the room was empty. It looked as if it had been cleaned to hide something. "Who was in here with you?" he asked. "Before I left for the supermarket, I heard you talking to somebody."

Father looked startled. "There was nobody," he said.

Narain saw the panic marching across his face and knew that he had guessed correctly. A woman was visiting Father. Having exposed Father's secret, he felt emboldened to reveal his own. He handed the newspaper to Father.

"It's all in Chinese," Father said.

Narain pointed impatiently at the grainy picture of men lined up along the street. "These are my friends," Narain said. "They are just like me." Father's brow furrowed in confusion as his eyes wandered over the foreign lettering. "They were caught on New Year's Eve at an underground club for being with men. They're homosexuals, Father. They're just like me."

This reality seemed to set like a dislodged bone clicking suddenly into place. Father recoiled at the word. "I didn't know how else to tell you," Narain said.

Father stared at the picture for a long time. When he spoke, his voice was hoarse but steady. "I was going to go out to the coffee shop to eat dinner," he said. "I haven't had roti prata in a long time."

"I'm not hungry," Narain replied. "You go ahead." He watched Father pick up his wallet and check for cash. "That's all you're going to say about this?"

"Narain," Father said, avoiding his gaze. "It is a new year. Everything can change."

"This is not something that will change. You have to accept this."

"Come with me," Father said. Exasperated, Narain followed him.

At the coffee shop, Father pulled out a chair for himself and told Narain to order. "One teh tarik for me. Less sugar. They always make it too sweet." Before Narain could leave to make his order, Father pushed a five dollar note in his direction. "And two plain roti pratas, and you order whatever food you want. I know you didn't eat lunch today."

A vendor came to them with a tray holding two steaming bowls of fish curry and two plates of crisp roti pratas. He hurried back to the stall and returned with cutlery. Father gave him a strange look and he placed the cutlery on the table before rushing off again.

"Who eats roti prata with a spoon and fork? You picked this up from that gorah country," Father said, ripping the pieces. Grease made his fingers glisten.

"I'm sorry I had to tell you in that way," Narain said. "I'm just tired of keeping quiet about it."

Father continued to eat. *Say something*, Narain begged. This silence reminded Narain of the days when he returned from the back lane. Each time, Narain had waited for an argument, even a cold slap on the face if that was what it would take for both of them to move on. But there was nothing. Since then, he had felt as if his sins were still accumulating.

"You were always different," Father said. "I just thought it was because you were so close to your mother. She wanted a girl, you know. When she was expecting you she kept saying she could feel you were a girl. Is that what you want to be?"

"No," Narain said. "It's not like that."

"I do not understand it, Narain," Father said. "I cannot even shout or scream because that won't take it out of you. This is not the behaviour of a Sikh man." He looked dejected. Narain almost pitied him. He reached out and touched Father's hand. Father looked miserably at his food and pulled away to continue eating.

A group of foreign construction workers descended on the table next to theirs, laughing loudly. They had dark skin and greasy parted hair. Their eyes were filmy and slightly jaundiced. Other patrons of the coffee shop barely noticed their noise—only Narain and Father opted for silence over the racket. The workers were sharing a bottle of whiskey. They raised their glasses and cheered. One of them, a man who wore a long-sleeved blue shirt with missing buttons in the cuffs, grinned happily at Narain.

"My friend wife. She come to Singapore tomorrow. We happy," he explained. The other workers turned to look at Narain and Father.

"Good for you," Father said in Malay, raising his glass of tea. The men laughed and clapped.

Taking Father's response as an invitation, they rose and descended like birds around him and Narain. "Come, come. You happy also," the blue-shirted man said. Father did not protest. The man called for two more glasses. His arms wobbled as he poured for Father and Narain.

Another man spoke up. His Malay was more fluent than the others'. "We all come from Bangladesh," he told Narain. "I was in Malaysia for many years—so were these two." He gestured at a pair of men who were talking to each other. "The others only left Bangladesh a few months ago. They are new here." He lowered his voice even though it was clear the others could not understand. "The government didn't let their wives into the country. All visa applications rejected. They are trying again. I say, why try so hard? There can be one wife in Bangladesh, one wife here. Everybody wins." He chuckled at his own joke.

"Which is better? Malaysia or Singapore?" Father asked.

"Singapore," one of the pair from Malaysia chimed in. "Better pay."

Father was proud. Narain saw his chest expand.

"More expensive," the other man complained. "One glass of beer costs twice the price it costs in Malaysia."

"You fussy bastard. You're getting paid twice as much here," another one argued. The other men looked baffled until those who spoke Malay translated. Then they nodded in agreement. Then one man said something in a language Narain did not understand and the rest broke out in laughter. They continued talking, their voices rising over the others in the coffee shop. Now people were turning to stare. They shot dirty looks at the workers.

The worker who was fluent in Malay spoke. "Too many rules in Singapore. Can't even make a bit of noise. There are signs everywhere—cannot do this and that. No smoking here, no stepping on this patch of grass. Piss on the street, get a $500 fine. So expensive just to take a piss!" Raucous laughter broke out again, turning more heads. Narain sensed Father's embarrassment at being seen with these men.

"Shall we go?" Narain asked him in English.

"Yes," Father said.

They were about to rise when one of the men said something to make them stop. "Pretty girl. Pretty Punjabi girl not so expensive."

"Let's go," Narain said. His voice sounded like it was far away, mingling with the clatter of cutlery at the next table. Father remained seated. Narain saw the heavy rise and fall of his breath. It was like he was in a trance.

The blue-shirted man dragged the bottle of whiskey to the middle of the table and gave Narain a wink. "There's a Punjabi girl who lives in that block over there, behind the closed shop. I forgot her name, or maybe she never told us. She's a very special girl. If you want, I can find her for you. We met her here last night. For a few drinks, you can do anything you want with her. Four, five, six of us at one time, just for half a bottle of whiskey. A special girl." He poured another round for everybody at the table. His hands were even more unsteady this time and his eyes were bloodshot. He shook the last drops of whiskey into Father's tea glass and then tapped the lip of his bottle against the glass.

Narain stared at the filmy mix of tiny specks of tea leaves, milk and whiskey. Drain water, he thought, thinking of the filth that used to surge through the island's veins, through the canals and the river. He was aware that he was shaking with rage, that he might reach over the table and smash a bottle over the head of one of these men. He uttered a quick prayer—a string of words memorised in childhood which came to him automatically. Then he noticed Father. Staring wide-eyed at the men like a child witnessing his first horror, Father had begun to cry. He did not bother to wipe away his tears and his lips curled and quivered, his shoulders shook. He wept and mumbled until Narain steered him away from the men whose glasses began clinking again only moments after they left.

Amrit

"WHAT IS HAPPENING is simple," Amrit said. Her new friends responded with wild laughter. She let out a high-pitched giggle as well. "No, listen. Listen to my idea."

"Your bullshit ideas," one man said loudly. His girlfriend placed an open palm over his mouth to shush him.

He twitched his nose and said something that made her retort, "You, lah!"

There were five of them sitting on the beach. The tide arrived like a furtive tongue against Amrit's feet, leaving grit between her toes. Amrit had an idea about this earlier, about the earth eventually eroding if she sat here long enough to receive the sand. Her feet, she told all of them in a frenzy of discovery, her feet were taking what belonged to the seabed. If she kept collecting it and didn't return it to the water, what would happen to the earth? That was when the laughing had begun, and it was contagious. The smell of beer on their skins mixing with the salty air, the blank night, made her feel braver, and she blurted out her every thought. She sensed their confusion, their bafflement and their impatience, but of course these people were not as clever as she, not even close.

"Hey, Amrit," the man in the red shirt said, "just now, ah, when we saw you sitting alone, we thought, this is just a quiet Punjabi girl. Sitting near the seaside, maybe praying to your guru or something." Laughter scattered across the beach. Amrit closed her eyes and felt the laughter rock her body. "We didn't know you have so many theories."

Behind her, one of the men was sitting and watching her. She could feel the heat of his stare spreading over her skin like a firm hand. There were too many things to be said. She found it difficult to concentrate but she kept talking. "I'm just saying. There's no such thing as no end. No end of the earth means that everything goes, bye-bye, done. But you really think everyone will allow it? And look. Look at the numbers. Today's date, next week—it's all the same as in the lottery. The lottery numbers follow the calendar. The lottery continues, so the world has to continue. If you just read the numbers correctly, you can predict everything that is going to happen, five, ten, twenty years from now." She pulled out the lottery tickets from her back pocket and spread them across the sand. One of the men whistled.

"How many did you buy?"

"Seventeen," Amrit said proudly. "I'll win seventeen times." Her mind was foggy with the details of her winning strategy because she'd been planning it when they approached her. She'd been sitting on the beach, her clothes and hair soaked after taking a dip in the water. *Clean me*, she'd thought, swimming fast strokes away from the shore. She wanted to emerge without a trace of all the men she'd been with but when she was drying off, this group caught her eye.

The man sitting behind her reached over to touch her back. She smiled warmly and fell into his hands. The others gave each other looks and turned away, their gazes sweeping deliberately over the black sea and the tiny lights in the distance.

"Where do you live?" the man whispered. Amrit closed her eyes. It had been so long since she had been home that she could almost forget where it was. The day before New Year's Eve, 30 December, had been the last time she remembered being home. She had woken up feeling a terrible sense of foreboding. The flat was empty; Narain was at work and the door of the master bedroom was shut. She had heard Father chattering away in his room. She went to his door and listened but only heard snippets of conversation. She knocked hard on the door and the noise from his room ceased. Amrit waited for Father to come out and scold her for interrupting him, and then it occurred to her that she had imagined all of it. She found a copy of the Yellow Pages in the storeroom and searched for the number for the Samaritans of Singapore. Her stomach twisting, she picked up the phone receiver, punched in the numbers and hung up on the first ring because she needed to rush to the bathroom. She called back several times afterwards and managed to stay on the line when a woman's voice greeted her but she did not speak. How could she talk to this stranger? What would she say?

"I live in Woodbridge Hospital," she joked, "for mad people." He chuckled and drew her closer. She had called them as well after she gave up on the Samaritans of Singapore. She had even spoken to a telephone operator about how to get a referral from a polyclinic doctor, but then the operator had asked for her name. Again, Amrit had found herself speechless. Imagine having to tell Father that she was now a lunatic, after all the shame she had already caused the family. Imagine Banu being unable to look her temple friends in the eye. Imagine Narain feeling defeated again. *I'd rather be dead*, she had thought.

Amrit heard the tide gently crashing over the sand and she couldn't separate one sensation from another—his hands, the water, the ground dissolving beneath her feet. She constantly thought about the end, and all the possible ways it would happen when this thrill finally wore off. Escape. There were many possibilities. To think she had once thought of marriage as the only means to depart! She could lean far enough out of her bedroom window to let gravity take her down. She could drink a bottle of whiskey until it drowned every cell in her body. She could slam her head against the earth and let the noise in her mind give way to a peace she had never known.

· · ·

Amrit woke to a clicking sound. A brief rush of wind cooled her feet and then left. The room became uncomfortably warm again. She forced her eyes open to the white morning light. This was not her room. The window grills were slanted bars behind a set of dust-coated blinds. The walls were covered in a tired shade of blue that made her think of hospital clothes.

There was also a mattress on the floor. A cartoon-printed sheet covered the lumpy shape of a person. Amrit was slowly remembering. It had been four—no, five—days since she left home with all the money she had and each morning, she had woken up somewhere different. Along the way she'd been to a string of pubs, the beach, the fancy club in town and more coffee shops. Sunlight streamed into the room, false and cheery. Amrit took in the white dresser with crayon lines scribbled across its side, and the pile of magazines on top. This was not a man's room. Should she feel relieved? She was a little sick of men, but they were familiar. They had that same smell. Their tricks were predictable. She could close her eyes and shut out her senses and be with a man. Men did not expect very much from her, whereas the women she knew were full of expectations. They were sharper and they could see right into her. She was afraid to tell them anything about herself because she knew what they would think of her. Loose and easy. Shameless.

The clicking started again. She thought it might be in her mind but it was too persistent. It was right behind her.

"Taufiq, stop it," the shape under the blanket hissed. The clicking stopped. Amrit turned to see a young boy standing next to a kitchen stool on which sat a box fan. His finger hovered over a button.

"I press this one and the wind go around," he told Amrit. "This one. Is R-O-T-A-T-E." She made an effort to smile. Her tongue tasted like ash. The boy turned and then bolted from the room. His feet were light as raindrops against the tiles.

"Hafiza," Amrit said, suddenly. The name just flashed into her mind.

There was a pause before the person under the blanket responded with a groan. "Still early," Hafiza mumbled. Amrit sank back into the bed. Hafiza. They had met yesterday in the Lava Lounge on Tunnel Street. Hafiza had a head full of dyed brown hair and she was there with a large man with a pierced ear. He kept a strong arm linked around her waist like an anchor, and he slowly rubbed the fabric of her tight black tank top with his thumb.

Amrit had met a Dutch man there. Jacob. Her heart skipped a beat. She dug her hands into her pockets and pulled out two bus tickets, a rubber band for tying her hair, and a crumpled business card. Jacob's phone number. He had told her to call him at some point. He was apologetic, she remembered, as he explained that she could not stay in his apartment. "But please call me some time. You can get me in my office." His parting kiss had been wet but not unpleasant. She felt it in her mouth now—his tongue against hers, his lips small but plump.

There was a clanging in the kitchen and then a heavy-set figure appeared in the doorway. "Hafiza! Hafiza, I'm going to work," she said in Malay. The woman, dressed in dark blue slacks and a white polka-dotted blouse stepped into the room. "Oi, Hafiza. I already gave Taufiq his breakfast. You take care of the rest."

"He's not going to kindergarten?" Hafiza mumbled. Amrit glanced at the calendar on the wall. It was Saturday.

"Hafiza, get up!" the woman shrieked. She kicked a toy truck. It skidded across the room and narrowly missed Hafiza's head. "And tell your friend this isn't a hotel." She glared at Amrit and stormed out. Amrit saw Taufiq trailing after her like a lanky shadow.

"I'll go soon," Amrit said. She got out of the bed. Her bones felt strangely stiff. She felt like she'd been running for days. Fragments of memories entered her mind. She remembered running, bursting out of the flat. She longed for that burst of energy now, that powerful rush of invincibility. So many friends made, so many jokes told. She remembered pitying people who were not like her. They were simply living, whereas she was electrified, magnified. She was fantastic. She wanted photographs taken of herself because she was certain her face glowed. Now she just felt worn and dull. Her hair was matted, her breath smelled terrible, her skin felt like it was covered with remnants of smoke and grease and last night's rain. She'd been gradually descending since last night at the club, where all the drinks suddenly made her feel sombre and hopeless. They weighed her down and made her sob into Hafiza's shoulder. "I can't go home. I can't go home," she had wailed as Hafiza stumbled onto the road and hailed a cab.

"I should really leave," Amrit said.

"No need," Hafiza said. She rose from the mattress. Her hair fell over the side of her face. She shook it away. Amrit studied her features in the light. Narrow eyes made to look wider with thick liquid eyeliner that curled around the corners, pointing to her temples. A wide nose. Small lips that looked like they were puckering even when they were not. There was a smudge of her blusher on the white pillowcase. The mattress was wrapped in an old sheet. It was faded yellow with squares and cartoon teddy bears.

"You don't have to go so quickly. She just loves to make a fuss. She'll be at work the whole day anyway. No rush." Hafiza surveyed her surroundings. "What time is it?"

"Don't know," Amrit said, searching the room for a clock.

"Taufiq!" Hafiza suddenly shouted. It was as if she just remembered him. "My son," she explained. "Mum gives him one breakfast and she thinks I should treat her like the bloody Queen. Big deal. Taufiq!"

Amrit tried to digest this information. Hafiza's mother looked no older than Hafiza herself. "Taufiq's father?" she asked.

Hafiza shrugged. "Don't know, lah. Useless bum." She called for Taufiq again. He entered the room and sank into the mattress. "Oh my boy. Oh my big, big boy," Hafiza crooned. "Oh my big, big boy. Smelly boy." Taufiq giggled. Amrit smiled. Hafiza held her nose. "Stinky, stinky, smelly boy," she said.

After he ran off again, Hafiza turned to Amrit. "He's easy to take care of. My mum just likes to nag. Climbs on top of my head, that woman."

"Mine too," Amrit said, trying out the complaint. "Always nagging." She tried to picture Mother hovering over her shoulders and telling her off. She tried to picture herself shaking off Mother and telling her to go away.

"They can't live without it, lah," Hafiza said. Then something occurred to her. "Eh, your mum's okay with you not going home?"

Amrit shrugged. "She doesn't notice."

Hafiza let out a loud laugh. "Doesn't notice? What the hell, you stay in a bungalow or what? Doesn't notice?"

Amrit laughed along with her. "Yeah, I mean she knows but she can't do anything, right? First time it happened she was upset. Now she's used to it." How easy it was to conjure a mother like this, Amrit thought. She could create a few anecdotes and Mother could be sitting in this room between her and Hafiza, a model to study. She remembered doing this in primary school once, walking along the corridors and animatedly telling her classmates that her mother sewed her an apron for Home Economics, her mother was a dancer, her mother told great jokes. Word had gotten to Narain somehow and he told her to stop it. "It's disrespectful," he told her quietly, although at the time she could not see how. She thought Mother was doing all these things in her absence.

Taufiq rushed back into the room again. "Can I watch cartoons?" he asked Hafiza in Malay.

"Can," Hafiza said, "but when I say it's enough, you shut it off, understand?"

Taufiq nodded and left. Amrit could see the entire corridor of the flat from where she was. "Where's your mother's room?" she asked Hafiza.

"She sleeps here. Taufiq also. You took her bed, that's why she's so grumpy today. She came home and found us two drunkards." Hafiza giggled.

"Oh shit. Sorry," Amrit mumbled.

"No need to be sorry, lah. Happens. She needs something to get angry about anyway. At least today it's you. She'll have to spend her whole day at work thinking of excuses to be upset with me." Hafiza switched from Malay to English. "That's why Taufiq television time also got limit. She see the electric bill—wah—big fuss, man. Like we suppose to live like animals or what." Hafiza shook her head. "Eh, yesterday I saw you with that ang moh guy. Not bad. Cantik. Usually

I don't like that kind, you know. Sly buggers. Come here and think they can screw every girl because they have white skin. But that fella was good looking, lah. Seeing him again?"

Jacob entered Amrit's mind in a sharp flash. She remembered the wiry hairs on his arms and the surprisingly rough way they grazed her skin as they bumped against each other on the dance floor. "You're not shy. My wife is shy," he had told her. His eyes were fixed on a spot far past her shoulders as he said this. He didn't look her in the eye.

"No," Amrit said. "Lost his number."

"Aiyoh. Stupid woman. Take, lah, next time. You never know. He might be rich." Hafiza studied her face. "What kind of house do you stay in?" she asked.

"Hmm?"

"Flat, semidetached, condo, what kind of home your parents have?"

"Flat," Amrit said.

"Must be nice. Five room? Must be. Must be five room. You went to good schools, right? I can hear it in your English. Last night. That's why the ang mohs like you. You can talk to them properly," Hafiza said, admiringly. She sat up and went closer to Amrit. "See. See your face." She raked her fingers slowly but with force through Amrit's hair. The knots came loose. Amrit's scalp stung. The shadows beneath her eyes and the uneven patches on her skin were more noticeable with her hair pulled away. She thought she looked haggard and worn, older than twenty-nine.

"Ah. There," Hafiza said. "Hold this, I'll get the mirror. I tell you, you put your hair like this, you look like somebody important. What job you want to have?"

"Always thought I'd be a lawyer. Or work in advertising. I'm good with words," Amrit said, gazing into the mirror. Hafiza had twisted a few bits of hair into tendrils and let them hang down the sides of her face. "Failed all my exams though. No chance. Can't even be a maid." She smiled to take the sting out of the words but she could not help remembering the stacks of applications she had sent in to advertising companies all over the island, even those who had no vacancies available. With each application, Amrit had included a portfolio of her own ideas for advertisements for household products. They surely trumped the unimaginative ones that repeated on television and bus stop posters, but nobody had replied. She finally gathered up the nerve to call one agency to ask them if they had received her application. On the other end, a tired sounding woman had told her that they were not interested. "Have you seen my drawings?" Amrit had asked.

"We hire people who are qualified to conduct business, not just draw pictures," the woman had said crisply.

"Better, lah. Can be model or actress or what," Hafiza scoffed. "And you're so skinny also. I tell you, I was like you until I got pregnant. After I gave birth, I went and bought this exercise thing." Hafiza crawled under the bed and began to search for something. Amrit continued to gaze at her own reflection. A sheen of sweat glistened on her cheeks. A row of fierce black hairs had sprouted up between her eyebrows and above her lip. Her eyes were bloodshot. She released her hair and let it fall loose. There was no reason to be showing her face.

Hafiza dragged a contraption out from under the bed.

It looked like a crossbow, with horizontal bars and a flat panel in place of the arrow head. Hafiza laid flat on her back and pressed the panel to her belly. She gripped the bars and drew them towards her. A large spring in the contraption creaked as she sat up slowly. "I tried sit-ups but they didn't help," she told Amrit between gasps. "This one, they call it the Ab-Flat. If I use it everyday, it helps to flatten out my tummy." She grinned.

"Let me try," Amrit said.

Hafiza readily passed it over. With a loud grunt, she fell back onto her mattress. "Finish already."

"Lazy bum. You only did five sit-ups," Amrit said.

"Oh, lazy me? You try. See how much you can do," Hafiza challenged. Amrit positioned the Ab-Flat on her belly and pulled herself up. "You have to pull down that part also," Hafiza told her. The spring creaked in protest. Amrit started giggling.

"Call me lazy! You can't even do it!" Hafiza shouted. Amrit shoved the contraption away, shaking now with laughter. Hafiza collapsed back in her bed, giggling into the pillow. "Gilas, both of us. Crazy women," she said. The statement brought more laughter from Amrit. Outside, the roar of the television abruptly stopped. Taufiq came back to the room.

"See, finish already," he announced in English to Amrit. He curled up next to Hafiza and laughed along with her although he did not know the joke.

• • •

Amrit left Hafiza's place only after eating an early dinner. She could not remember the last time she ate and she did not think she was hungry until Hafiza mentioned food. "Want to eat before you go? My mum works double shifts on Saturdays. She always leaves something." Amrit nodded and followed her into the kitchen—a slim counter, two cupboards and a fridge wedged between the sink and the washing machine. The only bathroom in the flat was in the corner of the kitchen, close to a window from which wet clothes and sheets clipped to bamboo poles flared in the wind like flags. The bathroom had a tin door; the lock was broken and replaced by a piece of raffia string looped through a small hole in the wall. Taufiq banged a spoon against the door as Amrit showered. The noise was like thunder.

"Thanks so much," Amrit said, before she left.

"Take care, yeah," Hafiza said, grinning. "Don't be naughty."

Amrit's hair was still damp when she left. The sun was making a slow descent and the sky was a bright and fiery orange. She sat down on the steps at the bottom of Hafiza's block and ran her fingers through her hair. This was what she had done on the mornings when she had no place to go: she sat on the steps and waited until somebody came along. A man always came along, especially in these types of areas with older apartment blocks, walls stained with dirt, tiles peeling off the floor. She was so familiar with this type of neighbourhood that she didn't need directions. There would be a string of provisions shops and hawker centres. The tarry smell of burned rubber would hover in the air, mixing with incense and the filthy water that bubbled in the canals. A few lights would flicker on as the darkness set in, but they would be too dim to illuminate the flats. Flat windows were like tiny screens, all on at the same time. Silhouettes darted past like characters in a puppet show. She'd spent many nights transfixed on those figures as they flitted back and forth. What were other people doing? She longed to find out and compare herself to them.

A man, curly-haired and pot-bellied, met her gaze. "You're lost?" he asked. The gold chain on his neck caught the last bit of daylight. A smile played at the corner of his lips. Amrit knew that if she smiled back, she would not have to go home for a while. He wanted that. But she did not have the energy. It had waned and now she was tired, she badly needed sleep, and she didn't feel like drinking or dancing anymore. She pushed herself off the step and darted off onto the sidewalk. The man called out weakly after her.

Amrit searched the street signs and bus stops to get her bearings. The number 77 was the only bus she recognised but it didn't even go to the interchange close to her place. It terminated only halfway there, where she'd have to switch to another bus. "It's too far," she wailed.

Two women sitting at the bus stop glanced at each other. One used her index finger to make a circling motion at her temple. "Siao," she mouthed to the other women, who nodded and threw Amrit a disdainful look.

"What? What? Was I talking to you?" Amrit snapped. The women looked at each other and began speaking loudly in Chinese. Their words—whatever they meant—were directed at Amrit. She swore at them and stormed off. The women shouted names after her. She broke into a run, feeling a short burst of energy, but she grew tired quickly. She stopped, caught her breath, and checked in at another bus stop. It was the same route. The sky was darker now. Streetlights were flickering on. She squinted and saw a hawker centre down the street, its fluorescent signs glowing. Her stomach rumbled. She stuffed her hands into her pockets and pulled out some change. There wasn't enough for a decent meal but she could call home. Narain would have to help her get home; she'd been gone for six days.

Approaching the hawker centre, she saw the same man she'd seen under the block. Had he followed her? She walked in the shadows and darted into a small lane. A spotted cat pranced past, its belly swaying like a pendulum. It was dark now. There was a pile of straw baskets in the corner. Bile collected in her mouth and she spat it into the baskets. As Amrit came out of the lane, the man was standing near a drinks stall. "One Coke," he told the vendor. As he twisted to get his wallet from his back pocket, he caught Amrit's eye. She kept on walking towards the payphone.

The phone rang for a very long time before it was cut off. Amrit pressed down the receiver and tried again. She looked over her shoulder to see if anybody was waiting in line and she saw the man again. He had taken a table close to the phone. With one leg crossed openly over the other and his arms stretched over two chairs, he watched her. There was that smile again, more certain now. He thought she was playing hard to get. She shot him an angry glare. The repeated rings of the phone agitated her. Were they deliberately not answering? This seemed like the type of thing Father would do until he gave in.

The phone was cut off again. When she tried a third time, the response was that same aggravating engaged tone. She slammed the receiver down so hard that it made the platform shake. A hawker came running out of his stall. "Don't break the phone," he warned, menacingly. He pointed to a sign on the wall: No Vandalism; Penalties Apply. She rolled her eyes at him and was about to storm off when she realised she had nowhere to go. It was dark now. She had Jacob's office number, but it was a Saturday—he wouldn't be there. He was a foreigner anyway—he wouldn't know the directions any more than she did. Her legs were rubbery. She remembered running; where had that energy gone? Why had it come to her in the first place? Why couldn't she summon it once more? She wanted to go back to three days ago when she felt as though everything she said was illuminatingly clever, when she knew exactly how to move so that the curves of her body showed through her clothes.

"Angry with your boyfriend?" the man asked. Amrit slumped into the chair across from him and placed her head on the table. She wanted a place to rest. She was aware, suddenly, of the tears that were running down her cheeks onto her T-shirt. She was too embarrassed to bring her head up but then the man came around to her side. "Shh," he said. "Never mind. Shh." Amrit kept her eyes open. She saw the damp floor and the legs of the table and a beetle making its way towards her feet. She shifted and looked up again. The lights hurt her eyes.

"My name is Amrit," she heard herself say. "What's your name?" The man's mouth moved but she could barely hear him. She just wanted to lie down.

• • •

The sky was pitch black when Amrit finally got into a taxi. It was 1am. As she mumbled directions, the driver kept his eye on her in the rearview mirror. "You okay? You okay?" he asked, concern edging into his voice. "You vomit in the car, I cannot drive you."

She told him that she hadn't been drinking. "I'm just tired, Uncle," she insisted meekly. He did not look as though he believed her.

"Where you come from?" he asked.

Amrit pointed out the window. The rows of apartment blocks in the distance were obscured by the shadows of tall trees on the concrete divider. The hawker centre lights were off and the chairs were piled on the tables. "My friend's house," she said. She rested her head against the pane and hoped he wouldn't be a chatty driver. Most of them were very curt but there was the occasional driver who tried hard to make conversation.

She'd only gone home with that man because she wanted to rest. He gave her money afterwards. She'd been asleep for most of it, only waking up when his heaving became too loud. A stinging soreness radiated through her body. "Please go quickly."

"Don't worry," the driver said. She slouched across the back seat. He continued with his questions non-stop, uninterested in the answers. "Are you Indian? How come some of you have fair skin? I thought Indians all got dark skin? You speak Tamil? You speak Malay? You look more like Malay because your skin fair. Or Eurasian. But not as fair as Chinese. That's why I don't know. You go dancing today is it? Why never go town? Town got better dancing."

"Hmm," Amrit replied. A row of figurines on the dashboard serenely watched her. A slim ceramic cat sat next to a jade Buddha. A turtle with springs attached to its head and legs jiggled silently as the cab took her home. She peered out of the window. In the dark, the most illuminated sights were the construction sites. There was rust-coloured scaffolding everywhere—great skeletons caging the unfinished concrete and brick structures that were filling the city. Signs posted outside each site described the project but it was too dark and they were going too quickly for her to be able to read them. Everything was filling up, Amrit thought morosely. It was a realisation that used to excite her as a young girl: possibilities would be endless in a city that kept on building. Now it made her miserable. The city didn't seem like it was expanding, but rapidly closing in on her, its niggling rules and watchful eyes making her escapes more troublesome.

"I hate this country," she said, venomously. The driver looked surprised before fear flashed across his face.

"Eh, don't say like that," he cautioned her. "Government, ah, you never know when they can hear you."

She crossed her arms over her chest and closed her eyes. Streetlights flashed dimly into her unconscious, as did a succession of quick images from her dreams. Mother was rubbing oil into the curls on her head. Mother was adjusting the strings on her salwar before going to the temple. Mother was lying down with an arm crossed over her eyes to shield her from the afternoon light. Mother was folding her clothes methodically and placing them in stacks.

When the taxi came to a halt, Amrit's eyes flew open. She gave the driver the $10 note, took the change and then climbed out. "Now you can sleep properly," the driver said, laughing. Amrit grimaced and walked towards her block. When she arrived at the door of her flat, she realised she was unprepared. She needed to look like somebody who had only stepped out of her home for an errand or a breath of fresh air. The more controlled she looked upon her return, the less time they took to forgive her. It was coming home drunk that got her family so upset. She was fine now; she was sober. She would be let into the flat without too much fuss, and she would devote herself to doing an endless number of chores until their anger subsided.

If they would all sit down and listen, Amrit would tell her family that she had reached a point where she didn't think she could change. She did not know the first thing about change. It was a large concept best left to those who built skyscrapers and filled the sea with sand, adding new edges to the island. It wasn't in her to put a stop to the rushing thoughts or the need to scratch every itch that prickled her body. She was not strong enough to refuse these impulses. All her family could count on was that she eventually ran out of places to go. She always returned.

Amrit found the key in her pocket and hoped that they had not changed the locks. She slid it into the gate and jiggled it before realising it was unlocked and open. Fear gripped her chest. Father was always careful about locking the doors at night before going to sleep. Had somebody broken in? Was that why the phone was cut off when she tried to call earlier? She gave the door a tentative push and slipped off her shoes. The lights were all off. Pale moonlight spilled through the windows. Amrit kept her fingers on the walls outside the kitchen to guide her through the corridor as she made her way past the living room and the dining table until she reached her room.

At first, she didn't see Father. She heard a noise and whirled around, shooting her hand out to the light switch, flooding the hallway with the sharp white light she had been trying to avoid. Father was sitting in his prayer seat, a wooden chair opposite the Guru's portrait. His head was bowed and his hair had come loose. Amrit couldn't remember seeing him with his hair undone. Long strings of black, grey and white spilled past his shoulders, their tips nearly touching the floor. Had he fallen asleep like this while praying? Then Amrit heard the sound again. A quiet whimper.

"Father," she said quietly. He didn't look up. She noticed his shoulders quivering. "Father," she said more urgently.

Father put his hands over his face. A loud, unashamed cry filled the air. At this time of the night when everything was so still, the sound seemed magnified and Amrit was certain the entire neighbourhood heard him. Her throat was painfully dry all of a sudden. She looked out of the window and saw the blocks of flats on either side of theirs. Almost all of them were dark now, the lights out, blinds and curtains shut.

Father stood up and came close to her. She barely recognised his face. His greyish eyes were wet and his mouth was twisted into an odd and frightening shape. Hair hung like a ragged curtain over his cheeks. She shut her eyes but a bare outline of his figure still loomed before her. She prepared to be hit. She was too frightened to know what else to do. Then, slowly, she felt his presence shift away. When she opened her eyes, Narain was coming out of her room, lugging two suitcases. He avoided looking directly at her as he told her, "I want you to leave." He set down the suitcases and waved an envelope at her. She could tell that there was money inside.

"I can't," she said. "Where will I go?"

"Where have you been sleeping?" Narain asked. "Go back there. Father's had enough." His voice cracked. "I've had enough," he added.

"You don't want me to go. Don't do this," she pleaded. "I've tried but I can't be better. I can't do what you do— what normal people do. Work, have a family, spend wisely. And I drink. So what? So I drink. Half the community does it. Women, too, they're just doing it in private." She straightened her back. "Hypocrites," she spat. "So what if people see me? They have their share of sins as well." She could hear Father shuffling through his room and the mattress creaking under his weight.

Narain shook his head and pushed past her. He opened the door and flung her suitcases into the corridor. One of them popped open and her clothes sprang out, littering the stairs. Narain bit his lip. He moved forwards as if he wanted to help, and then he turned back into the flat.

"No," Amrit cried as Narain began to close the door. She just wanted to go inside and get some sleep. "Let's talk about this. Look, Father is angry, I know, but you? You don't want me to go." The door remained slightly ajar. Through the gap, she could see Narain drawing in his breath.

"I do. I've had enough. I've been helping you, covering up for you, tracking you down for years now. My life revolves around you. What's Amrit doing? Where's Amrit going? Will she come back? You don't see how much you've done to this family." Narain opened the door again now and took a step into the hallway. He lowered his voice. "You didn't see Father this afternoon when those Bangladeshi workers started bragging about taking you all at the same time."

His words slammed into her chest, knocking the breath out of her. "What?" she whispered.

"You know what I'm talking about. Enough is enough, Amrit. I knew the rumours were bad, but even the biggest gossips in the community couldn't make up a story like that. Every time I heard something about you, I told myself, we all told ourselves, that it was an exaggeration. I thought everything you did was out of your control somehow, but this?" The disgust in his voice was thick and venomous. "This is no longer any of my business."

He opened the door and went back inside. The door slammed shut and Amrit sank to her knees, surrounded by her clothes. The other suitcase tilted towards her. She shut her eyes. Was this what Father wanted? To expose her to the neighbours, to humiliate her, and then to take her back in, only after witnessing her remorse? Then she recalled Narain's hard stare. She sprang to her feet and, leaving her clothes behind, tore at the gate. The clanging metal echoed through the corridor. Something clicked; a neighbour opened his door cautiously and peered through the crack before quickly retracting.

Amrit spun on her heels and ran down the eighteen floors until she was on the ground again. The sobbing made her body shake violently. Something between a scream and a plea kept getting caught in her throat, refusing to render itself in any recognisable language. She darted wildly into the main road, outrunning Narain's words and the image of Father crying. A set of lights flooded the street. She saw the car coming around the bend and she stepped onto the road. The horn blasted and the car switched lanes to avoid her. A taxi followed and then the street was momentarily lifeless. In the distance, she could see a bus slowly approaching. *Escape*, she thought, staring straight into its headlights.

PART IV
1990

Mother

AT DAWN, EVERY neighbourhood turned into a construction site. Teams of workers appeared in hard hats and khaki shirts. Their dark skin glistened in the sunlight. Like Dalveer, they were present but meant to conduct themselves as if invisible. She stood in the shade of an apartment block and watched them tend to their assigned spaces. Last month, she had witnessed the construction of a sheltered walkway that extended from one apartment block all the way to the nearest bus stop. It protected the residents from the monsoon rains so that they could go from their homes to whatever destination without feeling a single drop. How could they deny the rain, though? It would arrive again tonight, she could feel it. She anticipated the rain like it was its own festival. It threw the island off balance. People leapt over puddles and slipped on the sidewalks. Colours melted together, turning the sharp edges of the city blurry. She wished the rain would come now and send these workers scattering.

Today, the workers were mending yet another imperfection in a landscape that had already been tended to so many times that it resembled the town council's glass-encased model. Two men wearing yellow vests and gloves crouched over the pebble garden that bordered the playground. They removed the pebbles until nothing was left but bald concrete. Dalveer stared at the patch of ground. Surely they would not leave it that way. She had never noticed any trouble with the pebbles until a few days ago when two young boys got into a heated argument. One had picked up a pebble and thrown it at the other boy, who howled dramatically when he noticed a spot of blood on his collar. Dalveer had wanted to rush to the boys and ask them who their mothers were but, of course, her words would mean nothing to them. Somebody must have made a complaint, and now the pebbles were being removed. Dalveer shook her head and looked around, wishing she had somebody to complain to. Harbeer did not like to hear her lamenting the loss of the old island: the swampy earth and twisting bark, the constant hum of mosquitoes.

Another worker arrived with a contraption nearly as tall as he was. He clicked a switch and began to roll it over the concrete. Ribbons of smoke spun from the ground and a bitter smell filled Dalveer's nostrils. She recoiled further back as the fumes stung her eyes. The other workers paid her no attention as they began to place the pebbles back onto the concrete. Dalveer understood then. The pebbles were being cemented to the ground so that nobody could pick them up. The men were deep in concentration as they placed the pebbles at angles. Their supervisor, a Chinese man, came over and nodded, approving the spacing of the pebbles. Dalveer watched, dismayed, as a new unmoveable garden was laid before her very eyes.

Gurdev

IN THE DARK morning hours, a major earthquake ripped through Indonesia, tearing down houses and buildings. In Singapore, the tiniest ripple effects were being reported the next morning. Gurdev had felt nothing but he turned on the car radio to listen to updates. Rani yanked open the passenger door and plopped heavily onto her seat. "I still don't know why you won't just let me take the train," she muttered.

Gurdev turned up the radio. On the early morning train, Rani would be jostling and bumping against the boys from the neighbourhood school. He and Banu had agreed it was best that he drive Rani to school, but that she could ride the school bus home. "The school bus!" Rani had exclaimed, when they informed her of this plan. "The school bus is for all the *children*!" Gurdev, bewildered by this outburst, had demanded to know just what she thought a twelve-year-old girl was, but Rani had huffily turned away to end the conversation.

On the radio, experts warned of aftershocks throughout East Java; in Singapore, they would not be felt. Gurdev lowered the volume and turned his attention to Rani. "Do you have all of your books?" he asked.

"Yeah."

"All of them? You didn't forget anything?"

"Everything," Rani said. Gurdev noticed the way she shifted and drew her bag closer to her chest. A fog of unease rolled towards him, but this was commonplace nowadays. This year, Rani would sit for national exams that would determine her secondary school placement. From Primary One, Rani's exam results had only been average. A steady stream of tutors carved an avenue through their home to help raise her scores, but their impact was minimal. Each time Gurdev saw the exam dates marked on the calendar, he felt a familiar discomfort tying a knot at the base of his spine.

"You have maths tuition this afternoon so no staying back to chit-chat with your friends," Gurdev reminded Rani, as he pulled up to her school. He watched her shrink into her seat. "Go on," he said, firmly. She turned to him as if she might say something, but then thought better of it and grabbed her bag, exiting the car. He waited at the kerb, watching as she trudged through the gates.

At the office, Gurdev sought comfort from his worries in the columns and numbers that made up the day's work. Predictable and unchanging, they lured him into a trance-like state that was only broken when the office girls returned from their lunch break, bracelets and earrings clattering, high-heels tapping a steady beat into the tiled floors.

Jamilah, the new receptionist, stopped by Gurdev's cubicle. "For you," she said, handing him a pink plastic bag. Inside were three otak-otak—grilled fish paste wrapped in folded banana leaves, held together by toothpicks. "Your favourite," she said.

Gurdev smiled. "Thanks, Jamilah. So nice of you to think of me."

"Are these your daughters?" Jamilah asked. She pointed at the picture frame on his desk. "Very pretty. And that one is so cute!" She pointed at Rani.

"They are big girls now," Gurdev said. "Much older. My youngest is in Primary Six already."

"They're lovely," Jamilah said. Trotting back to her desk, she paused to check her reflection in the glass door.

Gurdev was tempted to ask Jamilah to explain what she saw in his daughters that made her so sure of anything. Gurdev had stood at the photographer's side when the photos were taken; sometimes when he looked at the photos he could sense himself in the background, aching at their innocence as the first flashes startled them.

At the time of the picture, it had been three days since the prize ceremony. One evening, when Banu began lamenting about Amrit's reputation, Gurdev could not bear to hear it. He made an excuse to go to the shops so that he could take a walk and think. Returning home no less confused, he checked the letterbox and found a glossy advertisement for a photographic studio. *Preserve your memories*, the advertisement urged. He booked an appointment for their earliest available session, which was the following afternoon.

When he and the girls had returned from the studio, Gurdev fell into a near comatose state to gain back all the sleep he had lost from worrying. He was only in bed for a few hours before the phone rang. Still groggy, Gurdev muttered, "Wrong number, wrong number," in response to a man's frantic tirade. Then he heard Amrit's name and a quick shudder roused him. The voice on the other end of the line belonged to Narain. "Narain, what happened?"

Exhaustion dripped off his shoulders like melting wax as the story unfolded. By the time Narain told him about Amrit running out into the road, Gurdev was wide awake.

"I told her to get out but then I saw the way she ran down the stairs. She didn't take the lift, she just ran all eighteen floors. I didn't know what to do. If I went after her, she'd come back to the house and I was still so angry at her. And Father, he couldn't even look at her without crying. Finally, I decided to go after her. I took the stairs too because I was afraid she might have stopped on one of the floors and started banging on the doors, asking for a place to stay or something. When I got to the ground floor I searched around and then I saw her figure in the distance. She was going out onto the main road. I started running and calling for her and a car came straight at her but the driver changed lanes. Amrit didn't even move, she just stood there like a statue. I screamed her name again but she didn't hear me. Then there was a double-decker bus and she just stood there like she was going to let it hit her. I shouted her name one last time and she turned around and I swear to God, Gurdev, if she had waited one more second to jump away…"

Gurdev pictured Amrit standing on that main road, the sky awash in headlights. What thoughts were running through her mind as she challenged death? He did not understand. He remembered his disbelief, and his wanting Narain to explain the whole incident again; surely there were parts left out.

"She's at home now. Sleeping," Narain said quietly. "I'm outside her room. Tomorrow she wants to go to see a doctor."

"A doctor?" Gurdev was puzzled. "I thought you said she

wasn't injured."

"A different kind of doctor," Narain said. "She wants to get a referral to see someone at Woodbridge."

The meaning of this slowly unravelled to Gurdev. Narain went on to tell him that Amrit thought she could be suffering from some sort of madness. Gurdev shook his head as if he could shake Narain's words away as well. He could not believe this—his sister, a madwoman.

"Why is she doing this to our family?" Banu wailed when he told her. "The whole world knows she drinks and sleeps around. Now she wants to be a mental patient as well? What haven't we given her?" Gurdev wept furiously at her side.

A week later, the photographic studio called Gurdev to tell him that the portraits were ready and he made the occasion into a small family trip. Under the frosty blast of the studio's air-conditioning, the girls chattered and giggled as they saw the glossy images of themselves. "You all look very nice," the photographer told the girls. Gurdev stared at each image until he was able to erase every similarity each girl shared with Amrit. Rani's sharp nose. Kiran's deep-set eyes. Simran's grin. He noticed Banu looking at the pictures with the same intensity.

In the following weeks, news about Amrit trickled into their home from Narain. He informed them that the doctors had a possible diagnosis for Amrit, and that she had been ill since her teens. "She could get better. Imagine, Gurdev, there's a name for Amrit's behaviour and we never considered it."

Gurdev rejected this. "Rubbish," he spat. "What kind of illness causes somebody to shirk their responsibilities in life, spend too much money, sleep around, and drink too much? If that's the case then this quack doctor can explain all of our laziness. Next time I want to take a round-the-world trip and squander my life savings on alcohol, I'll just say it's because I'm sick in the head. What a convenient excuse."

"It's not exactly like that," Narain said, defensively. "It's very complicated, and I know how it all sounds but what if there's a chance this might work for Amrit? The doctor explained the symptoms to her. Amrit says it makes perfect sense and she wants to be treated. She thinks she could recover from it. Isn't that what matters?"

"Amrit makes a lot of promises to do better in life, Narain. Haven't you at least learned that? She's tricking you."

"I really think this is different. I took the day off work today and I went to the library to read up on this thing. It's a…wait. I wrote down some things. It's a mood disorder. There's nothing Amrit could have done to prevent it, like any disease." Narain said. He dropped his voice. "I also read something about how it can run in families—"

As Narain attempted to read off a list of symptoms, Gurdev made an excuse to end the conversation and hung up. "That Narain is too trusting," Banu agreed. "Some doctors just search and search until they can tell a patient something—of course they'd find something wrong with Amrit! As if it is so easy to fix everything." Gurdev had avoided telling Banu what Narain had said about this madness running in families because the mere prospect made him slightly nauseous.

Now he wanted to prompt Jamilah again. "Tell me about my daughters." If he had the courage, he would seek her advice on the conflicts that had rattled his home recently. He would ask Jamilah why Simran wanted to work as a waitress—a waitress of all things!—in some restaurant in the city during her school holidays. He would plead with Jamilah to explain why Kiran wanted to transfer to a university in England when she had been bright enough to gain entrance to the law faculty of the National University of Singapore, where she was currently in her first year. He would ask her why Rani's school marks were not improving. These were the reasons that he left these young versions of them on display. In reality, the girls and their potential disasters had grown to proportions that he could not comprehend.

•   •   •

Gurdev preferred taking his lunch breaks later in the day, when crowds of office workers didn't clog the sidewalks. He crossed two roads and took a shortcut through a back lane. Tucked out of sight from the glistening high-rises was a row of dimly lit hawker centres and coffee shops. The floor was slick with both cooking oil and the soapy water that was occasionally thrown to keep the centre up to government cleanliness standards. Laminated sheets were posted up at each stall, declaring the grade given after the health inspections. Gurdev's favourite char kway teow hawker leaped to action when he noticed him approaching.

"Take the train today?" the hawker asked over the hiss of oil sizzling on the wok.

"No. I drive every day," Gurdev said.

"I take the train yesterday. Nice. Better than bus. Very nice," he said, gliding his hand across an invisible train track. Gurdev smiled. His local station had opened a few years ago and he had taken the girls on the inaugural ride. Seeing the island pass the windows, Gurdev had seen its foreignness framed like shots on a film reel. Vulgar pink bougainvilleas used to burst across the land; now they were draped across the overhead bridges to make the concrete look more welcoming. The Cinema-On-Wheels man used to push his rickety cart along the side streets and charge just 5¢ for a peek at still shots of cartoons; now cineplexes advertised Hollywood movies on flashy billboards. Memories arrived as quickly as the new island rushed below, tightening Gurdev's chest with a palpable sense of loss.

The noodles arrived. A rotating fan creaked on the wall behind him, sending a feeble breath of air across the back of his neck. "Wah," the hawker said, admiringly. He nodded into the distance. "Pretty girl." He grinned and walked away.

Gurdev turned to see Jamilah running towards the hawker centre, her knees bent awkwardly as she ran in her high-heeled shoes. When Gurdev saw the panic on her face, he knew. *It's the girls*, he thought. *It has finally happened.*

· · ·

The few facts that Banu was able to provide over the phone through her sobs turned in Gurdev's mind repeatedly on his drive home. Rani had not taken the afternoon bus home. A girl from her class claimed she had not been in school since recess and the busy class teacher assumed she had received permission to leave early from the school office. Banu had gone out to the neighbourhood police post to make a report before calling Gurdev's office.

Tears were pouring down Banu's face as she fumbled with the lock. Her hands trembled. "The police say it's too soon to make a report." The police. Gurdev suddenly remembered his argument with Father and Karam over notifying the police when teenage Amrit first went missing. *This is not a matter for the police,* Father had said. Now the same retort ran through Gurdev's mind but he avoided saying it. Banu was upset enough.

"We'll find her," Gurdev said, taking Banu into his arms. "Did you call her friends' houses?"

"All of them," Banu said between sobs. "I called almost the entire class. Spoke to all their mothers—so embarrassing. Asking them if they've seen my daughter. Nobody…nobody knows where she is." She buried her head in his chest.

"Shh," Gurdev said. He searched for more consoling words but found none. "Where are Simran and Kiran?"

"Simran's studying at the library. Kiran should be back soon."

The entire flat had become cluttered with the business of educating Rani. Eraser shavings and bits of pencil lead littered the floor, and loose sheets of paper caught the breeze and floated through the living room like leaves. They went into the room Rani shared with Simran, to search through Rani's things. Books were piled everywhere and her school diary gave no clues.

"What haven't we given them?" Banu asked, sitting on the edge of Rani's bed. Gurdev went to the window. Below him was an island that had been split open, thoroughly cleaned and redesigned. Imperfections were now highly visible. There were fewer of those dark crevices that he had often pictured Amrit falling into, but knowing this did surprisingly little to reassure him.

"You think she ran off with somebody?" Banu asked quietly.

"With whom?" Gurdev asked.

"*Somebody*," Banu said. "I see these girls nowadays hanging around the bus interchange, tightening their pinafore belts and talking to boys. Young girls, not much older than Rani."

"She's too young to be interested in boys. If she's with a boy, he's lured her somewhere." At his own suggestion, Gurdev became aware of the quickening beat of his pulse.

The gate rattled. Banu sprang from the sofa and ran for the door. Gurdev followed her. She pulled away from the peephole. "It's the other two," she announced.

"Both of them?" Gurdev asked. "That's strange. They came from different places."

"Quickly come in," Banu told them as they entered the flat and kicked off their shoes.

"Do either of you know where Rani is? She's missing," Gurdev said, once the door was shut. "She left school some time this morning, and nobody knows where she is."

The girls looked calm. A look passed between them but they did not seem surprised or upset. "We know," Kiran said.

Banu looked as if she might faint. "*You know?*" Gurdev asked.

"You did this? You two plotted with her to run away? Are you crazy? You know how worried we've been? I called all her school friends." Tears were streaming down Banu's face now. "Where the hell is Rani?"

"She's at Kavita's house," Kiran said. "She's fine. I took her there myself after my morning lecture. She's playing with Kavita's cats."

"What is she doing at Kavita's house?" Gurdev asked. Nothing made sense. Kavita was one of Kiran's friends from secondary school. She had no connection to Rani.

"I met Rani at the train station near her school and I took her to Kavita's house," Kiran said slowly. "Then I went back to campus for my afternoon lecture. Simran called every hour from school to make sure Rani was all right."

"Why did you take her there?" Gurdev asked. "Kiran, don't play games now. Tell me everything, or I will—" He stopped there. Kiran did not speak. Simran crossed her arms over her chest.

"You will do what?" Simran asked, softly. She did not have Kiran's cool confidence but she tried hard to replicate her demeanor: hard eyes; lips tight and upturned to indicate that he could not pry the words from her.

Gurdev started over. "Tell me—tell us—what's going on." He sensed a detailed plan here. The girls nodded as if awaiting this cue, and then they led him and Banu to the living room.

"We have a lot of things to talk to you about," Simran said. "And we've tried to discuss our issues with you but everything turns into a fight. Rani's got a lot of problems as well but she's too scared to tell you two what she's going through. She tries but then she ends up crying or causing a fuss. So we decided that she should do something else to get your attention."

"She decided," Kiran quickly corrected. "We didn't force

her to do anything she wasn't already planning to do. She was planning on running away by the way, Daddy."

"Not Rani," Banu said, shaking her head. "Rani would never come up with such a stupid idea. Where would she go?"

"I noticed she woke up early this morning," Simran said, "and I pretended to stay asleep while she packed her things. When she went off to the toilet, I looked inside her bag and found clothes. I don't know where she was planning on going—she didn't really seem to know. She just wanted to get out of school and not return. She begged me to promise not to tell anybody that she wanted to run away. I played along on the condition that she let me tell Kiran and then Kiran arranged to let her stay with Kavita."

"Why didn't you just inform me?" Gurdev asked.

"If we told you, you'd get angry and just give her another lecture about studying. If we showed her we were against her running away, she'd just panic and shut down completely and we'd never know what she was planning on doing," Kiran said.

"And we also saw it as an opportunity," Simran said.

"That's right," Kiran agreed. "Simran and I discussed it and we decided this would be a big wake-up call. For all of us," she added.

Gurdev pressed the bridge of his nose. He felt a headache coming on. "Let me get this straight. You two have kidnapped your own sister and you're holding her as some sort of hostage?"

Kiran tilted her head, considering this. "Yes. And our only request is that you listen to what we have to say." She exchanged a gleeful look with Simran.

Banu shook her head and glared at the girls. "You think this a joke? You think it's funny to scare us like this? You have no idea how worried we were. Your Father had to come home from work." She rubbed her face with her palms.

"We're very sorry for that, Mum," Kiran said.

"Sorry? You think sorry is going to restore everything? What did we ever do to deserve this?" A fresh wave of tears poured down Banu's cheeks. She stepped towards Kiran, smacking her first and then Simran. The girls graciously accepted the single smacks, which landed on their arms. Banu marched off into the bedroom.

"You deserved that," Gurdev said to them.

"We're really sorry," Kiran repeated. Simran rubbed the new redness on her arm.

"Okay. Okay." Gurdev tried to wave away the chaos. "What was so important that you had to give me and your mother a heart attack?" he asked.

"I'll start with Rani," Kiran said. "She's really stressed out, Dad. You put too much pressure on her."

"She's weak in school," Gurdev protested.

"Her marks are the only thing you know about her," Simran shot back.

Kiran reached into her bag and pulled out a piece of paper that had been ripped to pieces and then crudely taped together. "There's a girl in Rani's class who calls her Dumbo all the time. Did you know that? And she made the other girls on the school bus sign a petition banning Rani from sitting with them during recess because Rani let down the whole class. The teacher promised to buy ice-cream for the entire class if everyone got full marks and Rani was the only one who got six out of ten. Rani studied very hard for that test but somehow she couldn't remember the correct spellings on the day. She was hysterical when she came home. She had ripped up the petition but I put it together again and read it."

Gurdev felt a hot flash of rage at this bully but from the look Kiran was giving him, he knew that more was to come. "The girls have been teasing her for some time now. She mentioned it to you once. You told her that if she didn't want to be singled out for not doing well in school, then she should buck up and start working harder." Kiran could not hide the disgust in her voice. She passed the petition to Gurdev. Names were scribbled below a proclamation that Rani was to remain without friends as a punishment for being 'the biggest idiot in the world'.

"And then there's me," Simran piped up. "I want to work as a waitress during my school holidays."

"Out of the question," Gurdev said, looking up from the petition.

"Why?"

"Waitresses wear those skimpy skirts and they hang around with men," Banu called from the hallway. She came marching back. "What kind of job is that for a Punjabi girl? Have some shame."

"Waitresses in hawker centres and coffee shops do that sort of thing," Simran corrected. "I told you both that I wanted to work at one of the hotel restaurants in town. It's more like being catering staff."

"They wear pressed shirts and pants," Kiran offered.

Gurdev and Banu exchanged looks. Gurdev had to admit he did not know anything about the hotel restaurants. "Why do you want to do this?" he asked.

"For some independence," Simran said. "See—look at your faces whenever we say that word. Independence. You treat it with so much suspicion. Just because I want to make my own money doesn't mean I want to spend it on cigarettes and beer. I just want to know what it's like to work, make my own cash."

"Same here," Kiran said. "Just because I want to go to university abroad doesn't mean that I want to run wild in another country away from your supervision."

"It happens," Banu said. "Auntie Harminder's daughter went to Australia to study and she picked up smoking."

"Okay, another thing," Kiran said, irritably. "You have to stop thinking that we might do all the horrible things that other people's children did."

"If you're going to compare us to your friends' children, then you should hold up the ones who did good things as examples, too. Like Auntie Punam's son, who recently won some major grant for young entrepreneurs of Singapore. That could be me one day," Simran said.

"Or Rani," Kiran said. She looked Gurdev squarely in the eye.

Gurdev avoided the comment and focused on folding the petition. "I'll call Rani's teacher tomorrow and ask to meet with her. What is this girl's name?"

"Jessica something," Kiran said. "I forget. Her sister went to our secondary school. It's one whole family of bitches." Simran giggled. Gurdev opened his mouth to reprimand Kiran for her language but the girls had both started laughing now. He cleared his throat instead and looked on helplessly, waiting for them to stop.

· · ·

Banu gave the girls another scolding just before Gurdev and Kiran left to pick up Rani. "You could have given me a heart attack, scaring us like that. What were you thinking? When you all get home your father and I will discuss a punishment. No telephone, no television, housework every weekend until your backs are sore. Disgraceful you both are."

Kiran called her friend's house to make sure Rani was all right. She asked Gurdev if he wanted to speak to her. "I'll talk to her when she's back," he said, fearing that if Rani detected the tension in his voice, she might not want to come home.

He heard Kiran saying, "Don't worry about anything. No, no, he's not angry. We're coming over now, okay? Wait on the side facing the bus stop."

They didn't speak until they were in the car, halfway across the freeway that stretched over the city. The sky was a fierce shade of gold as the sun descended behind the city buildings.

"So can I at least look into universities abroad now?" Kiran asked quietly. "You didn't say anything about it just now. The transfer applications for courses in England close soon."

Gurdev sighed. "I still don't understand it. What's so bad about Singapore?"

"There's nothing bad about it," Kiran replied.

"You don't know how fortunate you are. When I was

young, this island was nothing."

"People in your generation always compare Singapore to the past. They don't compare Singapore to what the rest of the world can offer."

"What does the rest of the world offer, Kiran? You tell me. In Indonesia today, there was an earthquake which flattened villages. In London, New York and Sydney there are many places where you won't be able to walk around alone at night. People in my generation are grateful because we knew instability. We look at this country now and we feel proud of these clean and safe streets."

"It's a showroom," Kiran argued. "It's not real. It's so competitive."

"But you've done well in this environment," Gurdev protested.

"I've scored highly in all of my exams but I haven't learned very much. I just know how to take the government's tests. I memorised my textbooks. I look at Rani and I know how miserable she is. I hate the way they put students in academic streams based on their test results. They cast aside the ones who don't score well while grooming the high scorers in all the top streams. I saw the way my teachers treated our class and how they would compare us to the kids in the lower classes. They'd gush and tell us we were the hope for the nation, the ones bound to go to university and have successful careers; then they'd cluck their tongues and say there was less hope for the other children. What did they know? Based on one test, they behaved as if they had the authority to write every child's future."

"Kiran, this is a small country. We don't have a choice but

to be competitive."

"You don't think it's just a bit inhumane?"

"No," Gurdev said.

"Bullshit."

"Kiran!"

She crossed her arms over her chest and looked out the window. "Last weekend when we went out to that new Indian diner near the community centre you ordered a banana leaf dish and they brought it to you on a plate shaped like a banana leaf. Remember? You told the waiter you wanted an actual banana leaf and he said, "We don't have those." You tried explaining to him that the banana leaf adds a certain flavour to the rice and he just shrugged and said they were too messy. We were all laughing but I saw the look on your face. Like somebody took something away from you."

"Kiran, of course I miss the authenticity of certain things. But we have to sacrifice—"

"Just think about it," Kiran interrupted. "I don't need to hear a speech about the greater good. I've heard it all my life from my teachers."

Gurdev sighed. "Fine. I'll consider it, Kiran. Don't ask me about it for a few days. There are a lot of things your mother and I have to discuss."

"But you'll think about it," Kiran repeated.

"Yes." He felt her gaze warming the side of his face. "Don't get me wrong though, Kiran. I'm proud that you've done so well in school. A lot of parents have a hard time getting their children into the National University. We never had that problem with you."

"Or Simmy," Kiran said. "She'll do well in her exams."

"You think Simran will want to study abroad also?" Gurdev asked. A fresh wave of concern washed over him.

Kiran laughed and shook her head. "What, Simran? Simran can't even go away for a weekend without missing her friends and her hawker centres and her shopping malls. She's too comfortable here."

"Good," Gurdev said, trying to conceal some of his relief. "It would cost a lot of money to send the two of you overseas at the same time. And I'd have to save all over again for Rani in a few years. She might have to go abroad whether she wants to or not."

"She's not stupid, you know," Kiran said defensively.

"Of course she's not. I never said she was stupid. She just needs to work harder."

"She works very hard already. I've watched her doing her homework. She really tries."

"What are you saying?" Gurdev asked.

"There might be something…some reason she's struggling so much to grasp simple concepts. Like a learning disability or something. I saw a documentary about this boy who couldn't concentrate on his work and switched around letters and numbers in his head. He wasn't doing any of it on purpose, it was just the way his mind worked. Maybe Rani has that problem. You could have her evaluated."

Gurdev tightened his grip on the steering wheel. That word—evaluated. It immediately brought to mind images of Rani being surrounded and scrutinised by white-coated figures searching for a defect. Hadn't they done this to Amrit? He was not sure how the process of diagnosing her had taken place because Narain stopped updating him after that last conversation.

Gurdev remembered the week Amrit got diagnosed. It had been Gurdev's turn to take the girls to the library. While the girls picked their books for the fortnight, he wandered into the non-fiction section and found the row titled Psychology. Gurdev picked the first relevant title he saw—*Mood Disorders: Symptoms and Treatments.* He poked his head out to check on the girls. Returning to the book, he thumbed through the pages, surprised by the density of the text. Glancing at the shelf, he noticed several more books about mood disorders. He picked up a few more: *Quieting the Bipolar Mind—A Memoir* and *A Guide for Manic Depressive Patients.*

Gurdev only looked up from the books when the librarian brought the girls to him. "I thought they were lost," she said, smiling. "We're closing in five minutes." Hastily, he placed the books back on the shelves. Waiting in line with the girls, Gurdev could not stop thinking about the abundance of information about Amrit's condition. Like a dirt path paved into a clear city road, the baffling mystery of Amrit's behaviour had a name, a history, a presence in other people's lives. Was he meant to be comforted by this? He certainly didn't feel that way. Amrit's diagnosis felt less like a resolution than a new threat. After that visit to the library, Gurdev did not return to continue his research; he did not want to be burdened with more knowledge.

Now they were coming off the highway and merging into a series of lanes. Wide leaves and tree branches hunched over the road, splashing a pattern of shadows that shaded them from the sun. Kiran's suggestion about Rani echoed in Gurdev's mind. He was aware that Kiran was staring at him, waiting for a response.

"In my time there was no need to go searching for the roots to every problem," Gurdev said as they entered a multi-storey car park. "If you didn't do well in school, you were lazy or just not very bright. If you misbehaved and broke the rules, you were rebellious and foolish. Nowadays everybody wants to blame some underlying issue."

He pulled the car into a vacant lot and unbuckled his seatbelt. Kiran made no move to do the same. She was still peering at him and when he turned his head, their eyes locked. Very gently, she spoke. "It's not your time anymore."

Gurdev looked out onto the housing development. Painters on a metal platform inched their way up the sides of a building, applying coats of white onto the facade. It had not even started yellowing yet. A high-pitched wind whistled through the trees. It grew louder, and brought with it the screech of rubbing metal. He squinted and saw a train snaking through the buildings, its windows bright like eyes. *It's not your time anymore*, Kiran had said, like a consolation, like the chapter of a sermon. No, it certainly wasn't.

Narain

TO THE DIRECTOR of the Social Development Unit,

My name is Narain Singh Sandhu and I am writing in response to a letter recently sent to me from your organisation. To answer your questions in very simple terms: yes, I can confirm that I am unmarried and yes, I would like to find my life partner in the near future. However, my reason for never having used your services isn't due to a lack of awareness, so you can take me off your mailing list for flyers and events updates. I never signed up for this information that clutters my letterbox. I am sure you are sending these notices to all single Singaporeans within a certain age bracket so I shouldn't take it personally, but my reasons for not joining are valid. Before I explain them, I'd like to reiterate my request that you stop sending me information.

The first question on your recent correspondence was: "What do you really know about the SDU?" Like most Singaporeans, I know what I have read in the newspapers. The Social Development Unit was established by the government a few years ago to 'promote interaction' between the sexes. It is essentially a government-run dating agency for single Singaporean men and women. You must be aware that most Singaporeans have adapted the acronym to fit the term

Single, Desperate and Ugly. It is probably for this reason that your newer flyers contain photos of very attractive and vivacious-looking men and women mingling at barbecues and strolling along Sentosa Island.

When I first heard of the SDU's existence, I was not surprised. It seems very Singaporean for the government to sponsor and promote love. Then it occurred to me: twenty years ago, few people could label any behaviour as 'very Singaporean'. This country did not have much of an identity—we were still trying to find ourselves. Nowadays, everywhere I turn there are reminders of what a Singaporean is—or, rather, what we should strive to be.

On the buses, the National Courtesy Campaign posters remind us not to shove other passengers. Signs with penalty warnings remind us that the cost of littering is $500. Although falling in love and all of its excitement, along with its pitfalls and challenges, are not forbidden to Singaporeans, our government seems more concerned with legally pairing men and women who will eventually breed to fill the future population. I am writing today to tell you that love cannot be manufactured. This should be the most basic knowledge to anybody who claims love as their business. We do not always choose who and how we love. In my case, we do not always love the people we are supposed to.

I will never marry a woman. I am a homosexual. There was a time in my life, during my years of National Service, when my officers treated this with great gravity, as if I carried a contagious and dangerous disease that needed to be contained. They asked me to confirm their suspicions. I told them the truth because I did not think I could hide it. If two commanding officers who only knew me from basic drills could see right through me, what chance did I have of hiding this from anybody else? Over the years, however, I became more aware of the fact that hiding my homosexuality was the appropriate option.

I must admit that your recent marketing campaign has revamped your image significantly. If you catered to my population, maybe I would have attended your recent movie night or the Hawaiian *luau* or the picnic in Bukit Timah nature reserve. But after reading the Getting Started brochure and the registration form, certain questions would have turned me off. I would have sat down to write this letter regardless.

Firstly, the SDU is exclusively for university graduates. I fit into this category, which means that the government values my potential for finding a partner. So let's not deny why the SDU was really founded: the government's aim is to populate this island with the future offspring of university graduates in hope that we will have a more educated society. Clever people breed with other clever people and create clever children. Attached to this letter, you will find a photocopy of my secondary school leaving slip, with my results in every subject. My marks were always just above average and I was lucky to be accepted into a third-rate engineering program in America, where they were eager for the revenue from international student fees. I have a degree, but I have never considered myself an intellectual. A questioner, yes. An occasional reader, to combat my boredom on the commute to work. My father was a driven and self-motivated Indian immigrant who taught himself English with great discipline. Although he did everything to instil this same drive in me and my siblings, I narrowly passed my secondary school exams. My older brother was also an average student; he makes his living selling insurance now but two of his daughters have received countless awards, scholarships and prizes throughout their academic careers. There is no guarantee that an intelligent and studious man can produce carbon copies in his offspring, or that a less academic man is destined to have stupid children.

My sister Amrit is one of the most intelligent people I have ever met. Although I doubt she'd try joining the SDU. She would be rejected upon application. Amrit would not pass the screening on the grounds that she didn't go to university. But let's just say that she did. Let's say that Amrit graduated from the National University of Singapore with an honours degree in Law or Physics. She still would probably fail the SDU screening because of her record with Woodbridge Hospital (Question 7a: Do you have any history of mental illness? Please explain in the space below).

When I was getting ready to study overseas in America, my sister was fifteen and about to sit her O-Levels. She was what you would describe as a mischievous girl, a bit of a troublemaker. She was never a bad kid, just restless and curious. Yet at some point, Amrit changed for the worse. She began mixing with boys who skipped school, and doing dishonourable things. When Amrit first ran away from home, I knew that something serious had taken place. I also knew that it had been present in her all along. Since her adolescence, I had been trying to suppress this thing in Amrit that made her different—not just daring and rebellious but impulsive, overly excited and incredibly moody. I always knew that when I left, it would spring out and take over her, and it did.

By the time I graduated and moved back to Singapore, Amrit had already carved a reputation for herself for drinking, staying out late and mingling with the wrong company. She had trouble finding work and when she did, she was unreliable and frequently late. This continued, so my father tried to arrange her marriage but the engagement did not last. After that, things just became worse. Amrit would disappear for days on end and come back either drunk or hungover. Sometimes—mostly when she did not have any money—she would stay at home, but this was actually worse because we had to witness a different kind of disappearance, where it seemed as if Amrit's spirit had left her body and another one had replaced it. She talked rapidly and excitedly for hours about topics that had no relevance to each other. She had theories and ideas that made no sense. Then in the following days, she would be detached and incapable of speaking at all.

I look back on this period with a great deal of regret over how I handled Amrit's behaviour. In those days, I was blinded by the unfairness of this burden I had to carry. I believed that Amrit was holding me back and if not for her, I would be free to do whatever I wanted. I would have found love. I resented her. At the time I didn't realise that it was me—I was holding myself back. Whenever there was an opportunity for me to live a truer life, I saw Amrit as the obstacle that kept me from moving forward. I believed that

Amrit didn't want me to be free so she misbehaved and drew me back into my responsibilities.

Several years ago, everything began to make sense. Amrit vanished from our flat for nearly a week and during that time, I decided I wanted nothing to do with her. If she returned, I would padlock the gate and tell her to take her things and go back to where she had been. Certain events had occurred in the days prior that made me feel as though lying for another day would just be unbearable. I told my father that I was gay. He chose not to deal with it, but I was relieved anyway. I had told him. Moments later, we were sitting with a group of men at a coffee shop and they began to make jokes about a girl who lived in our building and slept with several men at a time for the price of a bottle of whiskey. We knew it must be my sister. My father broke down. I knew his tears were not just for Amrit. He was crying for everything he had lost, and I felt partially responsible for that. I was furious with Amrit for eclipsing this moment of my coming out, and for following her impulses with no sense of the consequences. In contrast to her actions, I had narrowly escaped jail just for 'dancing with men'.

I went back to our flat, and Amrit returned only a few hours later. I did not give her a chance to sneak in; I stood at the door and told her to get out. Then I took all of her belongings and threw them out of our flat. Amrit became hysterical and ran down the stairs of our apartment block. I panicked and ran after her. She went straight to the main road and planted herself in the middle of it. I screamed her name. In the surrounding apartment blocks, I remember a few lights flickering on but there was nobody out there but me and my sister. I don't know if she heard me. We both saw the bus approaching at the same time. Still running towards the road, I screamed out her name again and this time, she turned and stepped off the road.

The story, as Amrit would like to believe it, is that I pushed her out of the way. She claims she remembers my hands on her shoulders, pulling her out of harm's way. The psychiatrist she saw afterwards told her that it was common to confuse fantasy with memory after a traumatic incident. The truth as I witnessed it is this: Amrit saved herself. She stepped off the road, away from the bus, and collapsed into tears. I crouched next to her and, for a long time, we remained there in complete shock. Eventually, we returned home. Amrit looked as though she was still in a daze but her words were very clear. "I need help," she said.

Now I know that there are terms for what we just used to call Amrit's disappearances, and there is research to explain it all. We discovered these terms a short time after this incident when Amrit managed to get a referral to see a doctor at Woodbridge. He confirmed that she could not help her behaviour because she had a sickness that produced these emotional highs and lows. The doctor said that a steady course of medication and therapy would be the best treatment for Amrit. I certainly did not think it would be so simple, and I was right. Some pills made Amrit drowsy. Some made her sick. Others turned her into a zombie. At one point, Amrit decided it was better to go off medication altogether. She missed the highs she used to feel—the thrilling confidence and exhilaration—and she thought she would be able to control the accompanying lows now that she was aware of the illness. Luckily, the doctor talked her out of it and recommended another type of medication. He also persuaded her to increase the frequency of her visits to the psychiatrist.

Throughout this period, I did what I had done my whole life: I protected Amrit. The only difference was that I was now protecting her from herself. My only concern was that Amrit stayed on course. I took a leave of absence from work, citing a family issue about which my colleagues were thankfully polite enough to refrain from asking. The first few weeks of therapy were very taxing on Amrit. She came home each day looking drained, and she slept for long periods. The new medication had fewer potential side effects and the only one that affected Amrit was constant thirst. Then something happened. The books describe it as a turning point, when the right combination of remedies clicks into place. Amrit sat me down one day and told me that she was feeling a little bit better. It doesn't sound like a very promising statement but this marked the first time that Amrit could say she was making some progress.

Currently, Amrit works part-time at a shop for a woman who sells Christian religious figurines. This boss likes to remind Amrit that she is lucky to have any job at all considering her illness (which Amrit had to disclose). Amrit wants to find a new job but she also knows that her boss is right. Amrit wants to study. She wants to learn more about her illness but she is afraid of borrowing too many books about her disorder from the library because she does not want her name attached to that subject matter. My job is to convince her that she has nothing to worry about.

I wish I could do this with complete faith but I cannot. Letters from organisations like the SDU remind me that we are being monitored and judged in the most private aspects of our lives.

When Amrit was switching medications, she went through a period when she just wanted to give up trying. Everything made her miserable, and chances of a cure were nowhere in sight. I found myself reminding her that there were no neat solutions to such a complex problem. At the time, I said this out of desperation because I was very afraid that Amrit would slide back into her old ways. However, this became a daily reminder to myself as I noticed a disparity between the government's initiatives to civilise this nation and the actual signs of civilisation in our people. Courtesy campaigns and the banning of chewing gum are superficial solutions. People should be kind to each other for the sake of kindness. People should understand that sticking chewing gum on elevator buttons is disgusting. In the government's efforts to advance the people of this country as quickly as the skyscrapers are rising, they are forgetting that we are people. We are complex and diverse and will learn better through trial and error than through mandates. If you think I am wrong, step out of your office and look closely at the people. Peep into the government flats, take a stroll through the estates, eavesdrop on a hawker centre conversation. Everywhere, we cling to superstition and old beliefs. I entered a public rest room recently to find the muddy imprints of two shoes on a toilet seat. An older man from my father's generation must have squatted on the seat, not knowing that he was meant to sit on it, despite the illustrated Ministry of Health instructions pasted on the back of the door.

The old ways are rife in my own family, despite our modern surroundings. When Amrit informed my father of her diagnosis, I came home to find him sitting on the balcony counting his fingers. He said, "A man is supposed to have as many misfortunes as the fingers on his hands." He counted his fingers many times, looking genuinely puzzled. He had ten fingers but so many more misfortunes.

I worry about Amrit. Frankly, I don't know how anybody can survive in a society so eager to place each person into a category and close their file, without sacrificing their fundamental humanness. It is now my job to make sure Amrit does not believe she is only worthy of marginal things. Of course, this means that I have taken on another impossible responsibility but I can't live my life any other way.

On the SDU application, there was a space for me to write down what I wanted in a partner. If it were possible for a man like me to join the SDU, I would stipulate that my partner must accept that I would always take care of Amrit, even though she is learning to take care of herself. This is my reality. I will always wait for her phone calls, check on her, take down her doctor's number and follow up on her appointments to track her progress. This has nothing to do with what my family has assigned me to do. I want to support Amrit because I know how it feels to be defined by what I have not accomplished.

Initially, I wanted to write to say that I could not join the SDU because I have other responsibilities and duties, and they take precedence over finding a partner—but this is not true. My responsibilities towards Amrit are not more or less important than finding love. They are equal. If I can't show my sister the fullest support, then I can never hope to do the same for anybody else. Furthermore, my duties involve caring for somebody whose country does not consider her worthy of love. I want the government's attitude to change and I want Amrit to have the same opportunities as everybody else but I fear that, instead, this country will continue rapidly growing and changing in impressive ways that will make little difference to the humanity of its people.

For these reasons, I will not be sending this letter. I would rather send a simple note asking that you take me off the SDU's mailing list. It is enough that I have written the above sentiments, and that I keep this as a record of my opinions. Perhaps one day I will be able to read this again and see that something has changed.

Sincerely,
Narain Singh Sandhu

•   •   •

Narain blinked at the pages that were spread before him like a gambling deck. He stacked them together and stretched his neck and arms to ease some mild soreness. A long confessional had not been on this morning's agenda—he had only meant to inform companies to take him off their mailing lists.

It was not the first time this had happened. He recalled that hectic period during Amrit's in-patient treatment at Woodbridge. In between his visits, he had scribbled frantic notes in the flimsy pad he kept in his pocket to keep track of the names of medications and doctors. He still had that notebook, although its pages had long been filled with outraged rants at Gurdev for thinking Amrit's illness was a figment of her imagination, and with drafts of speeches to Father explaining the diagnosis in a way that he would accept. Each time Narain opened it, those feelings returned. So many words remained trapped within the margins of those pages.

As he contemplated a hiding spot for this letter, Narain noticed Amrit crossing the hallway past his open door. Her hair was neatly brushed and pinned up, her slacks ironed the night before. When she first started working for Ms Rosario, he supervised each of these tasks. Amrit had not liked it. "I'm not disabled," she had said exasperatedly one evening, after Narain reminded her to set her alarm clock. At the time, Amrit did not like hearing him explain the importance of setting routines.

Narain had known that Ms Rosario would not be kind to Amrit—he had met her himself when he accompanied Amrit to fill out her job application. Correctly predicting that the job offer would come with a catch, Narain was not surprised to see Amrit come home in tears one afternoon, declaring that she would give notice the next day. "No, you won't," Narain said firmly. "You have to work through it." Taking her through the tasks of laying out her clothes and setting her alarm clock for the next day, he was struck by the paradox of Amrit's situation. If she stayed, she had to put up with Ms Rosario's snide comments and suspicions about her character; if she quit, she would have to grapple with a sense of failure and a long wait until she found another employer willing to take her on. Even the smallest periods of idleness were dangerous—routines helped to close the gaps through which she might slip, especially in a crisis.

There she was again, her shadow flitting past Narain's door like a moth. He pushed the SDU letter into his dresser. Its contents felt private, even though Amrit knew him better than anyone else in the family.

Amrit poked her head in. "Is Father home?" she asked.

"Probably not. I heard him leave after eating breakfast," Narain replied. "Are you ready for work?"

Amrit nodded quickly. "I just have, uh… something to do," she said. "Where is Father exactly?"

"Taking one of his walks," Narain said. Father spent most early mornings on foot, travelling from one housing estate to the next and returning home with anecdotes brimming. He did not speak these stories to Amrit or Narain but, late at night, mistaking their flat for a home with wider dimensions, the muffled sound of his voice could be heard.

"What do you need from him?" Narain asked. Amrit did not answer. He looked up to see her opening the door to Father's room. She looked over her shoulder as if she knew that Narain would be right behind her. He repeated his question but Amrit said nothing as she entered the room and headed straight for Father's desk. Narain went after her, stopping at the door to jiggle the doorknob—Father had made no move to repair the lock, which had broken last week. Considering how much Father used to value his privacy, that was strange.

Amrit shuffled through Father's papers. She seemed intent on finding something, and Narain knew what it was. "Amrit," he said, placing his hand gently on her shoulder. She whipped around to face him.

"I heard him speaking to her again last night. I could actually hear what he was saying. He was blaming her for messing up the order of his papers. Look at them—they're all over the place. He said she had forgotten to dust during her last visit." Narain looked around the room. Dust motes swirled in the shafts of light that shot through the room from the gaps in the curtains. The blades of the ceiling fan were outlined in black grit. When was the last time anybody dusted this room? He had suggested hiring a part-time maid, but Father refused.

Amrit pulled up a pile of papers. "There you go," she said. "He mentions visits from Mother. She used to sneak in through the back door of the old Naval Base house, and after we moved into this flat, he would let her in through the main door. I remember hearing him going to the main door on some nights when I was awake. I thought he was just checking that the locks were secure—you know how he likes to be sure." Amrit clutched the letter to her chest. "I have so many questions that only he can answer, Narain. These supposed *visits* have been going on since we were children."

"Amrit, not today," Narain said, firmly. He held out his hand for the letters. During Amrit's hospital stay, Father had refused to visit her. He spent entire days cooped up in his room, scribbling fervently. When the scratching of his pen stopped, the night whispering began. Soon Father's words became distinct, the static clearing around his words and delivering a rant. "You wouldn't understand how hard it's been to raise the girl. You left us. I had to take care of her myself. Now they're saying she's mad. Harbeer Singh's daughter is in a mental hospital, everybody will say. How about you? She's your daughter too, but you just slip in and out of this flat whenever you please. It's not your name at stake." The realisation had made Narain recoil from the door: Mother was in that room.

Amrit was holding the letters close to her chest now. "I can't wait any longer. I want to talk to him about it today," she insisted.

"I know you do," Narain said. "But remember, one thing at a time. You wanted to talk to Ms Rosario about that promotion today. That's enough confrontation to deal with for one day."

"Yes, of course," Amrit said impatiently. "I haven't forgotten about that."

"Have you consulted Dr Chow about speaking with Father?" Narain asked.

"I've spoken to him countless times."

"Have you told him you want to speak to Father *today*?"

Amrit's expression soured slightly. "No."

"Why not?"

"It's my decision, Narain."

"It's not a good idea. Not yet."

"When then?" Amrit asked, exasperatedly. "You keep telling me to put it off but I can't take it anymore. He's not even trying to hide any of it. He practically left his door open and his papers within easy reach. Don't you see? He wants me to know. Just the other day, Dr Chow recommended a book to me. "It will answer your questions about those genetic links," he said. I picked it up from the library—there was a chapter that described this family so clearly it was like reading our family's story. I came home and heard him whispering in his room and it took me everything to stop myself from charging into that room and confronting Father, waving that book in his face. I just want him to understand that we share this illness. He's not alone, and neither am I. Shouldn't he know this by now? Shouldn't he hear it from me?"

"These visits from Mother have been going on for years, Amrit. Do you think that one conversation is going to make Father realise that he's been imagining Mother all this time?"

"She's not imaginary to him," Amrit argued. "He thinks she's real."

"She is real," Narain snapped. "To him," he added, because he caught the flicker of hurt on Amrit's face. There was no need to remind Amrit that she had never known Mother, that even though Narain's own memories were fragmented, they were fuller than any image Amrit might try to conjure. When they were children, Amrit would pester Narain for stories about Mother—what did she look like? How tall? How long was her hair? Facing Amrit now, he saw the same hunger in her expression, but he could not let her approach Father like this. She would scare him with her forthrightness; he would retreat and never speak of Mother again. "I know you must be full of questions but you have to tread this gently and pick the right time," Narain said.

"When are you going to say it's the right time?"

Was there ever a good time to call your father a madman? At first, Narain had taken great pains to keep it a secret. Between this discovery and Amrit's diagnosis, he felt as if the ground beneath his feet was made of flimsy planks. He ignored the hushed whispers from Father's room, telling himself it was the radio or the wind. When Amrit returned home, the whispers stopped temporarily but Narain found himself listening, ready to make excuses to explain them to her. He lost sleep as the truth gradually presented itself to him in their tensely silent flat. Finally he decided to see Dr Chow himself.

Sitting in the waiting room, Narain had wanted to distinguish himself from the other people—the patients. After all, this was a family member debriefing, not a therapy session. Yet throughout their hour together, Narain began to relax, slumping in his seat as if he were in therapy himself; there, he confessed to Dr Chow that he knew where Amrit's illness came from. Dr Chow, an eloquent psychiatrist whose early grey streaks made him look distinguished rather than worn, simply listened. When Narain was finished rambling, Dr Chow had said, "Mental illness is not like a virus, Narain. You could not have prevented Amrit from catching it."

It was those words that gave Narain the courage to explain it to Amrit one night, two years after her diagnosis. She had been on the balcony hanging clothes out to dry when she heard Father scolding somebody for breaking his mug. "Who is he talking to?" she asked Narain, alarmed. Father must have forgotten she was home, or otherwise, he had started becoming careless, wanting her to know. Narain had explained it to her but he warned her not to bring it up with Father. At the time, Amrit was shocked but agreeable; she spoke to Dr Chow who reminded her that the focus was on her recovery, not exploring its heredity.

Lately, as she returned to normalcy, she seemed anxious to want the same for everybody around her. Just last week, Narain had to convince her not to rush into her discussion with Ms Rosario to ask for a promotion. "It could go badly, so wait for an opportune time," he had reminded her. "You don't know what she might think." The truth was so discouraging to Amrit that she turned her proposal into a resignation letter. Narain knew to walk her through her routine again: alarm clock, clothes, ironing.

"Amrit, one day I'm sure he'll be willing to talk to you about it. Let him bring it up first. If you demand the truth from him when he's not ready, he'll just lose his temper and say hurtful things. Remember, I'm moving out in a month—"

"I know."

"Well, I just told Father about it yesterday."

"What? When?"

"In the morning. He obviously wasn't pleased about it. He asked me who I was going to live with."

Amrit studied him. "What did you tell him?"

"I told him the truth," Narain said. A glimmer of excitement crossed Amrit's face. Narain smiled. He could tell she wanted to give him a hug but she was still annoyed at not having her way.

"Fine then," Amrit said. She pushed past him and gave him a friendly nudge in the ribs. He could not help the grin spreading on his face. He remained in the hallway and shifted his position, first left, then right, then a bit more left. There was a particular spot in the flat where he could see a bit of each of its areas—the bedrooms, the balcony, the living room and the kitchen. At sunset, this vantage point was easier to find. Rays of fierce light shot through the flat, illuminating the spot in rich gold. It was nearly 7.30am; time for Amrit to go. After she left, he would go to the balcony and watch her miniature figure cross the walkway and reach the bus stop. She would wait for the 73A bus to take her to the train station and then she would make her journey to work.

Narain checked his watch. The car from his car-pool would arrive in twenty minutes and he had not showered, but there was still time for a short phone call to Andy. He went to the living room and called the operator, glancing at the number in the black address book only once as he recited the long string of numbers that would connect him to America. Andy's firm in Singapore had sent him to Chicago for three months, to manage one of their building projects. Narain pictured Andy sitting on a plush sofa and reading a book, his eyelids heavy. He missed him. When they first started seeing each other, cautiously and quietly even though it had been nearly two years since the New Year's nightclub raids, Narain had missed Andy even when he was sitting right next to him. He had cynically wondered if this meant Andy would not last in his life—perhaps he was preparing for Andy's departure. But when he confessed this feeling, Andy gently smiled and explained that this was what love felt like sometimes. "Like risk," Andy said.

Three rings and then Andy picked up. "I knew you'd call now," he said.

"How could you possibly know that?" Narain could not keep the smile from his voice.

"I just knew," Andy said mysteriously.

Narain laughed. "I can't talk for long. I have to get ready for work."

"All right," Andy said. "You're up early." He stressed the R and dragged the word, making Narain laugh once again. Narain had noticed a few Americanisms in Andy's expressions, and since Narain had pointed it out, Andy took it upon himself to exaggerate the accent.

"I had some things to do," Narain said. He told Andy about his unintended letter to the SDU.

"A manifesto," Andy said. "Make sure you keep it."

"I've hidden it away," Narain said. He thought about the letter sitting in that drawer. There were spaces all over this flat where he could tuck away such letters. "I think it's the first of a series of letters I'd like to write. I just wish I could send them."

"One day, Narain. Things might change." It might have been the firmness in his tone or the words themselves that filled Narain with emotion. Andy was relentless in reminding Narain to hold onto his ideals. On their first date, Narain had told him about the raids, and about how he had given up on his social justice quest after his group had fallen apart. It had all just been a reckless experiment in rebellion, he told Andy, dismissing the flyers and the underground movement. "You're telling me all of this!" Andy had said. "We barely know each other. How do you know I'm not an undercover policeman? There's still a campaign to punish homosexuals even though they've relaxed with the raids and canings. I could be waiting to arrest you at any moment." Narain had been surprised at his own response—a shrug—to which

Andy responded, "Exactly. You cannot stop believing in the truth. No need for flyers or groups to promote it. It's always in you, Narain."

Now he asked Narain what else he wanted to write about. "Tell me," he said. "Unless you'll be late for work?"

Narain pictured Andy sitting back, closing his eyes and tipping his head up as he did when he listened to music. "I'll write to those police officers from the New Year's raid. I'll tell them about my key," he began. He could practically see the unabashed grin stretching across Andy's face as he chattered on about the key Andy had given him within months of knowing him. Narain spent a few nights a week there, searching for spots to place his own things. It was not difficult to find those empty spaces; it was as if Andy had found the place years ago knowing that Narain would arrive, their lives neatly fitting together. Before leaving for America, Andy had presented Narain with a copy of the lease. "I would tell them all about the apartment. I would even send them a copy of that lease with our names next to each other: Mr Narain Singh Sandhu and Mr Andrew Tay Hok Kim. I would tell them it's the only official document the government will let us get away with."

"For now," Andy reminded him. "Things could change."

Narain pressed the receiver so close to his lips that he could feel the pores in the plastic through which Andy's voice emerged. "I would tell them that too," he said.

Amrit

THE TRAIN RIDE was smooth, as usual. The handles swayed gently above her head but Amrit didn't need their support; she had a steady place near the doors, where the windows were widest. She took in the view of the island. Treetops and buildings rushed beneath her feet. A Catholic school's church steeple met her at eye level, reminding her of those days at school when everything towered over her.

As the train arrived at Toa Payoh station, it suddenly jolted. Arms shot out in every direction, reaching for the poles, but Amrit's hand flew straight to her heart. She clutched the fabric of her blouse, crushing it between her fingers.

The elderly man standing next to her shook his head and shot a glare in the direction of the main car. "Why train driver go so fast?" he asked. "Go so fast then when want to stop, got problem. Make passenger all fall down for nothing." He rubbed his eyes and blinked quickly several times.

Two youths in school uniforms exchanged a surreptitious smile. The man continued mumbling to nobody in particular. Amrit wondered what was wrong with him. The teenagers seemed to be asking the same question. One of them rolled his eyes and spun his finger in circles next to his forehead. The other chuckled softly behind his hands. Amrit shifted away from the teenagers and closer to the doors.

More passengers entered at the next stop, and then the announcer's voice came on. In all four national languages—English, Chinese, Malay and Tamil—it was made clear that the train would reach its final destination at the next stop. A pair of young women squeezed in behind Amrit and grabbed the railings above her head, leaving her facing their armpits. As she twisted away, one of them was saying, "She thinks she's so special, that's what I can't stand. She thinks she can get more annual leave by wearing thick eye shadow and short skirts."

"Damn cheap," the other woman agreed. "This kind of people, ah, they cannot make it, lah. Just wait. Few months down the road and boss will get fed up with her tricks."

Amrit's instinct was to freeze. They were talking about her—yes, of course they were. They were calling her names. They didn't know her but they could see inside her and they knew everything that she was. Her body felt tight, as if it was being squeezed. Just as the panic began to set in, she recalled Dr Chow's words: *sometimes you will think everything is a message for you, but it's not. Your mind is tricking you again.*

The first time Amrit heard that explanation, it was hardly consoling. It was reiterated throughout her diagnosis and during the multitude of counselling sessions that began to blur together. The words lost their effect quickly; the idea that her own mind could turn against her was not something she could easily grasp.

"Think of this as any other kind of illness," Narain urged her after her diagnosis. "The body which becomes vulnerable to the flu, for example, has been betrayed by its immune system." He had been so eager to make such comparisons, but they did little to soothe Amrit. Textbooks and studies had been written on this illness, and doctors had been trained to recognise its symptoms. This demon inside her had been given a name years ago, but she had only found out after years of believing that she was not fit for a meaningful existence.

"What I wouldn't do to trade this for a physical illness," she had told Narain after the diagnosis. One of the recommended books had outlined a list of physical symptoms expressed by people in cultures that did not have the word for 'depression' in their vocabulary. Stomach pains. Whole body aches. Numbness. Disappearance of the spirit. Amrit's comprehension had been somewhere between the ignorance of a village woman and the cultivation of a modern British-educated woman. But, as Dr Chow pointed out, even the most educated people were not necessarily aware that mental illness had so many different shades.

Shades. Amrit liked the word; it gave her a place on a spectrum, a spot among a hierarchy of patients. There were those at the very bottom—the stark raving mad: the girl she'd seen at the temple whose face hung slack as she rocked back and forth next to her mother; the man pacing a local shopping centre muttering obscenities and lugging a satchel of yellowed legal papers that he distributed to strangers; the patients she had envisioned staggering and moaning beyond the gates of the mental hospital, waiting to greet her like a band of zombies. Then there were people at the top—the normal people with an occasional hobby of moodiness: the misfits. Squarely in the centre, perhaps teetering occasionally, was Amrit. Most of the time she felt grateful to be treatable, and to be able to pass as a normal person. She could walk down the street without so much as a limp or an odd facial expression and nobody would know the difference.

However, sometimes she wished that her behaviour fit people's expectations of insanity: banging-head-against-the-wall; shrieking; fetal position; inconsolable. Nobody would have any questions—they'd take one look at her and shake their heads and say, "Pity". The downside of being only moderately mad was being doubted. Everybody was reluctant to believe in her illness. If she could behave normally sometimes then why couldn't she always control her emotions? Who ever heard of an illness causing rebelliousness? Was every alcoholic, thief and loose woman suddenly deserving of therapy?

The train jerked to its final stop and the man began to grumble again, this time softly. His eyes caught Amrit's but she quickly turned away. Did he see it? Did it show, a flash in her eye, a signal? She moved with the current of passengers onto the platform and the man dissolved into a cloud of shirts, bags, arms and chatter. Had he actually been there in the first place? She searched for the youths. There was no proof of anything. The tiled floors gleamed under the bright station lights. Amrit wanted to sit down for a moment but the crowd was falling into neat formation at the escalators and if she turned back, she would cause a brief disruption. After passing through the turnstiles, she found the closest wall and leaned against it with her eyes shut. *Stop*, she told herself. She had taken her medication this morning and there was no reason to believe that the illness was slowly creeping back. "You're too conscious of it now," Dr Chow had told her when she described her constant panic lately. It distracted her and made her irate, which was why she had been so impatient with Narain this morning. The doctor had advised her to take a break from reading all those books about her condition, and to focus on goals that could be achieved. In her purse, carefully tucked into a side pocket, was a thin square of a notebook. It contained a list of everything she wanted to do. Despite Narain's attempt to dissuade her this morning, there were two tasks she planned to carry out today. Each time she felt the shape of the notebook in her bag, her heart began to race.

●　●　●

It was a short walk past a row of coffee shops, minimarts, private doctors' offices and a sportswear shop. But by the time Amrit reached Block 55, she was already tired. Construction barriers cordoned off the straightest path to her workplace. Fluorescent orange nets and steel poles turned her simple routine into a construction maze, where dust-covered workers pointed out the new route.

Amrit checked her watch and quickened her pace as she approached the Staff of Life Christian Bookstore, which was on the third floor of a low commercial building. On the bottom floor, an Indian sweets and magazine shop occupied two lots, and adjacent to it was a hairdresser. The second floor was filled with two competing tuition centres and a single dry-cleaning business, which sat squarely between them, a neutral divider. Children in their school uniforms held books in one hand and swung their water bottles from the other.

"You're late," Ms Rosario said, as Amrit slunk in.

"Only by one minute," Amrit said. "The construction workers blocked off the road."

Ms Rosario waved away her excuse and motioned for her to approach the cash register. "Look at this," she said. Amrit saw nothing, but she nodded anyway.

"You see it, or you're just nodding?" Ms Rosario asked.

"I don't know what you want me to look at."

Ms Rosario sighed and walked away. "I'm going to the toilet. When I come back, I want you to explain what happened to my cash register." She headed out the door and then turned back. "Do you have tissues?" she asked.

Amrit pulled out a packet of tissues from her back pocket and Ms Rosario took it. "I want an explanation," she said, warningly, as she left.

Amrit had been in the job eight months, nearly nine. After she decided she was well enough to begin working again, she began a job search that repeatedly brought her home in tears, much to the dismay of Narain, who thought another breakdown was on the horizon. She finally found Ms Rosario, who was willing to take her on, even after she revealed her record at Woodbridge. The only catch was having to put up with Ms Rosario's belief that Amrit, like her other two employees, was suffering from a lack of godliness. Ms Rosario had taken it upon herself to change their fates with an eventual conversion to Christianity. She placed leaflets strategically across counters, and offered an employee discount on figurines and wall hangings inscribed with Bible quotes. She became more persistent during the off-peak season, when her stream of customers dwindled. Outside of the major Christian holidays, the shop didn't offer anything new, and the few who knew of it had already bought everything they wanted. *What would I possibly buy from here*, Amrit wondered in her first week, staring at the shelves full of devotional books and plaques inscribed with Scripture. Once she spotted a bunch of gaudy plastic flowers in a teal vase. She could almost see it brightening the flat in a space next to the television, but when she picked it up, she discovered a crucifix clumsily affixed to one side, globs of dried white glue hanging like frozen tears.

Ms Rosario returned with a smile. "Well then. You want to tell me what happened?"

"I still don't know what you're talking about," Amrit said. "I didn't take any money from the cash register, if that's what you're saying."

"Look at this," Ms Rosario said. She took hold of Amrit's elbow and steered her closer to the cash register. Amrit squinted, seeing some lettering lightly scratched into the surface. *Fuck you*, it said.

"I didn't do this," Amrit said. "I wouldn't."

"Maybe you did," Ms Rosario said, with narrowed eyes. "Maybe you did and you don't remember."

Amrit stiffened. "I would remember," she said.

Ms Rosario shook her head. "I once saw a movie about an American boy with multiple personalities. It's based on a real story. He gets up in the middle of the night and tears apart the whole kitchen and then goes back to sleep calmly, like nothing happened. When his parents wake up, he tells them some story about aliens coming in and doing it. He blacks out and doesn't remember at all that he did it himself. He's the aliens."

Some employers left a space on their forms under the

question about illness to allow the job applicant to specify. The space was minimal—just enough for Amrit to squeeze in a few words. She had never tried to explain bipolar disorder to Ms Rosario, knowing that it would only be used against her.

"It must have been somebody else. I'm not the only one who works here," Amrit reminded Ms Rosario. She cast a glance at her bag in the corner and remembered her list. She could not anger the woman today; she had to reason with her.

"This is what I get for giving you a chance," Ms Rosario muttered, shooting her a look from the corner of her eye. She tossed Amrit's tissue packet across the counter and went to the farthest corner of the store. Ms Rosario only hired people who she could blame for her own state of disarray. The vandal was probably another worker. There were two more employees: Jeremy, a vibrant 20-something-year-old with spiky hair; and Yee Ling, a frighteningly fragile girl whose long floral skirts had to be pinned to the hem of her blouses or they would fall off her bony frame. Ms Rosario only had this to say about Yee Ling: "The girl never eats. Every time I offer her a little bit of lunch she looks like she's about to cry." Her lips curled with disgust each time she had to mention Jeremy. She had nothing to say about him, only that they were remotely related.

Amrit and Ms Rosario did not speak for the rest of the morning, which passed laboriously, with only two customers appearing to glance at the shelves and leave, realising they'd mistaken the shop for something else. She busied herself with wiping down the ceramic angels. Dust collected in the crevices of their elbows and eyelids, and Ms Rosario insisted they simply couldn't be sold in that condition. Amrit pulled out her cloth and folded it to a sharp point that would fit into the tiny nooks. After the angels, she had inventories to sort out and phone calls to make for a fundraiser Ms Rosario was planning for her church.

During her lunch break, Amrit hurried to the town centre coffee shop, clutching her bag. She ordered a rice plate from a Malay stall and chose beef rendang and stir-fried long beans to go with it. As she ate, she pulled out the notebook from her bag and read the first item on her list. "Propose suggestions to Ms Rosario about improving business." On the other side of the page was the list of suggestions that she had brainstormed with Narain's help many months ago, when she first started working for Ms Rosario.

Soon her lunch break was over but her plate remained full. Amrit was concerned about the list. What if Ms Rosario got annoyed with her? What if her ideas seemed silly? She didn't know the first thing about business but if she had a chance to learn with experience, maybe she'd be able to put those skills towards building a career. She began to walk back to the shop. Ms Rosario was probably still annoyed with her, so maybe today was not the day. She passed the library, where she used to spend her lunchtimes before the doctor advised her to take a break from researching her illness. Then she looked at the list again and stuffed the notebook back into her bag. She had written it months ago, knowing that there would be a day when Ms Rosario's judgement became unbearable enough for her to take this risk. It had to be today, and then she could go home tonight and confront Father. She was ready for his rage; she had prepared for it, and time was running out. This was what she could not explain to Narain this morning. She was planning on moving out as well—renting a one-bedroom flat of her own. The first step was gaining this promotion—the next, confronting Father. Narain did not believe that she was ready for either task. She sensed that when he looked at her, he saw the teenage girl he had left behind in that Naval Base bungalow when he set off for America. He did not see her as she was now. Faint creases appeared in the corners of her eyes when she smiled. There was a thickness to her waist and limbs that many associated with the pitfalls of age, but Amrit didn't mind it. She looked and felt like an adult, and she should be trusted to live like one.

Ms Rosario glanced at her bag when she returned. "No books?" she asked.

"No," Amrit said. "I didn't go to the library." Whenever she borrowed books, they bulged through the bag. Ms Rosario had asked her about the books before and Amrit always lied, saying they were novels, not manuals on how to cope with bipolar disorder.

"Well, while you're not reading anything, I think you're ready for this," Ms Rosario said, handing her a leather-bound Bible. Amrit was surprised by its weight. She opened the front cover and delicately turned the first few pages, aware of Ms Rosario's scrutinising gaze. Each time she casually handed Amrit a new pamphlet or recited scripture, Amrit saw her fierce and urgent hope that her purpose would not be lost here.

"Thanks," Amrit said, closing the book and stroking the embossed lettering. "This is lovely," she added, at the hint of Ms Rosario's smile. Amrit cleared her throat. "I was wondering if I could talk to you about something."

Ms Rosario nodded.

"Umm…on my way over here, you know what I was thinking? You can hand out leaflets at the train station. So many people going in and out—I'm sure you'll get better business. I've collected a few leaflets myself, for tuition centres and restaurants mostly. I think I have a pretty good idea of how to organise the information and make it look presentable," she said. She looked down and cleared her throat again, wishing she had memorised a speech.

Ms Rosario let out a long sigh. "You can't just go around handing out advertisements. You have to get permission," she said, impatiently.

"Yes, I know. But I can research how to do that and I can obtain permission from the town council or whoever it is." Now Amrit was beginning to speak too quickly, but Ms Rosario looked more interested. "Also, I was thinking maybe you'd want to advertise in churches, and maybe look at expanding the merchandise. Greeting cards, balloons, inspirational books, things like that. I could help to research those opportunities too."

Ms Rosario remained silent. Amrit looked at the Bible and ran a hand over its cover. "Anyway, those are just my suggestions. You probably have plans for the shop and you've probably thought about all of these things." She bit her lower lip. Ms Rosario was watching her carefully, slightly amused. Amrit could feel her face flush. "It wasn't me," she blurted out. "I didn't do that to your counter. I would never do something like that. I've never even called in sick, I often stay behind to help after my shift even without pay and I follow every instruction you give me. I always wanted to work in advertising. I can sell things and convince people. I'm good with words." She looked around the shop helplessly. A row of angel statues with their heads cocked at the same angle stared back at her, but she was finished now. She wanted to sit down.

Ms Rosario finally spoke. "The punishment for vandalism nowadays is very severe. You saw that in the papers? Those hoodlums who used spray paint on those parked cars? Six strokes of the cane. Our government wants to send a message loud and clear." Then she looked away. "I know it wasn't you. Just now while you were on your break, that useless Jeremy called. He told me, 'I left you a message in your shop. Did you get it?'"

Amrit almost smiled.

"That one is nothing but trouble. He's lucky he got spared a caning. You know he was arrested once? For repeatedly urinating in lifts." Ms Rosario's face scrunched up in disgust. "First time they caught him, they fined him, but he wouldn't stop! He thought it was funny or something. He was caught on camera and the police came to arrest him in front of all his neighbours. I know his parents—we're distant relatives. Very distant. But in the Eurasian community, everybody is sort of related, huh? Even if you're not cousins or uncles you just say you are because it's better to pretend to be family than be like strangers. Except when something goes wrong. Then you realise how small the community is. That's what happened to Jeremy. People found out, his parents' church friends began talking about them, he was ostracised. I took him in! I let him work here, and you see what he's done to my counter? All because I told him to read the Bible." Ms Rosario nodded at the copy she'd placed in Amrit's hands. "Better to give it to somebody who actually reads books.

That boy is useless. He's not coming back here." Ms Rosario suddenly looked distraught. "This means he's not going to change," she said, sitting heavily on the stool next to the cash register. "I can't save him."

"You did what you could," Amrit said encouragingly. "It's not easy. Not everyone understands how to help."

"He is such an idiot. Why urinate in a lift? There are two functioning toilets in his flat." She shook her head. "When he was young he was always picking fights in school. His poor mother. I've told him so many times to think about her when he's about to do something stupid. How did she feel, seeing the police show up like that?" She squinted at Amrit. "How did your mother feel?"

"Excuse me?"

"Wasn't she sad? Wasn't she humiliated? I know you said you couldn't help having this, this disorder, but didn't you think about how your mother felt when she found out?"

"I did," Amrit said, sparing Ms Rosario the truth.

The entrance bell clanged as a customer entered. Thin, tall, with a crew cut. He glanced curiously at Amrit. "Do you sell stickers?"

Ms Rosario beamed. "Yes, we do," she said, ushering him to the crafts section. Amrit's kara banged noisily against the counter top. She took it off while dusting because it had caught on a figurine's arm once and nearly toppled the entire ceramic collection. Ms Rosario always eyed it, once telling her that a rosary ring was much less trouble than this cumbersome Sikh bangle. "Even your men wear it?" Ms Rosario had asked, her incredulous tone telling Amrit just what she thought of that.

The customer paid and left. Ms Rosario asked Amrit if she had seen him before. "He was looking at you," she said. She reached out unexpectedly and pushed the curls out of Amrit's face. "You have lovely skin, Amrit. Makes you look younger than you are."

"Thank you," she said, and in the same breath, she handed the Bible back to Ms Rosario. "Thank you for this as well," she said, her voice gentle but firm. "But it's not for me." Might as well resign now, she thought grimly, seeing the pinched look of insult on Ms Rosario's face as she took the Bible back.

The rest of their day passed with only fragmented conversation. Amrit dusted the shelves, showed customers to the things they needed and, at the end of the day, counted the cash, under the watchful eye of Ms Rosario. "So, tomorrow you can start a double shift because Jeremy won't be here," Ms Rosario said, casually. "If you want to stay back after your shift today, we can talk about your ideas. I'll pay you for the time."

Amrit nodded. "I'm happy to learn," she said, perhaps too eagerly, because Ms Rosario looked up sharply and scanned her face for traces of sarcasm. Her gaze eventually softened and she looked away.

• • •

By the time Amrit left the shop, the neighbourhood was bustling with the return of commuters from the city. She dropped in at the local bakery to pick up some steamed red bean buns for Narain, a peace offering for being so curt with him in the morning. Now that Ms Rosario had agreed to give her the promotion, she was less anxious. On the train, she began to think about what she would say to Father. She would sit down with him in his prayer corner and ask him when he last saw Mother.

"What if he tells you the truth?" Dr Chow had asked when she told him of her plan. "Are you ready to hear it?"

Conversations with Father were not so simple. He would become irate quickly, and ask her what she was talking about. He would tell her she was trying to cause trouble. These were the reactions she had been preparing for. "Where is Mother, Father?" she pictured herself asking, sitting tall and proud. Trying to understand. He would point wildly in every direction. Mother was in the shower, using up all the hot water. She was in the kitchen, dropping another plate by accident and failing to sweep away the tiniest specks. This was the part that Amrit always struggled with in her enactments. She could not pretend that Mother was alive.

It had been Father's job to tell her what happened to Mother all those years ago but all he had said was, "She is gone, Amrit. She went away right after you were born." That euphemism had been so common throughout her life. As a child, before learning the specifics from Narain, Amrit was plagued by images of a fleeing woman, not a dying one. It was time for Father to address this. If he admitted nothing else, then at least explain that Mother's departure was unintended.

Father

HIS FEET WERE still sore, even though he had returned from his walk hours ago. Limping slightly, he moved from room to room in the flat, searching for that Chinese balm that Dalveer had once urged him to buy. It came in a small green pot and gave off the smell of eucalyptus, which reminded him of their first days in Singapore, when everything was novel.

When Amrit returned, he was sitting in the prayer corner with his eyes shut, rubbing the balm into his feet. He heard the rustling of plastic bags being set down on the kitchen counter and the patter of Amrit's feet across the tiles. It was the same sound her feet had made when she was a child.

"How are you, Father?" she asked, when his eyes opened.

"Fine."

"What happened to your feet?"

"I was walking and they started to hurt," he said. "I think I walked too much."

Amrit approached him. "Your toenails are too long. They need to be cut. They're probably digging into your skin and making it more uncomfortable."

"They're fine," Harbeer said. He knew his toenails were too long but his fingers weren't dexterous enough to wield the clippers. Each time he leaned forward, he felt the stiffness in his back. "They don't need any cutting." Amrit ducked into her room before he had a chance to protest any further. She came back with nail clippers. "I told you they don't need to be cut," he said sternly. He turned away from her and picked up a prayer book.

"Father," Amrit gasped. "Your hands just touched your feet."

Harbeer dropped the prayer book back onto its stack immediately. He leaned towards the book and kissed it as an apology. He noticed Amrit looking away as he did this. Had any of his children ever witnessed him making such a mistake? He noticed his hands were shaking slightly. He started to pull himself to his feet and waved Amrit away when she tried to help. She followed him into his room.

"I brought red bean buns for tea," Amrit said.

"It's almost dinner time."

"We can save them for breakfast tomorrow then."

He lowered himself onto the edge of his bed. "Good," he said. "I don't think I'll have dinner tonight anyway."

"Father, I got a promotion at work today," Amrit said, suddenly. "Ms Rosario says she wants me to help her market her products. I'm going to start taking more shifts."

"Good," Harbeer said. He had to force a smile but could not help the next words from escaping his lips. "You'll move out of this flat soon then. This is what your mother did when she had the chance. She left."

"She died," Amrit said calmly. "She died when I was born. She did not choose that." She looked away for a moment. "Unless she told you something different."

Harbeer caught Amrit glancing at the desk. She continued. "I know you think…I know she comes to see you. I know you think it's her spirit but actually…" Her voice trailed off as Harbeer stood up and took a step towards her. She shrank away, but he was not trying to harm her—he wanted to inspect the order of his papers on the desk. When Amrit realised this, she went on, her words gaining momentum. She talked quickly about hallucinations and delusions, those so-called medical terms similar to the ones that echoed through the flat after her diagnosis.

"You looked through my letters," Harbeer said. "You broke into this room and looked through my letters."

"The door was unlocked," Amrit said. "Father, there are people who can help you."

"Help me?" he cried. "Help? Everybody wants to blame me! You think I gave this problem to you? You think that's what I did? Your Mother is the mad one. She left us because she wanted her old life. She thought she could run back into the past and stay there. She left me with you." He swung his arm into the air and brought a clenched fist down on the table. Some of his letters tumbled onto the floor, grazing his feet. He searched the room, wishing Dalveer would burst in and show herself to Amrit, but she was never willing to appear for anybody but him.

•   •   •

At first, Harbeer had believed it was just death—simple, and part of an incomprehensible system of balance: the arrival of his only daughter for the departure of his wife. The doctors had had to explain it to him several times, and despite his strong English, he was a novice at the vocabulary of Dalveer's exit. High blood pressure. Complications. Renal failure. Seizure. A nurse handed him the bundle that contained Amrit, and he received a slip that contained details of the birth date and time, to apply for her birth certificate. A pause, a mere pause, and the nurse sorrowfully handed him another slip for Dalveer's death certificate. The dates and times were nearly identical.

After the cremation, members of the Punjabi community arrived at their home offering their assistance, along with their condolences. Men came unannounced with their wives holding pots of dahl and containers of fresh rotis. Women came to attend to the newborn Amrit. At first, Harbeer graciously thanked them, expecting the stream of visitors to wane as the effects of the tragedy faded. After all, their help was appreciated while he was trying to settle his sons into a routine of cooking and cleaning. But weeks after Dalveer's death, the visitors were still constant, appearing at his doorstep punctually, as if it was their duty. Conflicted between feelings of puzzlement and gratitude, Harbeer began to evade them. "Please, this is plenty. Do not trouble yourselves any further," he would say.

A comment from one wife settled his confusion. "Brother, what trouble is this? You have a daughter who will never know her mother. Something will always be missing in her life." Those words haunted Harbeer. He was new at fathering a daughter; he only had the vaguest sense of what the girl would need over the years. Concerned about Amrit's welfare, he put aside his grieving and searched for a solution. Several members of the community offered to arrange a new marriage for him but few parents in India were willing to surrender their daughters to immediate motherhood in a foreign country. He briefly considered moving back to India, where his sister and female cousins could step in and take turns helping to raise Amrit, but he thought against it; some departures were not meant to be reversible. The first few years of Amrit's life were a blur, as he and the boys took on shifts to attend to her. Narain was especially gentle towards his sister. He smiled at her and cradled her as Dalveer would have. During those difficult colicky months when Harbeer grew exasperated with Amrit's constant mewling, Narain patiently picked her up and rocked her until she calmed down.

When did Dalveer return? Harbeer remembered thinking he was seeing her silhouette on the edges of the room when actually they were just shadows cast by low branches. Then one day, he thought he saw her peering through the window, but when he rushed to her, she scurried away. That night he heard her whispering through the window, a sound so distinct that it could not just be the wind. She had returned to him.

It defied all logical explanation. Didn't he have a death certificate? He retrieved it that night from the depths of his desk. He read it carefully, his heart filling with sadness at the scant information brought over from Dalveer's village life. Her date of birth was unknown. Her name in the official English hardly gave justice to its Punjabi phonetics. He had looked up to find Dalveer standing at the edge of the room. Speechless, Harbeer could only crumple the death certificate in his hands. When he recovered from the shock, he asked Dalveer why she had left in the first place. She did not have an answer. She did not speak very much—she made gestures and murmured incoherent sentences. One condition of her visits was very clear, however. He was not to tell anybody about her.

There were only two instances when he mentioned Dalveer's presence in front of the children. There was an afternoon when he was at a loss to explain to the toddler Amrit why she should not publicly scratch between her legs. Feeling a blush creeping into his cheeks, he pleaded but Amrit's hand kept on travelling to that region. "Stop it," he snapped finally, advancing towards her. Amrit ran into her room. Dalveer's shadow slipped along the window outside, catching his attention.

"Your mother does not like you doing that." The words just slipped from his mouth but they were successful in making Amrit freeze. Gulping back a sob, she looked at him strangely, pondering this sudden introduction. "Your mother says it is very bad." Dalveer approved with the quietest murmur.

On the eve of Amrit's first day of primary school, Harbeer was sitting at his desk looking through the bills when Dalveer arrived, the bells on her anklets ringing so faintly that he initially mistook them for the jingling collar of the neighbour's cat. With nothing but worry etched into her face, she reminded him that Amrit's uniform needed to be ironed. He waved her off—her visits had become frequent to the point of being inconvenient and annoying. She inched closer to him. The fabric of her cotton kameez brushed his fingertips as she leaned towards the desk. "Fine," he said, as he shot up from the chair and went to the closet to retrieve the package from the uniform tailor. Keeping his voice low, he read the date from the receipt to remind Dalveer that he had bought the uniform far in advance, so prepared was he to educate the daughter that she had carelessly left behind. She sat on the edge of the bed and looked distractedly at her hands while he pulled apart the plastic wrapping. He laid the uniform flat on the bed next to her, feeling a rush of warmth as his eyes took in the small sleeves, and the short belt that would encircle Amrit's little waist.

Dalveer inspected the uniform, and gestured for Harbeer to look. Deep creases from the folding intersected the blouse and pinafore in the wrong places, cutting an arm and giving the appearance of two waists. Harbeer laid out the uniform on the ironing board, wishing it was not too late in the evening to call the local errand girl. He aimed the iron, pressing down hard on the creases, but they stubbornly remained, marking his daughter's body in unnatural bends. He increased the temperature on the iron. When he lifted it, the creases were hardly noticeable but Dalveer was not satisfied. On his third try, the fabric hissed in protest. He lifted the iron to find that he had burned a streak through the fabric, making permanent what he wanted to erase.

"Stupid woman!" he shouted. Dalveer scuttled away, frightened as a mouse. "You made me do this. The uniform was fine before—now look what I've done! Stupid village woman!" He had heard footsteps, and then Gurdev and Narain arrived to see him holding the iron and ranting at what seemed to be an empty room. He explained weakly that he had had a bad dream, and dismissed them before they could ask any questions.

Why Dalveer had begun to sabotage him, Harbeer

did not know. Whenever his domestic inadequacies were exposed, he blamed Dalveer. When a splinter from a stray piece of rattan lodged itself into Amrit's heel, Harbeer cursed Dalveer for leading him to buy the lowest quality broom from the local shop's wide selection. When the errand girl took a day off and he brewed tea with two heaped spoons of salt instead of sugar, he rampaged through the house, certain Dalveer was hiding somewhere.

The sabotaging lessened as the children became older. Dalveer became a more willing partner, coaching him in the housework and demonstrating the order of things. Harbeer began to see himself cleanly divided as two parents. Every clutching sense of panic he felt was Dalveer's. Every intellectual argument was his.

This was the period that inspired Harbeer's first letters. Something had changed in his mind—a fog had lifted and unearthed his brilliant and original ideas. While Dalveer was busy wringing her hands and worrying about household issues, he wrote detailed letters to newspaper editors and leaders of the nation, making known his ideas. At times, his thoughts became so rapid that his pen could not catch up and he scribbled so hard that his hand cramped. For this, too, Dalveer was to blame. She hovered near him, watching him form a script she would never learn to read. Her presence often distracted him mid-sentence. So many letters were incomplete because of Dalveer. They all sat wrapped in rubber bands in shoe boxes stacked behind starched shirts in his closet. The sight of these boxes created knots of regret that tightened every time he heard closet hinges creak anywhere in his home. He would curse Dalveer, heaping the worst of insults on her for weeks, driving her back into the shadows. Then he would allow himself to grieve, because when the rage wore off, it seemed to be the only function for which his body was designed. The stomach that normally rumbled for food contracted instead and produced sobs that rose through his gullet and exploded from his mouth. The broad shoulders for displaying confidence curved inwards to shelter his heart. Dalveer did not appear in those days; she was gracious enough to let him grieve for her on his own.

• • •

Now, Amrit was still talking, but Harbeer would hear none of it. Still staring at the mess of his desk, and at the papers lying close to his feet, Harbeer felt his rage grow. He spread out his fingers and raised his hand into the air again. "Stop it," he warned. When he turned to face Amrit, he froze. She looked different. All of the questions that used to cloud her wide eyes were gone, and there wasn't a trace of fear on her face.

"There is nothing wrong with me," he said. "I gave you opportunity, food, education. And you have the nerve to tell me that I gave you madness."

"I'm not here to blame you, Father. I'm just concerned about you. She's not real. I can't see her. Nobody can see her but you. Doesn't this bother you?"

Harbeer did not reply. He looked past Amrit's shoulder, where a shadow had begun to form. What would anybody understand? Dalveer was here, gradually taking shape.

"I think I will have to move out," Amrit said. "I'll let you know when I've found a place. I'll come back on weekends if you need me to help with cooking or anything."

"Narain will be here," Harbeer said.

"Narain is also leaving soon." Harbeer had a hazy memory of Narain telling him this, and of seeing a lease with the name of his son and another man on it.

"I will have no problems living without you two," Harbeer told Amrit. "Go whenever you want."

Crouching on the floor now, Dalveer picked up the papers and did her best to arrange them. *You will always be here,* he thought. Dalveer did not acknowledge this as she continued her work, levelling the papers with her hands.

Mother

DALVEER PAUSED BENEATH the awning of the textile shop, watching the street as daylight dimmed over Little India. Shrill violin notes from old Tamil songs floated in the distance. A fortune teller spread a set of cards on a table and instructed his parrot to pick one for the customer. The air was ripe with the mix of sweat, sandalwood and jasmine incense.

She followed Harbeer into the shop. The walls were lined with crooked shelves crammed with trays of glittery costume jewellery. While Harbeer searched for Rani's birthday present, Dalveer's eyes roamed. It was a decrepit shop, with chipping paint and the distinct smell of cumin that seeped through all the walls. In the shop owner's tiny bedroom and kitchenette upstairs, there was bound to be beings like herself. Spirits thrived in these dusty old shops, their footsteps delightfully noiseless on the creaking floorboards.

Harbeer frowned as he picked through the trays. All of the bracelets and earrings probably looked the same to him, but Rani was becoming an age where colours and patterns were significant. He picked up a set of thin bangles with tiny bells attached and Dalveer saw his thoughts: he was uncertain about them. He turned to her imploringly and she felt herself emerge in full colour. Their bronze shade was too sober for a young girl. Gently, she guided his hand towards a tray on the centre of the shelf. It was a set of bangles in alternating baby blue and pink, and a matching pair of earrings. Rani would sparkle in those colours.

Under his breath, Harbeer grumbled about the prices. "Of course she makes me pick the most expensive one," he said, to nobody in particular. Dalveer pressed closer to let him feel her warmth.

He took the set to the counter and gruffly asked the shopkeeper in Malay for his best price. The shopkeeper wearily shook his head and said something in English. Harbeer barked back in Malay. The shopkeeper replied, shaking his head. Dalveer knew she had to interfere. She brushed her fingertips against Harbeer's elbows and directed his gaze towards details of the shopkeeper's haggard appearance. His fingernails were dirty and chipped, and the half-moons under his eyes were swollen and shadowy from a lack of sleep. Harbeer continued his rant until he was satisfied that the shopkeeper had learned his lesson. Then with a great show of pain at the injustice of the inflated costs, he pulled out his wallet and paid the full price for the bangles.

"No more. We've spent enough time and money," Harbeer announced, as they walked out of the shop. A couple standing nearby watched him curiously but he didn't seem to care. Deep in these lanes of Little India, where chaos still reigned, a man talking to himself was acceptable.

"He wanted three times as much as we needed to pay. These shopkeepers jack up all the prices and don't recognise the difference between the tourists and those of us from India," Harbeer continued.

They were walking in the shadows now, and the lane was bumpy with smashed fruit. In the distance, the street lamps had been lit. Harbeer charged purposefully towards the main road but Dalveer lingered, stepping in the potholes, letting her sandals slip loose from her feet. She made excuses so that Harbeer would slow down and stay in the side lanes, so they could remain on this tiny portion of the island that already seemed like a memory.

Dalveer remembered dying. It had felt different from the way she had imagined it would: not a sensation of sinking into the unknown depths, but a gradual, exhilarating sense of floating on her own. As the doctor's fervid commands to the nurses faded away, Dalveer had felt, tangibly, the world drifting away. The bed slid from her back, the doors moved off, the walls drew together and then exited. The hospital, the street and the island all pulled out from underneath her, leaving her untended and utterly free. An understanding overcame her: she would remain like this forever. But only moments later, there she was with her daughter, aged five, cowering in Harbeer's presence after having tested his temper.

Dalveer appeared to her husband willingly, knowing that he would not be able to cope on his own. She had tried to appear to her children as well, but they didn't see her. Yet, they knew her presence. She could hear them calling upon her in their deepest thoughts when they struggled, and she felt them leaping into her arms when they experienced triumph. For these encounters, however sporadic, Dalveer had continued to roam through their rooms and sit between them during dinner. At times, it pained her that she couldn't be there in the flesh to reprimand or reassure them, but Harbeer was diligent about expressing her thoughts.

Finally, they emerged on the main road and Harbeer flagged down a taxi. He held open the door and waited just for a moment to let Dalveer scoot in before he entered. Inside the car, a sharp wind from the airconditioner blasted her face. She blinked uncomfortably and turned away. Harbeer gestured for the driver to direct the vents elsewhere. An upbeat Chinese song played on the radio and a jade Buddha on the dashboard tipped towards Dalveer. His smile was familiar to her—she had seen his expression on the faces of spirits during the Hungry Ghost Festival. Dalveer wished for a Punjabi tradition that honoured the dead and invited them to feast with the living. It would be an occasion where Harbeer would not be the only person to acknowledge that she breathed, ate and slept. These days, she did not encounter other spirits very often. The island used to pulse with their presence. In the old swamplands, Dalveer would encounter them draped over palm tree branches and bathing in the muddy waters. In the evenings, their chatter used to buzz excitedly alongside the chirping of crickets, as families settled down to eat their dinners. Then the island changed—the tangled weeds were combed through to form neat bouquets and square hedges. This was no longer a home for spirits.

Looking out of the taxi window now, Dalveer saw that they were passing the river. Small boats bobbed gently from the weight of the tourists, and the water glowed with the melted lights of the restaurants along the banks. Through the crack of the open taxi window, Dalveer breathed in the air but did not catch a whiff of the water's pungent stink. It was something different now, something unwelcoming. Harbeer disagreed, of course. "This is what a river should be," he would argue. She was tempted to lean closer to the window and make a show of her sorrow over this loss. Harbeer would struggle to maintain his composure and resist scolding her in front of this taxi driver. Yet Dalveer often felt remorse when she forced this conflict onto her husband; it wasn't right that anybody thought he was mad for acknowledging her presence. Even their children regarded him with apprehension, and Dalveer felt the injustice of this as strongly as Harbeer did. She reached out to squeeze his palm and felt him gripping hers back tightly.

When they arrived back at the flat, Dalveer went to Amrit's room first. Amrit wasn't there, and the room was a mess of books and clothes. A suitcase had been dragged out from the storeroom and next to it, two cardboard boxes overflowed with hangers, shoes and photo albums. For a week now, the flat had been clanging with the sounds of Amrit's impending departure. Dalveer led Harbeer into the room and they both sat on the edge of Amrit's bed. She placed Harbeer's palms over the wrinkles in the sheets, calling to his memory the press of the iron over Amrit's school uniform.

Together, they remembered the softness of Amrit's hair as Dalveer guided Harbeer to braid it each morning. Harbeer's eyes glistened. Soon he would jerk away from her and march out of this room, grumbling about her sentimentality. *Your unnecessary tears*, he would scornfully call them. Alone in his room, he would get dressed and they would wait for the flat to fill with their children. Banu would bring the birthday cake and Gurdev would hover over the candles, making sure his daughters did not get burnt. Narain would stay close to Amrit all night, chatting and laughing in their own secret world. Throughout the evening, Dalveer's heart would fill to the point of bursting, so grateful was she to be surrounded by her children. Softly, she would lament that the family only came together for special occasions, and Harbeer would grumble to the children that their mother was being tearful again. "She can't just enjoy a nice evening. She must spoil the occasion," he would say. He would go on about their differences—men and women, like adults and children. Where she was weak, he was strong. Where he was practical, she was full of emotion. Later he would retreat to his room to write a letter, confident in his ideas, while Dalveer stood aside, tending to her simpler tasks.

But for this moment Dalveer and Harbeer were the same.

Acknowledgements

Thank you Mum, Dad, Manmeet, my grandparents and my extended family in Singapore and Malaysia. Thank you Paul for being my favourite reader.

My sincere thanks to the following teachers: Suzanne Kirk, Pinckney Benedict, Pauline Kaldas, Inman Majors, Richard Bausch, Steve Goodwin and Susan Shreve. Your feedback and advice over the years have been invaluable.

I was also very fortunate to be given the space and time to write this novel at the University of East Anglia. Special thanks to the writers and administrators who made me feel most welcome during my stay in England.

To Anna Power, who had the patience to read through multiple drafts, provide detailed notes and push me to consider what this story was really about—thank you. Louise Swinn and Zoe Dattner: without your infectious enthusiasm and compassion for this story, I would not be able to call myself an author.

Thanks to Edmund Wee and the Epigram Books team for publishing the revised edition of this novel and for being such strong advocates for Singaporean literature. Special thanks to my friend and editor Jason Erik Lundberg.

About the author

Balli Kaur Jaswal is also the author of *Sugarbread*, a finalist for the 2015 Epigram Books Fiction Prize, and a story about fitting in and confronting the past. Born in Singapore and raised in Japan, Russia and the Philippines, she studied creative writing in the United States. She has received writing fellowships from the University of East Anglia and Nanyang Technological University, and was named Best Young Australian Novelist of 2014 by the *Sydney Morning Herald*.

Kevin is a young man without a soul, holidaying in Tokyo; Mr Five, the enigmatic kappa, is the man he happens to meet. Little does Kevin know that kappas— the river demons of Japanese folklore—desire nothing more than the souls of other humans. Set between Singapore and Japan, *Kappa Quartet* is split into eight discrete sections, tracing the rippling effects of this chance encounter across a host of other characters, connected and bound to one another in ways both strange and serendipitous.

ISBN: 978-191-2098-72-9
Publication date: May 2017

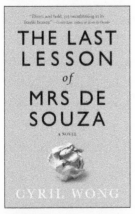

One last time and on her birthday, Rose de Souza is returning to school to give a final lesson to her classroom of secondary school boys before retiring from her long teaching career. What ensues is an unexpected confession in which she recounts the tragic and traumatic story of Amir, a student from her past who overturned the way she saw herself as a teacher, and changed her life forever.

ISBN: 978-191-2098-70-5
Publication date: July 2017

During the Christmas holidays in 2004, an earthquake in the Indian Ocean triggers a tsunami that devastates fourteen countries. Two couples from Singapore are vacationing in Phuket when the tsunami strikes. Alternating between the aftermath of the catastrophe and past events that led these characters to that fateful moment, *Now That It's Over* weaves a tapestry of causality and regret, and chronicles the physical and emotional wreckage wrought by natural and man-made disasters.

ISBN: 978-191-2098-69-9
Publication date: July 2017